TO THE EDGE OF ATHENIA

A HOUSE OF HYRAX NOVEL

ARCADIA RAYNE

TO THE EDGE OF ATHENIA

A House of Hyrax Novel

Arcadia Rayne

To those of us who have never had main character energy but still have stories worth telling.

And to my family and loved ones who have supported the start of the House of Hyrax series with more love and encouragement than I could have ever imagined.

CONTENT WARNING

Please note this is an Adult/New Adult fantasy novel written for a mature reader.

This story includes scenes of sexual content, dishonesty regarding pregnancy, war trauma, murder, violence, portrayals of insanity, references to potential domestic violence, torture, and harm to a pet. Please read at your own discretion.

Your mental health still matters.

PRONUNCIATION GUIDE

Characters

- Iris – (EYE-ris)

- Rankor – (RANGK-or)

- Camilla – (kuh-Meel-ah)

- Kent – (kent)

- Lorelai – (LOHR-uh-lie)

- Walric – (WAWL-rik)

- Elaijah – (el-AY-shuh)

- Alina – (uh-LEE-nuh)

- Seralyn – (SER-uh-lin)

- Joliette – (SHOH-lee-ET)

- Nikolai – (NIK-oh-lie)

- Gentry – (JEN-tree)

- Kreyana – (KREY-ahn-uh)

- Kressida – (KRES-uh-duh)

- Helena – (HELL-uh-nuh)

- Erilea – (ER-i-LAY-ugh)

Gods

- Hyrax, God of the Dead – (HIGH-racks)

- Zion, King of the Gods – (ZYE-uhn)

- Palaemon, God of the Water & Oceans – (puh-LAY-mon)

- Delia, Goddess of Pregnancy & Childbirth – (DEE-lee-uh)

- Hypatia, Goddess of the Earth – (hi-PAY-shuh)

- Arto, God of Violence – (AHR-toh)

- Athene, Goddess of Wisdom – (uh-TEE-nee)

DESCENDANT LINES
OF THE HIGH GODS

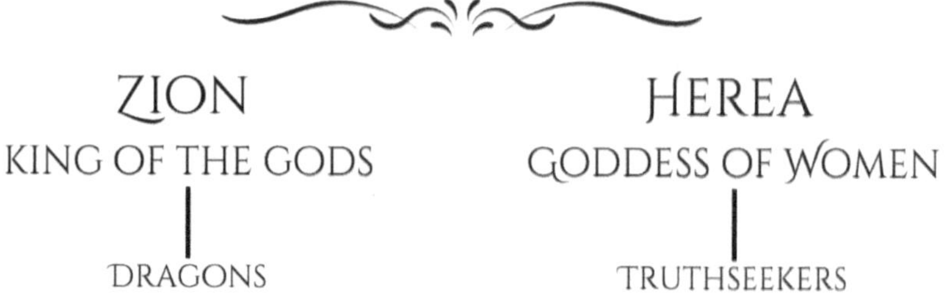

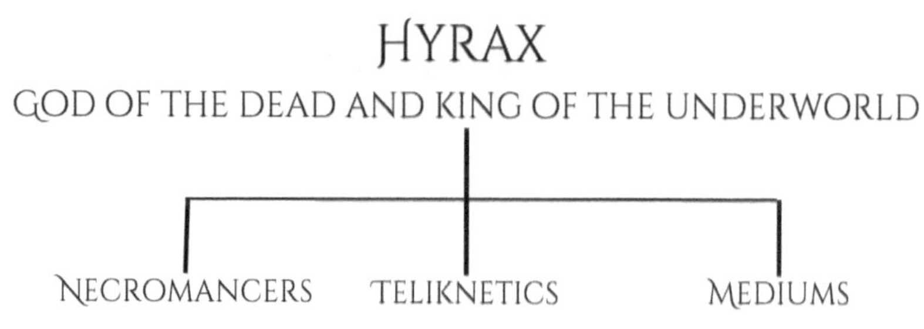

ADDITIONAL DESCENDANT LINES

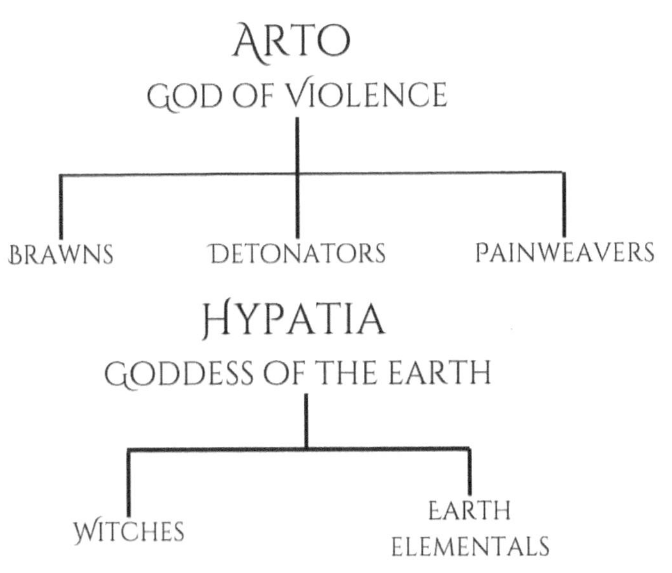

PASNIA
GODDESS OF MADNESS

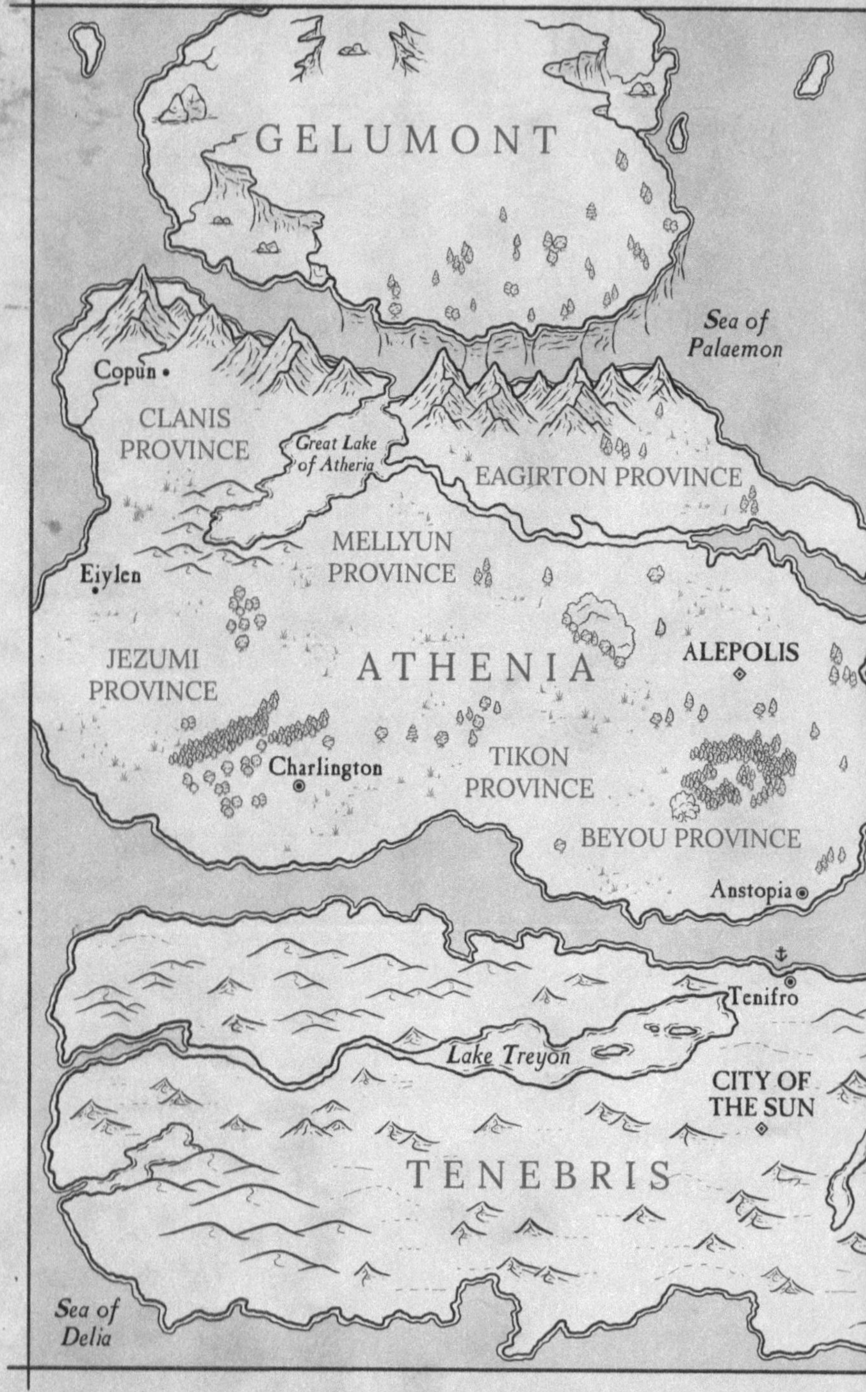

GELUMONT
Sea of Palaemon
Copun
CLANIS PROVINCE
Great Lake of Atheria
EAGIRTON PROVINCE
MELLYUN PROVINCE
Eiylen
JEZUMI PROVINCE
ATHENIA
ALEPOLIS
Charlington
TIKON PROVINCE
BEYOU PROVINCE
Anstopia
Tenifro
Lake Treyon
CITY OF THE SUN
TENEBRIS
Sea of Delia

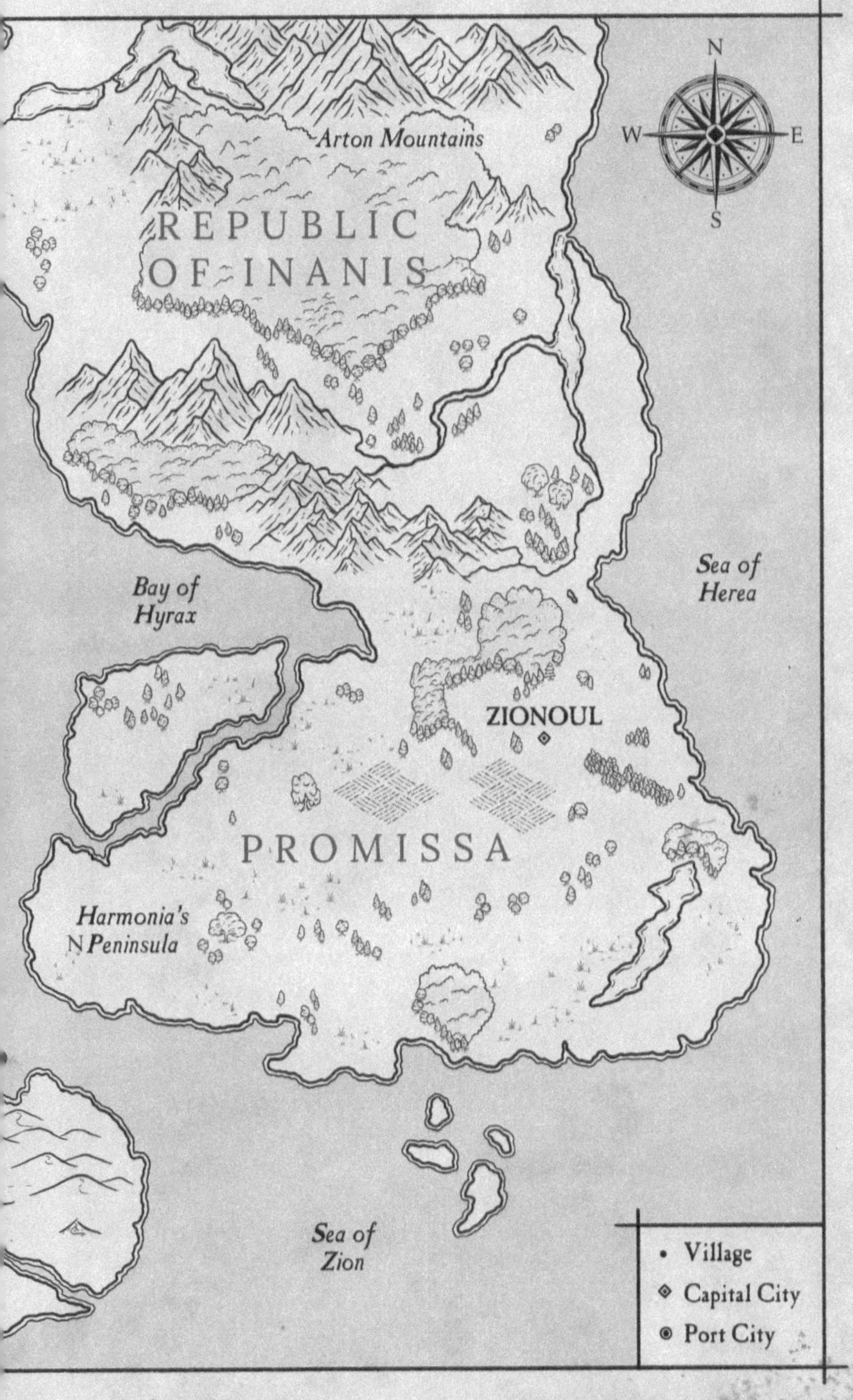

N
W
E
S
Arton Mountains
REPUBLIC OF INANIS
Sea of Herea
Bay of Hyrax
ZIONOUL
PROMISSA
Harmonia's Peninsula
Sea of Zion
Village
Capital City
Port City

IRIS

LOYALTY TO THE ORDER

"I win!" Iris cheered, laying her cards down proudly on the table in front of her.

Clay only sighed heavily and tossed his cards haphazardly down next to hers before he ran a hand tiredly over his face. He was dressed as elegantly as ever in his emerald jacket and tailored pants, but Iris couldn't help but notice the dark shadows under his eyes, betraying the fact he hadn't gotten enough sleep last night.

It wasn't hard to guess why. He'd been with Camilla last night, she was certain of it.

"Oh, what's wrong, your grace?" She asked sarcastically, eyebrows raised. "Not sleep well?"

He narrowed his slate grey eyes at her, but a playful smile danced on his lips as he bent to clean the cards and tuck them into a neat little pile. "My attention was otherwise occupied last night, but you won't find me complaining about it."

She tilted her head as she sent him a withering glare. In truth, Iris wasn't quite sure how she felt about Clay and Camilla's relationship. She loved them both individually, of course. Clay was the only consistent family she'd ever had, and Camilla was one of her oldest friends. She wanted them to be happy. But something about the two of them together seemed wrong, like the impossible mixture of oil and water. They were two people that simply didn't seem to mix well.

Out of respect for their privacy, she tried to stay out of it, but from an outsider's perspective, it was clear that any romance between them was doomed. Camilla didn't look at Clay with passion, and Clay looked at her with a little too much. She suspected Camilla was using him for his title and that he was using Camilla for...

Well, Iris didn't want to think of her cousin *like that.*

She shook her head to clear her thoughts and moved to her dressing chamber to find her slippered shoes. They would need to leave for dinner soon. Tonight was the quarterly dinner where the Dukes that presided over the six provinces of Athenia came to meet with the Dragon and deliver reports of their territories. Clay's father insisted he attend and so Clay had insisted she attend so that there was at least one person in the room he could get along with. It wasn't exactly her idea of a good time, but he needed her.

She was always there for him when he needed her.

"And what about your love life?" He called from the other room. "Still no one who has caught your eye?"

Iris laughed softly, tossing her cerulean curls over her shoulder as she hinged to slide on her pale pink shoes. Clay watched her, leaning back in his seat with his hands crossed easily behind his head.

"Too many people have caught my eye."

Iris had never been one to tie herself down, always bouncing from one lover to the next. She had yet to find someone who really captured her in a breathless sort of primal way. She'd admittedly been crushing on their friend Lorelai for a few years off and on, but she'd never acted on those feelings, too afraid of taking that step and ruining their friendship.

And now Lorelai was too good for her.

She was far too pure to handle all the darkness that had grown inside of Iris since she'd joined The Order.

Once she had secured her shoes, Clay stood and offered her his arm. Together they walked, arm in arm, out of her suite and Iris couldn't help but shiver as the door swung shut behind them.

Her apartment at the castle was new. She'd always had a room here, of course, a generosity offered to her simply because she was the prince's favorite playmate, but since she'd started working with The Order, so many things had changed for her. It had started with an upgraded suite, this one complete with sweeping windows with a mountain view and an extra large bathing tub. Then they had delivered fine silk gowns and sparkling jewelry to her. Then a ridiculously large assortment of weapons had shown up.

Iris had loved it all.

She'd always lived a fairly privileged life in the castle because of her closeness with Clay, more privileged than even some of their other friends, but she had never deluded herself into thinking it would stay that way forever. When her parents had fled the country years ago, they had left her with a limited amount of funds that had dwindled long before she was of age to provide for herself.

Eventually Iris found herself at a crossroads. She would either have to find a way to support herself here in Athenia, or she would have to leave and join her parents.

Ultimately, she couldn't bring herself to leave Clay and her friends behind.

Joining The Order had brought that much needed coin into her life, but it had also brought her a level of respect she'd never experienced before.

She was no longer just the prince's non-royal cousin; she was a member of The Order, the most elite society of spies and assassins within Athenia, sanctioned by the Dragon himself.

"You're quiet," Clay noted, pinching her arm gently. "Surely you're not dreading our meal that much?"

Iris rested her head against his shoulder as they walked. "Why would I ever dread a meal with the stuffy old nobleman?"

"Is that sarcasm I detect?"

"And here I was beginning to believe the rumors that the Crown Prince wasn't too smart."

He glanced at her from the corner of his eye, and she giggled, playfully pinching his arm in return as they entered his father's suite where the dinner would take place.

Clay's father, the Dragon, looked at them immediately, and she stiffened. The Dragon's graying hair was combed away from his face, but it was probably the only part of him that looked orderly. He'd already unbuttoned his shirt several times, leaving small patches of dark chest hair to poke out and his eyelids hung heavily. He quickly shifted his gaze from Clay to Iris, and then to the place where their arms were entwined before his mouth puckered into an irritated frown. With an irritated sigh, Iris lowered herself immediately, hating every second that passed where she had to keep her head bowed and wait for him to give her permission to rise.

"Father," Clay greeted him, voice tight.

The Dragon only turned away to return to his drink and the nobleman.

"He's already drunk," Iris whispered.

"I'm not surprised. Cryan arrived early."

Ice spread over her skin. Cryan, the Duke who presided over the Jezumi Province of Athenia, was a boyhood friend of the Dragon's and now, as a man, was nearly as abominable as the Dragon himself. He was the kind of leader who was so bloated with power that he hid all of his faults behind his abuse of anyone who displeased him—which explained why he and her uncle got along so well.

"So then I tell her to bend over and show me what I've paid for!" Cryan laughed, his voice too loud.

The Dragon smiled. "I believe I said something similar to Valentina the night I wed her."

Iris wanted to be sick. She turned away from where the men were drinking in the parlor to graze on the food that was scattered across the table. The feast of roasted boar and steamed vegetables was untouched, although the men had clearly already made startling progress drinking their way through the bar cart. It had likely been going on for hours already. The Queen was also notably missing. It was rare that the Dragon let her out of his sight, which likely meant one thing.

He had left her in the care of the palace healers again.

She bit her lip and worked to school her face into an expression of neutrality.

"You're doing it again," Clay sighed.

Iris frowned.

"You're assessing the room. Your eyes went to the dinner knives the second we entered and started scanning the room. I'd bet you have a running count of how many people have come in and out since we arrived."

She smiled darkly. "Four servants are working. One kitchen boy who's carrying in the heavy dishes, two women responsible for serving and one girl barely older than sixteen responsible for refilling the cups. She's currently standing in the parlor with your father and the four noblemen who have already arrived. There are, however, eight dinner knives on this table. If the Queen was coming, she would be here already, so someone else is late."

Clay shook his head as a shadow fell across his brow. With a huff, he picked up one of the knives on the dining table and twirled it easily through his fingers, an old habit that came out when he was nervous or upset. "They're changing you."

He didn't need to explain his point, and she didn't need to deny it. The Order *had* changed her. They'd taught her to expect the unexpected. They'd trained her to be prepared for anything. Their lessons had been brutal and unrelenting. Of course it had changed her.

"You changed when you went to war," she reminded him, thinking back to those moments she would see her cousin in between battles of the Great War.

He'd left for the army as a boy, he'd come home as a man. A future king.

"We're not at war, Iris."

"The Order can help make sure it stays that way."

"The Order is dangerous. They're killers."

She twisted away from him, less than eager to have this conversation with him again. Through the window, she could see a hawk circling through the sky, hunting for its prey. Its heavy wings beat through the air with an unspent energy that it needed to release onto a target. That was the way of life.

What she was doing was no different.

"Do I need to remind you that the Dragon commissioned The Order himself?"

Clay's eyes darkened as he grasped onto the knife tightly and balanced its tip onto the carved wood of the table. Iris knew well that with just a little pressure, he could burrow that blade into the wood. It wouldn't take much. Even dinner knives could slice through a thick surface if one applied pressure in the right place.

"And that makes it good?"

She sighed, ignoring the sudden urge to both laugh and cry. It's not like anything he could say to her now would change what was already done. Joining The Order was irreversible. Joining The Order meant making a lifelong pledge of loyalty and service that could never be rescinded.

Besides, Iris had joined The Order for a reason. That's what she reminded herself every time sparks of doubt rose within her.

She had needed the coin. She had needed a reason to ignore her parents' demands that she return to them and look for an eligible suitor. She had needed a reason to stay in Athenia.

The Order gave her one.

As a member of The Order, she was now an entirely independent person. She always had a warm welcome within the castle and neither the Dragon nor her parents would ever force her to marry. She could stay here, with Clay, Lorelai, Kent, Rankor and Camilla, for as long as she wanted.

It had been the *only* option for her.

"Let us eat!" The Dragon demanded, clapping his hands together and pushing his guests towards the table.

Clay's eyes lingered on Iris even as he addressed his father. "Are we not awaiting another guest, father?"

The Dragon responded with something about not caring to wait for the chronically late Duke of Eagirton, but Iris didn't bother to listen. She didn't need to hear confirmation that her assessment had been correct.

The Order had trained her to never make incorrect assessments.

I ris picked at her food miserably, terribly uncomfortable. Clay did his best to chat with her and distract her from the lewd conversations happening all around them, but she could tell he was just as miserable as she was.

She stabbed through her roasted carrots and glared at her uncle, wondering if that was why he insisted Clay come to these gatherings. Obviously, listening to conversations about Duke Crede fucking his way through the city of Alepolis wasn't teaching Clay to be a better ruler. Did the Dragon just get some sort of sick satisfaction in knowing that his son didn't want to be here? Probably.

"So." She turned to Clay. "I think it's fair to say you owe me for coming to this with you."

He gave her a crooked smile. "And how would you like your payment?"

"Well, I believe a new gown with that shimmering orange fabric we saw in the market last week should be suitable."

"Don't you have enough gowns by now?" Clay shook his head incredulously.

"Clayton, dear." She raised her hand to her chest in mock offense. "Do you know nothing of women?"

He raised a brow at her with an expression filled with innuendos and male smugness, and she fought the urge to smack him. Her uncle certainly wouldn't appreciate that. Although, the Dragon was already slurring his words, so it's highly possible he wouldn't even notice.

"I'm just saying the quickest way to a woman's heart is through a new gown." She pulled her wineglass to her lips to hide her smile as she watched him ponder over her words.

"That's really all it takes, huh?"

Iris rolled her eyes dramatically. "Well, that and a little *romance,* of course. Asking Ruthie to make any old gown as a thank you for me is perfectly fine. For a woman you truly want to fall for you, you'll need to pay attention to detail. You get her a gown that shows you know the color and styles she likes or a gown that shows you've thought about what she feels comfortable in and what she'll look beautiful in. She'll swoon not because of the present, but because of the thought behind it."

He ran a hand over his mouth, scratching the stubble on his jawline as if he were really considering her words.

"Try it with Camilla," Iris suggested, knowing his reaction would tell her everything she needed to know about the blossoming relationship between the two of them.

Clay snorted. "Camilla has enough gowns."

There it was. The truthful admission that Clay didn't truly want to be with Camilla. Iris sighed heavily, surprised by how conflicted she felt about that. On the one hand, she had known there was nothing deep happening between them, and yet she felt disappointed. Clay and Camilla both deserved love. It wasn't completely ridiculous to think that the torture the Dragon had inflicted on both of them may have brought them together. Out of everyone in their circle of friends, Clay and Camilla had faced the most hardship at the hands of that man. Iris wanted them to find happiness after all this time.

Iris longed for that sort of love herself. The kind of love that would leave you breathless, both on edge and comforted at the same time. The kind of love when you can trust that the person would choose you above all else.

And she was sure she would never find it.

"Perhaps you'll have to save that tip for whatever woman you do want to make fall in love with you."

Clay's eyes were distant, and she noticed that his hand grasped his dinner knife tighter than necessary.

"Love is a useless notion for someone like me," he muttered.

Iris opened her mouth to protest, to argue that he deserved love and affection more than anyone she knew, but the door to the Dragons' suite burst open suddenly, the wood crashing against the wall with force. Iris' instincts took over within a second. Without thinking, she had grasped both her dinner knife and Clay's and stood. Before anyone else had even moved, she was across the room, one blade against the throat of the new guest and the other poised against his crotch.

"What in all of creation do you think you're doing?" He growled, wide eyed and infuriated.

The Dragon's booming laughter pulled her out of her trance, and she felt Clay's hands wrapping around her wrists, pulling her back.

"That's the Duke of Eagirton," Clay whispered, taking the knives from her.

"Finally, my niece is useful for something!" The Dragon cheered. "You see how The Order of Athenia operates! They are ruthless. They act on pure instinct to protect and serve me."

Iciness settled over Iris as she tried to reacquaint herself to her surroundings. The Dragon was right. She had responded without thought, every instinct in her pushing her to protect her king and prince. Maybe Clay was right, and The Order had changed her in less than desirable ways.

"You arrive late to my dinner and could not manage to find time to bathe first?" The Dragon questioned his new guest.

It was only then that Iris took in the Duke's appearance. Blood coated his arms and his tunic was torn in several places. His haunted eyes were swollen and though he tried to tuck his hands behind his back, Iris still noticed the way they shook.

"Your majesty." He heaved, out of breath. "There's been an attack in Eagirton."

The Dragon sobered instantly, but remained seated. The fleck of gold in his eyes was the only visible sign that this news affected him. With pursed lips, he scanned over the Duke. "Continue."

"I was preparing to join you when vagrants ambushed my estate! I had already sent many of my guards to their homes as I prepared to leave. By the time they came for us, there were dozens of them to only my handful of protectors."

The Dragon raised a brow, his expression lacking sympathy. "Could you not defend your own home from a group of untrained thieves, Anton?"

"Your majesty," Anton's voice cracked, and a sudden dread settled over Iris. Clay had gone still next to her. "They knew the manor was unprotected. There was nothing we could do. They... they killed my son, your majesty. And they have taken my wife."

The silence that fell over the room was suffocating. Tension coiled within Iris' muscles and she suddenly longed for one of the dinner knives once more, as if the weight of the blade in her hand might help to ease some of the discomfort.

The Dragon sighed and began wiping his hands on one of the cloth napkins on the table in front of them. Without a word, he sent a deadly glare to the kitchen girl, who rushed to refill his glass once more before promptly bowing and fleeing from the room. The Dragon sipped from it slowly, calculation clear in his every move.

"Do you only come to me with tears and news of your failure?"

Anton sputtered, "Your majesty, please. Someone must have informed these thieves about my plans. Anyone who betrays me also betrays you. I implore you to take action. We must avenge my son and save my wife."

"You expect me to intervene with such little information?"

Anton's eyes flickered between the faces of the room, desperate for some assistance, but Iris could feel her uncle already losing interest in the conversation. He was on the verge of sending the Duke away, which would mean the man's poor wife would be lost forever.

"Did you take prisoners?" Iris asked him.

"Iris." Clay's voice was sharp and Iris suspected he knew what she was thinking, what she was planning.

It didn't matter, though. Iris already knew what she had to do.

The men in the room stilled, all staring at the girl who had dared to speak out of turn. A few years ago, it might have made her uncomfortable. Iris wasn't just the girl cousin of the Crown Prince anymore, though. She was deadlier than most of the men in this room and that gave her more than enough confidence to take control of this situation.

"A woman," Anton said. "I brought her with me. The guards took her to the palace cells when I arrived."

"Transport her to the dungeons of The Order. We'll take over from here."

"I wasn't aware you were far along enough in your initiation to be speaking on behalf of The Order," the Dragon snapped at her, every word dripping in poorly disguised disdain.

"You tasked The Order with protecting you, your majesty. As the Duke of Eagirton articulated, a traitor in his house may quickly become a traitor in yours. I believe you would agree with me in deciding that there's only one course of action in dealing with traitors. Therefore, I believe I am well within my rights to decide this is a matter for The Order."

The Dragon's golden eyes assessed her. "And have you had your first mission with The Order, Iris?"

She fought the urge to shiver. "No, your majesty. I have not."

The grin that spread across his features was venomous, and she felt his words in her bones long before he spoke them. She'd known when she joined The Order that the day would come when she heard these words. She just hadn't expected it to come so soon.

Clay tucked his hands under the table before anyone else could see the skin beginning to darken.

"Well then," the Dragon cooed. "Consider me convinced. Iris Carleton, you've been called to service by your king."

RANKOR

Wicked and Beautiful

"Another!" Rankor demanded, slamming his empty pint onto the bar top.

The bartender looked at him suspiciously. He was already piss drunk, and she knew it. She was a small woman, with a thin waist and breasts that seemed a remarkable size, given her otherwise petite stature. Her dark eyes scanned over him as she perked an eyebrow.

"You're going to drink me dry, soldier."

He winked. "I'm going to try, Arabella."

"Fetch him some ale, Bella!" Elaijah demanded, clapping Rankor heavily on his shoulder. His younger brother was possibly drunker than he was, which was saying something. Elaijah was eight years younger than Rankor, but fancied himself a man already. Rankor suspected that had to do with the way their mother constantly coddled him.

At least, the way she had coddled him when she was alive.

Arabella must have seen the flash of pain across Rankor's face. She refilled his glass without protest and squeezed his hand slightly as she passed it to him. He gave her a small smile of appreciation.

"I don't know how you managed to bed her," Elaijah mused, watching as she walked away to wipe down some of the newly emptied tables of the tavern. "She's too good for you."

"She is," he agreed, watching her.

Rankor and Bella weren't necessarily *together*, but they often found their way to each other any time he visited home, which had become more frequent in the past few months while the sickness had taken his mother. Bella had been kind to him and his mother both. She had often sat with the older woman, holding her hand when the fever had left her hallucinating.

It had been a fortnight since his mother had passed.

He was handling it as best he could, mostly by drinking during the day and losing himself inside Bella at night. Rankor was no stranger to death. He'd lost countless friends during the Great War when he'd served as a general in the Athenian army. After a while, he'd started to feel a bit desensitized to it all. This experience wasn't much different to him.

He mourned his mother, of course, but it wasn't like she'd been a routine presence in his life, anyway. He'd gone to live at the castle with his father as a young boy and his mother had stayed behind with Elaijah. Rankor had visited them from time to time, but they had never felt like family to him. Not truly.

Clay and Kent were more like brothers to him than this boy ever would be.

"Another one for me too, Bella!" Elaijah called to her, swallowing the last of his ale in a greedy gulp and running the back of his hand across his lips.

"You have most certainly had enough." She didn't even bother to look up at him.

Elaijah pouted for a moment before reaching for Rankor's glass, which the older man pulled from his reach with the kind of speed only a trained soldier like himself could have mustered.

Rankor had been humoring Elaijah in the days since they'd lit their mother's funeral pyre. His younger brother had certainly gone through a growth spurt since he'd last saw the boy. He was now nearly as tall as Rankor, but still lanky and somewhat uncoordinated. His hair was the same deep brown as Rankor's, but he kept his cut short. A slight shadow covered the skin above the boy's lip, where he likely was waiting for hair to fully sprout before finally shaving.

Still, just because he was starting to look like a man didn't mean he was one.

If pretending to be like his older brother was helping him process his grief, then Rankor supposed there was no harm in giving the boy a little leeway. That leeway, however, ended after two drinks.

"Go home Elaijah!" Arabella instructed, smacking his hand with a dish-towel as he reached for one of the bottles she kept behind the bar. "You're trying my patience and my tavern is officially closed."

Elaijah looked at his brother with a comically disappointed expression. "She can be a real stick in the mud, you know!"

Rankor grabbed the boy by the shoulders, spun him gently, and gave him a soft shove towards the door. Elaijah's heavy steps echoed through the room as he made his way out.

"You sure he can get home okay?" Arabella asked, coming to stand by him and wiping her hands on the towel as she watched Elaijah go.

He turned to Arabella, grabbed her by the waist, and gently pushed her, pinning her between his body and the bar top, not wanting to think of his brother any longer. She went willingly, even grinning softly, but her eyes still trailed to the door.

"I'm serious Rankor!"

He sighed heavily into her throat. Rankor had spent the entire day entertaining the boy. Right now, he wanted to be able to focus entirely on her. Couldn't she feel how hard he was for her. By the Gods, he simply wanted to rid her of this dirty gown and spread her bare body atop the counter like a personal feast.

"His house is just across the way. He could stumble there with his eyes closed and hands bound."

"You could try being nicer, you know," she reminded him as he began nipping at the delicate flesh at the hollow of her throat. "He is your brother."

"Would you rather he be the one bedding you tonight?" Rankor groaned impatiently.

Arabella made a snorting noise in the back of her throat. "Of course not. I'm just saying he was close with your mother. He's trying to impress you, his war-hero older brother, but I've caught him wiping away tears on more than one occasion. He needs you to look after him now."

A pain in his right shoulder flared suddenly, and he pulled away from her to knead at the knot of tension. That spot had been causing him quite a bit of grief over the past week. Arabella sighed before moving to stand behind him and take over the job of massaging the tight muscles.

"I can't look after him, Bella," he reminded her. "I'm barely his brother, and I'm certainly not his father."

"You're all he has."

"Then he has nothing! Have you somehow forgotten the reason my visits to this village are so short?"

Arabella's eyes flashed with a hot temper and Rankor briefly wondered how close she was with his younger brother to have developed such a maternal protectiveness over the boy.

"Do you expect me to pretend that I don't know you've been on leave for months? That I'm not already aware you've been traipsing through the country side bouncing from one whore's bed to the next? Tell me, Rankor, is that more important than your own flesh and blood?"

Was that jealousy that was turning her cheeks pink? Rankor ran a tired hand over his face. This wasn't supposed to be happening. There were no ties between the two of them; he thought she had understood that. He had never sought her out before for words of comfort or advice, and she had never demanded more from him than he was willing to give.

That doesn't mean there weren't suggestions of something *more* for them, of course. Rankor knew the village members talked about how fitting they looked together - her petite frame against his tall, muscular stature. Even Miralena, his mother, had once suggested that the two of them would make beautiful children.

It's not like he didn't feel attracted to her. The aching heaviness of his cock and balls was a testament to how fucking beautiful he found her. As a non-royal Descendant, he could even marry her if he chose to.

Still, he couldn't bring himself to tie himself to another when his life may very well be fleeting.

Both his parents were now dead, after all, as were so many of his friends from the army. Rankor was a warrior first and a lover second. He was one poorly timed sword blow away from joining his loved ones in the Underworld.

He wouldn't pledge himself to a wife just to leave her as a widow.

If Arabella had misunderstood the arrangement that existed between the two of them, then he needed to end it immediately. It was for her own good.

He ran a hand through his overgrown hair and turned to face her. "Listen Arabella, I care about you. I really do but-"

"Oh, you brute!" Her hands flew out suddenly, smacking him on the shoulder and chest as she began marching him towards the door. "I do not care who you share your bed with. I only mean to point out that your responsibilities now include that young boy. And maybe if you actually took some time to get to know him, you might find that there is one more person in this world that's worthy of your love!"

She let the door to the tavern slam closed in his face and it was all he could do not to walk back in there and continue arguing with her.

Arguing would get him nowhere tonight, though, and it certainly wouldn't ease the heat that burned in his lower stomach. So, with an exaggerated sigh that sounded more like a growl than he intended it to, he turned on his heels and began making his way back to the small house his mother and Elaijah had lived in for most of Rankor's life.

As he did, he prayed to his Godly ancestor, Arto, that Elaijah would already be asleep by the time he arrived. He would need a fair bit of privacy to ease the fire Arabella had left behind.

Wicked, beautiful woman.

CAMILLA
WITCHES' PURPOSE

Camilla stared at the wall in front of her, choosing to look anywhere else than at her grandmother's reflection in the water bowl in front of her crossed legs.

She wondered if she could simply blow out one of the candles, sever the communication spell, and blame it on an open window. Maybe if she chose the candle on the far left, her grandmother wouldn't be able to notice her doing it.

"Are you even listening to me?" Alina hissed through the water.

Camilla sighed and turned her attention back to the bowl. "Of course, grandmother."

Alina huffed. "I don't understand what's taking so long, Camilla. You've been inviting the prince to your bed for weeks now and yet there doesn't seem to be any indication that he might consider engagement?"

"Perhaps he's looking for more in his future wife than just a willingness to have sex?"

Her grandmother rolled her eyes dramatically. "Nonsense. He's a man like any other. You *need* to do this, Camilla. I have fought tirelessly to gain respect for our family throughout the years. It's time for you to step up and support our line. I'm losing my patience. Get the job done."

Her grandmother's image faded from the water bowl instantly, and Camilla fought the urge to throw the dish across the room. It didn't matter to Alina that Camilla didn't particularly *want* to sleep with Clay. It didn't matter that she'd only ever seen Clay as a friend and hadn't ever felt any sexual desire for him. Alina only cared about one thing: status. She saw her granddaughter only as a tool to help her gain more.

Camilla stood and began trying to clean up the remnants of the spell as her thoughts wandered briefly to how she got herself into this predicament. She'd barely been seventeen when she'd first proposed moving to the castle full-time. Like many girls approaching womanhood, she had been desperate to escape home. She was so desperate, in fact, that she didn't even stop to question why Alina had agreed so readily. She'd just considered herself lucky and happily moved into Lorelai's suite. That had been her first mistake.

The idea of living in the castle had seemed magical at first. She'd be with her friends all the time, she'd be able to go to all the parties and balls, and, best of all, she *wouldn't* have to be on the receiving end of her grandmother's anger anymore. On the surface, it was everything she wanted.

And the first few months living in the castle had, in fact, been magical. She'd spent every free second with Iris and Lorelai, laughing and getting into trouble, her bruises from her grandmothers beatings faded, and she finally had the freedom to explore her powers freely without the pressure to do the spells and incantations that her grandmother wanted her to learn.

But then she'd turned nineteen.

Her grandmother had sent her a gown to wear to her birthnight celebration. The dress had fit her like a second skin and its shimmering emerald fabric had brought out the color in her eyes. The neckline was dangerously low over her breasts and the slit had stretched high on her hip, leaving quite a bit of her tanned skin on display. Lorelai had struggled to find kind words to say when Camilla had initially tried it on for the first time, and Iris had only laughed and insisted that Camilla must be 'trying to get lucky for her birthday.'

Turns out that had been her grandmother's exact plan. And, for the most part, Alina's plan had been successful. Camilla had just ended up catching the attention of the wrong Dragon.

The next morning she'd woken with a card shoved under the door of the suite she and Lorelai shared, inviting her to the Dragon's private office. Lorelai had dismissed it as him just wanting to wish her a belated happy birthnight, but Camilla was well-aware of the Dragon's reputation by then.

She went to his office painfully aware of what was about to happen and she came back a changed woman.

She became one of his favorites after that. He was known to have three or four women at a time that he would choose as his favorites and keep them on a constant rotation. Still, he showed a particular preference for Camilla. As sick as it was, part of her had always wondered if that was because he knew she was friends with Clay. He seemed to always have some weird need to ruin anything that brought Clay joy.

Still, it wasn't so bad after a while.

Camilla knew how to take terrible situations and make the best of them. Eventually she learned that if she acted the way the Dragon wanted her to - if she dressed the way he liked, said the things he wanted to hear, did the things he wanted to do - then she could at least manipulate the situation to benefit her. After a few months, he gifted her a private suite in the castle, larger than what was typical of a bloodline that wasn't known for being particularly powerful, and absolutely unheard of for someone who wasn't somehow in service to his majesty. She was gifted with gowns and jewels. Sometimes, she would just return to her suite with bags of coins.

Her grandmother even seemed... happy. Somehow, the old woman convinced herself that the Dragon would make Camilla his new queen. The thought had been as laughable then as it still was now. The Dragon cared about bloodlines as much as Alina cared about status. There was no way he would get rid of his perfect Dragon Queen who had given him three perfect Dragon daughters in favor of his Hypatian whore. Camilla had just let the old woman think what she wanted.

Until it all stopped.

Eventually, the Dragon got bored with her and stopped sending invitations. She got to keep all the stuff he had gifted her along the way and no longer had to deal with his perversions. Win-win.

The only downside was that her grandmother's delusions about joining the royal family only got worse. Alina set her sights on the Prince instead, hence the near constant communication spells demanding *updates* on how things were progressing.

After everything Camilla had been through, having to provide regular details on her sex life to her grandmother might have been one of the worst.

A knock on the door sounded and Camilla sat the spell supplies down on her dining table to answer it, running her hands through her long, dark hair to muss it slightly. She pinched her cheeks to bring color to them and pulled down the neckline of her sheer nightdress.

There was only one person who would come to her room at this hour of the night.

And there was only one reason he would do it.

She opened the door slowly, taking the time to wrap her fingers around the frame and gaze up at him through her lashes.

Clay looked a bit ragged. His perfect hair was out of place and he didn't even bother to look at her before he pushed past her into the room and reached to pull his shirt off.

Straight to business then.

Camilla fought the urge to sigh as she followed him into the bedroom.

"Hello, your grace," she greeted him. "What's got you so intense and broody?"

"I am not broody."

She laughed. "You're always broody. It's one of your most identifiable personality traits."

The look he shot her was venomous, filled with equal parts of love and distaste.

That was the thing Camilla's grandmother didn't understand about her relationship with Clay. They had been friends, sure, but she was far closer to Iris, Lorelai and Kent than she had ever been with Clay. They were the kind of friends whose relationship primarily consisted of bickering. Alina insisted that the best relationships were often born out of the passion that followed hatred, but Camilla knew that wasn't what was happening here. There were no romantic inclinations lingering underneath their sarcastic barbs.

"Iris has been called to service."

Camilla's bitter heart sputtered slightly.

The Orders missions didn't always end in death and murder. Officially, after all, they were considered spies. Everyone in the kingdom knew the truth about the Dragon's little pet project, though. They were a group of assassins. If Iris had been called to service, it meant she was being sent to kill someone.

"Where?" Camilla demanded, her voice surprisingly sharp. "Who?"

Camilla and Clay rarely talked much during these nighttime visits, so there was an air of awkwardness as he sat shirtless on the edge of her bed and looked at her. She was painfully aware of how visible her body was under the barely there fabric of her nightgown and felt the urge to slide on a robe from her dressing room.

She didn't, though. Clay had already seen all she had to offer and her grandmother would be furious at hiding her most "convincing offerings" from his view.

"Eagirton, I think." Clay ran a tired hand over his face, his own discomfort visibly obvious. "The details are unclear."

"When does she leave?"

"She already did."

"What?"

She had obviously known the day was coming when Iris would be called into service. Their group of friends had been mentally preparing for it since the day Iris joined The Order, but she had never expected that it would happen with no warning. She hadn't even had the chance to say goodbye. What if something happened? What if-

"Camilla, I really don't want to talk about it."

Her attention snapped back to Clay. Of course, he didn't want to talk to her about it. He was just as worried about Iris as she was, and he didn't come here for words of support or to talk through his feelings. Clay came to her for a distraction. So, that's what she would be for him.

She went to him, rested her hands on each of his shoulders, and sat herself in his lap. His hands roamed over the curve of her ass almost instantly, lifting the hem of her dress and seeking the warmth of her skin. Bowing his head, he pressed his mouth to the hollow of her throat, eager to move things along, and she released a small, somewhat disingenuous, feminine whimper.

"Let's not talk anymore then," she whispered, and she pushed his shoulders until he fell backward on the bed, pulling her with him.

And thus, all speaking ceased. They kissed and moved together until Clay fell asleep next to her. Camilla thought of Iris' safety throughout the entire night, but in the silence after Clay had dozed off, she couldn't help but think about how much life had changed for all of them. Gone were the days of hanging out by the lake after a long day of lessons.

The lives of each of her friends had changed. They all had responsibilities now that were pulling them in different directions.

All of them except Camilla.

Camilla's only purpose was getting Clay to fall in love with her.

She hugged her knees to her chest as she looked over at the Prince. Deep down, she knew she would never marry him. Or rather, he would never marry her.

So what else did she have to offer the world?

KENT

The Beacon

Kent hadn't been prepared for such a sudden trip home, but when he'd gotten Seralyn's message, he had dropped all of his other responsibilities without a second thought. It was quite unlike him to leave so suddenly, in fact. Kent was the kind of person who liked plans, so much so that he abided to them to a fault at times. It was one reason he'd been a good leader in the army, though. Kent thought through everything meticulously, made effective plans, and carried them out without deviating from their structure.

There was only one person in this realm that could make him abandon that need for rigidity.

He'd spent the morning packing what he needed into sacks that he could easily attach to his horse's saddle. It wasn't much. He only needed enough clothing to get him through the short trip. He would likely be gone for no more than a week. Long enough to greet his mother, check in on his sisters, and watch the love of his life get married to someone else.

His stomach had been twisting since he'd read the wedding invitation.

It had been years since he'd seen Seralyn, long enough that he'd grown into a man since the last time they'd been in each other's presence. In truth, he should have known this day was imminently coming. Seralyn was beautiful after all, and well-liked, talented, easy-going. It had really only been a matter of time before some other man from their village asked for her hand.

Still, when the messenger arrived inviting him to the wedding of Seralyn Mercer and Jaxon Tried, his heart had damn near fallen out of his stomach.

He didn't even know Jaxon. The army had recruited Kent when he was so young that he remembered little of what his life had been like in the village. Flashes of memories would occasionally come to him. The grime that would coat his father's hands when he returned from a day at the fishing docks. The smell of his mother's freshly baked bread. The way his sisters would reach for each other in their crib. Everything else was a bit of a blur.

Everything except Seralyn.

The memory of her had always been perfectly clear in his mind.

She'd been his first friend - his only true friend in that small fishing village. He had spent his mornings walking to her family's cottage near the dock to greet her before school and had spent his afternoons roaming the village streets with her, looking for trouble to get into.

Seralyn had always been everything he wasn't. She was outgoing, while he was reserved. She was boisterous, while he was quiet. Perhaps it was that contradiction that pulled them to each other. She had been a beacon to him, and he'd been drawn to her long before he ever knew what attraction or love could feel like.

When General Brigham had arrived at his house seeking a Siren for the army, Kent had known he had no other choice than to agree to go with him. Kent's father had died a few years prior, and his mother had worked tirelessly as a seamstress since. No amount of long hours was enough to bring in the coin she needed to support three children, though. The army offered Kent a chance to make sure his mother and sisters never had to go without dinner. Even at just twelve years old, he'd known that without his father, it fell to him, as the man of the house, to take care of them. So, he'd agreed to go without a second thought.

Still, leaving Seralyn that first time had been gut-wrenching. He'd brought her to a small oak tree on the outskirts of town to tell her he was leaving, and her big, beautiful brown eyes had misted over with tears. She'd launched herself at him, wrapping her small arms around his neck and kissing him.

That had been his first kiss.

Those first few years of training for the army had been intense. Academic lessons were constant, sleep had been limited, and physical training was brutal. He lost himself in it completely, but along the way he found Clay and Rankor and they'd become his brothers in those early days in the training barracks.

It wasn't until he was sixteen that he got the first chance to take leave and return home for a visit. His sisters had grown in that time. He'd left behind toddlers and came back to children with more life and energy than he'd expected. His mother looked miraculously younger than when he had left her, the stress of having to provide for them no longer weighing her down.

And Seralyn... well, Seralyn had changed too. Her short, straggly, auburn hair was suddenly long and shining, hanging neatly past her now sizable breasts. As a girl, she'd been cute. As a woman, she was now undeniably shapely. When he'd gone to visit her cottage and she'd stepped into the warm sunlight and greeted him with a familiar smile, his blood ignited.

That had been the first time he'd known what it was like to *want* a woman.

By then, the Great War was in its height. He returned to his station, pent up with sexual frustration. General Brigham had seemed impressed at how his trip home had reinvigorated him, not even suspecting that it was lust that drove him to become more aggressive and ruthless in battle. Rankor had urged him to bed any barmaid or nurse that was willing to help ease the burden of his desire - the Gods knew Rankor had no problem taking partners - but each time Kent even looked at another woman, all he could think about was Seralyn.

The army gave Kent clearance for leave again the year after and he went to her immediately, desperate to spend as much of his week long break by her side.

When he went to her then, he found she had changed once more. At nearly eighteen, she was more rebellious than he remembered. She'd taken him to a tavern, stolen two bottles of liqueur and led him to that same oak tree. As they laid in the grass staring at the midnight sky, she demanded to hear story after story of what the rest of Athenia was like and what he'd seen of war. When he finally ran out of stories to tell, they sat in silence until she announced she hated she had spent her entire life in that village and never traveled more than a few yards from its borders.

Then she'd pressed her lips to his, guided his hands to her breasts, and let out a soft mewling sound that had hardened every part of him.

That had been the first time he'd lain with a woman.

In the morning afterwards, he had woken feeling more complete than he ever had, but when he turned over to kiss her, he found himself alone under that oak tree.

He rushed to her home only to hear that she and her mother had gone to visit her aunt and would be gone for several days.

As he found himself on the front lines once more, though, replaying the memories over and over of what it had been like to move inside of her, he had questioned if that night had meant something different to her than it had to him. To him, Seralyn was his light. She was the face he saw in his mind when he felt convinced he couldn't continue fighting any longer. For him, that night had been the culmination of years of desire and emotion.

And even though he wanted to look back on that moment in time as pure perfection, he questioned whether that night had been born out of a special connection between them or if it was just another way for her to seek adventure in an otherwise monotonous life.

The Peace Treaty went into effect shortly after that visit home and in the war's aftermath, the army promoted him to general. Clay's mother had just died, Iris' parents had fled the country, Rankor's nightmares woke him nearly every night, and the Dragon had just started calling Camilla to his chambers in the evenings. His new family had needed him more than Seralyn or his mother and sisters did.

So, he didn't ever return home.

He wrote to his mother, sisters and Seralyn regularly in those years after the Great War ended. But while his mother and sisters always responded to him, eventually Seralyn stopped responding. So he stopped writing to her. He found companionship in other women and moved on with his life.

At least that was what he had thought.

So why did the announcement of her marriage feel like a blade straight to his heart?

Kent knew he had no place at that wedding. He knew that the best course of action was to send his regards and to remain at his post at the castle. Clay and Camilla had told him as much when Kent had shown them the invitation.

Still, after all these years, Seralyn was his beacon, and she was calling him home.

LORELAI

FORBIDDEN ROMANCE

The countryside of Athenia really was quite beautiful in the spring. Each year, right when the flowers bloomed, Lorelai traveled from the castle to her family's summer estate to spend a few weeks tending to property and preparing for her annual Spring Soiree. She didn't typically enjoy traveling much, and otherwise stayed close to her home in the castle, but there was no denying that venturing to the edge of Athenia while the air turned warm and the earth came alive with a rainbow of flowers and foliage was one of the few times in her life that she felt truly alive.

Usually, at least.

This year, however, was different.

This year she had been in the middle of testing cake flavors for the party, which her favorite pastry shop had personally delivered, to her when four messenger birds had all arrived somewhat simultaneously.

Turns out her friends weren't able to come to this year's soiree.

Rankor needed to help his younger brother settle into a new home. Kent was traveling for a wedding. Iris was busy with *confidential business,* and Camilla's grandmother had insisted she stay at the castle with Clay.

Lorelai had other friends, of course. Her Spring Soiree was always the most widely attended event of the year - outside of the palace balls, of course. But what fun is it to have a party when the people you actually cared about seeing couldn't come?

And so, for the first time in nearly a decade, Lorelai had cancelled her party.

She'd spent nearly two days moping about it. After she sent out the notices that she was cancelling the event, she locked herself inside her family home, sent away all of her help, and spent her days eating all the delicate sugared sweets she'd bought for the event. She'd even spent nearly two hours simply staring at the dress Ruthie had made her for the soiree.

Oh, it was a beautiful dress.

When she'd seen the lovely lilac color of the fabric, she knew it was absolutely perfect for the soiree, and then she and Iris had hunted the market for the perfect shimmering crystals and gems to adorn it. Lorelai had designed the entirety of the gown herself. The gauzy fabric hung off one shoulder and fell in waves of tulle to the ground and Ruthie had arranged the gems across the bodice to appear like sparkling flowers.

Gods, when Ruthie had given it to her, Lorelai had just sighed happily and thrown her arms around the small woman, ignoring when the seamstress grumbled in protest.

And now no one was going to see it!

Without the party to look forward to, Lorelai's house had been too quiet, too lonely. So she'd packed away her gown, sure that she would find some other event at the castle to wear it to, and ordered for her carriage to be brought around.

"Miss Pelland," the stable hand protested. "We were not planning for you to depart today. The carriage is not fit for riding."

Lorelai frowned as she looked at it. "It has four wheels. The curtains appear to be clean. The horses have been watered. How is it not fit for riding?"

The stable hand, Gentry, was an older man. He'd been working at the Pelland estate since Lorelai was just a little girl, and he had long since become accustomed to Lorelai getting her way. Still, he ran a tired hand over his face as she propped her hands on her hips and motioned for her trunks to be loaded into the carriage.

"We try to inspect your carriages before long trips like this," he explained. "For safety's sake."

Lorelai waved a hand at him dismissively as she lifted her skirts and crawled into the carriage. Gentry was simply operating under her father's guidelines, and her father was nothing if not overprotective of his darling daughter. The carriage was brand new though - purchased from the finest craftworker just last summer. Her father had spent more than an adequate amount of gold on it, so there was nothing to worry about.

"The carriage will be just fine, Gentry. I do not wish to stay alone in this manor any longer. I'm quite sure the gardens at the castle have started to bloom by now, so we cannot delay. It's been years since I've been able to see the palace gardens at their peak and if I must miss my annual Spring Soiree, then I might as well get back home to the castle immediately."

Gentry's hand wrapped around the carriage door as she went to shut it, effectively stopping her. His hazel eyes bore into hers with such intensity, she almost had to suppress a shiver. "It's not just that, Miss Pelland. You sent away much of the staff. We don't have enough men to accompany you."

For the briefest of moments, Lorelai felt a sliver of doubt, but she pushed it aside just as quickly. She'd made the journey back and forth from her manor to the castle dozens of times, maybe even hundreds, and there had never been any problems. She'd never had a carriage break, and she'd certainly never run into any bandits. Gentry was worrying himself for no good reason.

"If I cannot convince you to stay a few days longer, then at least allow me to accompany you," Gentry pleaded.

Gentry was nearly her father's age, but while her father had spent his life living in luxury, Gentry had spent his days working hard. Even though his hair had grayed around his ears, his chest was still broad and his muscles still strong. He was an air weaver, not a strong one, but powerful enough that his presence would be a comfort to her.

With a small smile, she nodded at him. "Very well."

Gentry's lips parted into a relieved smile and he stepped away from the carriage, closing the door tightly before approaching the driver to share that he would be joining them. Lorelai leaned back onto the plush purple chair of the carriage and opened the book she'd been flipping through for the past few days. It was an entertaining enough story, a romance about a gallant knight who managed to steal the heart of his princess. Lorelai was a sucker for forbidden love stories.

Perhaps that was because all of her own love stories had been forbidden to her.

She had always been quick to love. All it took was a single longing glance and she would fall helplessly. She adored the rush of it. She craved the tingling energy of trying to discover if they returned her feelings. She dreamt of the moments after a first kiss when the world seemed to shift until all that mattered was the person standing in front of you.

And yet, none of her loves had ever lasted.

She had only ever felt affection like that for other women, and her father had absolutely forbidden it. Lorelai wasn't held to the same marriage restrictions as the Council. There was no law saying she *had* to marry another Truthseeker, and yet her father insisted on it. He was the patriarch of their House, by far the most powerful Truthseeker in the country, and he refused to pass off that power and status to someone else. He wanted Lorelai to take his place, and then he wanted a grandchild to take hers.

It had happened twice so far that he'd happened upon her and one of the women she had developed feelings for. The first time he'd been gentle in explaining why she could never engage in that kind of relationship. The second time, he'd been less forgiving. Lorelai had fallen head over heels for a cook named Amarani who worked at her family manor. Within days of finding them pressed together in one of the dark halls of the estate, he fired Amarani and made sure that no other home within the nearest twenty miles would hire her. Amarani had to pick up her life and leave, and Lorelai hadn't seen her since.

The coach door opened once more, distracting from her thoughts, and Gentry climbed in. He had to practically hinge in half at the waist to climb in because he was so tall, and as he sat, he balanced a somewhat rusted sword on his lap. He noticed her glancing at it and gave her a bashful smile, rubbing a hand over the back of his neck.

"It's been some time since I've needed to carry a blade on me," he explained.

Lorelai gave him a reassuring grin. "Well, I'm confident that our journey will go entirely as planned, with no difficulties, so I doubt you'll even be needing it."

Gentry banged fiercely on the wall three times and Lorelai heard the faint sound of the whip cracking outside before the horses started trotting and pulling the carriage along. They bounced slightly as they went along the uneven dirt road, but she hardly noticed, far too accustomed to it at this point in her life. Gentry was silent as they went, staring out the window and holding his body in stiff attention. Lorelai stifled the urge to chuckle behind her hand and turned her attention back to her book, content to lose herself in the story buried within its pages.

"Let us hope, Miss Pelland."

IRIS

BECOMING THE BIRD

I ris hated The Order's dungeon.

The area where the Crown kept its prisoners at the castle was clean, well-kept. The Order preferred to keep their dungeons a bit more... antiquated.

The Order had constructed the dungeons deep underground, where not even the slightest beam of sunlight would reach a prisoner, leaving the space unbearably cold and damp. They threw the prisoners into cells with nothing more than a dirt floor and a single bucket. The location of the dungeons was one of the closest guarded secrets in the kingdom. Only the members of The Order knew exactly where they were. It was a secret that they had carefully kept for decades.

At first it had seemed odd to Iris that The Order had dungeons separate from that of the palace, but she'd learned quickly that the difference between these dungeons and those at the castle were in their purpose. This wasn't a place that people were sent to serve time as a punishment. No one who was sent as a prisoner to this place ever left.

As she climbed down the steep staircase, she had to go slowly, her feet constantly threatening to slip out from under her with each movement.

The air was frigid, but she didn't dare shiver, not when Walric, the leader of The Order, was with her.

Walric was strict with his initiates, never failing to remind them that any sign of weakness would get them killed. He had been close with her father when her parents lived in Athenia, so Iris suspected he had a soft spot for her deep down. On the day she'd shown up in The Order's wing of the palace asking to sign her name to the seal of intent he had looked at her with such disappointment it had nearly been enough to convince her to turn around and return to where she had come from. Nearly.

Since then, he'd shown her no mercy. He wouldn't start now.

"We've gotten a great deal of information from the prisoner," he said as they walked. "Some we knew already."

"And my task?"

Walric grinned at her over his shoulder. It was easy to identify him as a member of The Order. Even if he didn't have their insignia embroidered into the breast of his doublet, it was clear in the way he carried himself. Walric always stood tall, even though he already towered over everyone else around him. His dark eyes scanned every room he entered and his hand never strayed from the sword strapped across his hip. He had long since shaved the hair from his head after having it once pulled during a fight and now had inked an enormous eye onto the skin on the back of his head.

Staring at it always left Iris feeling uncomfortable, and she supposed that was the intent. The message was obvious. He was watching you even when you didn't think he was.

"The Duke wasn't the most forthcoming with the details of the attack, claimed he had a foggy memory of the details because of a blow to the head. His men apparently found the prisoner in the fields behind the manor, running towards the house after the assailants had already left with the Duke's wife."

"You said we know of her already?"

He nodded, beckoning for Iris to walk ahead of him as they reached the bottom of the staircase. She saw it for the test it was. He wanted to be sure she was checking her surroundings, looking in each cell, assessing every inch of her landscape before stepping into it.

"Her name is Joliette. She's the daughter of the Serpent."

Iris hissed a gasp through her teeth. The Serpent was an infamous leader of one of several gangs that ran rampant throughout the country. While The Order had been quick to eliminate the poorer organized groups that popped up in the more impoverished areas of Athenia, the Serpent's people were meticulous. They were ruthless, of course, but they were smart too. With more money and influence than they should have, they had been impossible to completely locate and exterminate.

Worse than that, his rivalry with the gang leader known as Nikolai Legum had caused far too many deaths of innocent people. The capture of Joliette offered a genuine opportunity to finally end the reign of the Serpent.

Although that raised the question of...

"We find it a bit odd that the Serpent may have been involved in a simple robbery at a Duke's manor," Walric mused, giving voice to the thoughts in her head.

They slowed as they approached the thick steel door at the end of the hall. Its twisted handle was reinforced so much that only the strongest members of The Order could even push against it and move the lock out of place to open the door.

Walric opened it for them, grunting as he pushed it wide, and stepped aside to allow Iris to enter first.

She hadn't bothered to change out of her court dress before coming to the dungeons and she frowned slightly as the emerald fabric of her skirts caught on the muddied floor. Sighing, she bent to lift the hem off the ground before turning her attention to the center of the room.

Joliette sat chained to a chair, her head lolled back and her bottom lip swollen and bloody. Shallow cuts ran over the expanse of her arms and chest, some of which had scabbed over and others of which were still dripping fresh beads of scarlet blood. Her midnight hair was damp, sticking to her pale forehead, and her dark eyes trailed Iris' movements as she walked into the tiny room The Order reserved for torture.

Her father might be a snake, but Joliette has the dark awareness of a raven.

"My Gods." Iris chuckled as she raised a hand to pinch her nose. "You do not smell fresh, my dear."

Joliette's face flashed with disdain as her thickly accented voice rang clear through the room. "*You* are who they have sent to break me?"

Walric stood at the door to the room, thick arms crossed against his chest. He didn't bother to respond to Joliette and Iris knew it was because he had officially handed off the responsibility of Joliette to her. This was officially her mission now.

"I'm not here to break you," Iris sighed, wishing there was a clean space in this room to sit or lean against the wall. "You see, my colleagues and I understand that not everyone can be broken. We are, after all, trained to withstand any manner of interrogation ourselves. So, when we see that level of tenacity in someone else, we respect it, and we adopt alternative strategies."

Iris didn't miss the way Joliette flinched suddenly and bit down on her inner cheek. The girl was afraid. She seemed young, perhaps only nineteen. As the daughter of the Serpent, she had likely been treated as well as royalty for most of her life.

Which meant this steely expression of hers was nothing more than an act.

Iris let her gaze roam over the injuries that painted Joliette's skin. "That sure looks like it hurts. I think about it sometimes, you know. How I'd like to die, that is. Not that I want to die, but we all have to at some point, don't we? Anyway, I think I'd like to die propped up in my bed wearing the most incredible gown you've ever seen. I want my friends to be there too. And I know everyone says they don't want people to cry when they die, but I think I do. I want all the tears. I want to have such an amazing personality that people simply can't imagine their lives without me in them."

Joliette sighed dramatically. "Do you intend to break me by all this yapping?"

"I'm simply saying that of all the ways to die, death by a thousand cuts is probably one of my least favorites."

Her eyes widened slightly at the realization of what they were doing to her. The Order had long since decided they wouldn't get the information from her they wanted. Those cuts up and down her arms weren't an interrogation tactic anymore... they were a means to an end.

"I would take a thousand more cuts if it meant I no longer had to hear your voice."

She grinned wildly at the venom in Joliette's words. "Oh, thank the Gods you have a bit of spunk to you. I was actually quite worried you'd be boring or quiet."

Walric cleared his throat softly behind her and Iris sighed, annoyed at being rushed through this. This conversation might seem frivolous to him, but it was actually quite useful to her. She had already learned that Joliette was a terribly frightened little thing, but hid that behind a false sense of bravado. She had a tendency to widen her eyes just so slightly when alarmed, and her left finger had a nervous twitch. Her voice was generally low-pitched but rather melodic.

"It would seem my friend here agrees with you that I talk too much."

"I will tell you nothing!" Joliette insisted.

"I know, dear. That's why we're no longer asking you any questions. We're resorting to alternative methods, as I said."

This girl really wasn't paying attention. Not that Iris could blame her necessarily. This situation had to be terribly overwhelming for the poor thing.

Joliette failed to fully suppress the shiver that ran down her spine. Try as she might, the sound of her chains rattling against the metal of her chair was undeniable.

"Now for the fun part!" Iris smiled.

This was dirty work to be sure, everything The Order did was drenched in blurred lines of morality after all, but she could never feel bad about the feeling of magic that rushed over her skin as she willingly loosened her grasp on her form and let it mutate. The sensation was indescribable. There was a moment of utter weightlessness as she and the surrounding air melded into one single specter before her bones lengthened, before her skin lightened, before her hair straightened and darkened into that same dark hue of Joliette's. Her lips flattened slightly, her breasts shifted, her hips narrowed. Joliette's figure was lengthy and petite. For a moment, the utter foreignness of it filled Iris with a sense of dizzying confusion before she felt herself adjust to her new identity.

This is why The Order had wanted her in their ranks. This was what she could offer them.

"Demon!" Joliette hissed, eyes wide.

"Demon!" Iris echoed, forcing her mouth to curve and her voice to hitch in the same slight accent. She turned to Walric. "Not too bad for a first attempt?"

He grunted. "It'll do."

That might be the closest thing she would ever get to a compliment from him. A smile tugged at the corner of her lips. He liked her. He didn't want to admit it, but she knew he did. She glanced back at Joliette as she left, feeling an overwhelming sense of pity for the girl.

Joliette hadn't asked to be born to the Serpent, and now here she was paying for his crimes. It was too late for Iris to save her from what The Order had planned for the girl, but she could at least make Joliette's death meaningful. She could eliminate the Serpent and save countless lives in doing so.

Iris' steps faltered as Joliette's haunting laughter suddenly echoed around her.

"You think you are prepared to be me? You have no idea what he will do when he finds you."

Iris glanced over her shoulder at Joliette. "I'm going to kill your father."

Joliette only laughed harder.

Admittedly, this wasn't the best plan that The Order had ever come up with. Since they didn't know the Serpent's location, though, they had little to go on. And so, they'd dropped off Iris, now parading as Joliette, in the woods surrounding the Duke's estate. She'd donned the dress Joliette had been found in, a frilly thing made of folds of white lace that was stained with mud and dried blood. The gown had surprised her when she'd first seen it. In her brief interaction with Joliette, she'd imagined the girl in more of a darker colored ensemble.

Still, she put on the gown, mussed her hair, and set about roaming through the woods with nothing but the hope that she would stumble upon someone who would recognize her and escort her to Joliette's father.

Her hope turned to pessimism, which turned to frustration after her first few hours of stumbling through the woods. And then the rains had started. It was the kind of downpour that only came in the early days of spring, one that soaked through your clothes until you were sure that even your bones felt the droplets pelting down against them. She tolerated the wet clothes just fine, but it was the feeling of dampness in the soles of her shoes that nearly drove her out of her mind. That and the coldness of it all.

After a while, she found a small tree stump that was just shaded enough by some of the foliage above to protect it from some of the rain and sat upon it. She let herself give way to the shivering that threatened to overcome her and lost herself to doubts about whether joining The Order had been the right move after all. She was only a few hours into her first mission and was already feeling like a failure.

That was when they found her.

Strong hands wrapped around her, one over her mouth and one around her waist. Her instinct pushed her to throw her weight forward, hook a foot around the ankle of her attacker and push him over her shoulder, but she suppressed the urge, adopting Joliette's persona with false bravado instead. She thrashed against the arms so intently that the hand around her mouth slipped.

"Get off of me this instant!"

She was acutely aware of the sound of shuffling leaves and heavy steps behind her. She'd guess four, maybe five, additional men. Her assailant ripped at her arms, tugging her so intently that her feet tangled in her dress and she stumbled ever so slightly as he spun her to face the others.

"Well now," a voice over her shoulder called. "What a pleasant surprise."

Hands ripped at her, spinning her around so violently that she fell forward onto her knees. From the ground, she lifted her head and suppressed the urge to shudder when she finally looked up and met the hazel eyes of Nikolai Legum.

Iris' heart beat wildly as she took in the sight of him. She'd seen drawings of his likeness before, of course, but none had done him any justice.

He was positively beautiful in a steal your breath and leave you feeling entirely off-balance kind of way.

Nikolai was remarkably tall and lean figured, wearing crisp leather trousers and a thin grey tunic with the sleeves cuffed over his forearms. Golden rings adorned each of his fingers, which rested easily on the golden scabbard of the blade strapped to his hip. His hair, a dark copper, hung in gentle waves over his ears and curled just so slightly under his sharp jawline. When she met his gaze, his lips twitched into a crooked smile.

"I've found my little bird," he said.

LORELAI

TRUTH & LIES

The ride back to the palace was long. Lorelai lost herself inside the pages of her book for a few hours and when she flipped over the last page and read *The End,* she sat the book next to her and closed her eyes, content to listen to the sounds of the birds chirping outside. At some point, the smooth motion of the carriage must have lulled her to sleep, because she woke sharply when a bump in the road sent her head bouncing against the carriage wall.

Numbly, she rubbed the injury on her head as she blinked and took in her surroundings. It was darker than she had expected. Could it be night already? She frowned as she listened to a steady patter against the windows, rhythmic and oddly comforting. Rain. She hadn't been aware it was meant to rain.

"Have we almost arrived?" She asked, clearing her throat to shake off the hoarseness that lingered in her voice from sleeping.

Gentry was pale, looking out the window with an intensity that left Lorelai uneasy. Quickly she reached across herself, pulling the window curtain back and peering out to glance upon the woods.

That wasn't right. The road back to the palace should have taken them through villages and fields.

"The main road flooded," Gentry explained, as if reading her mind. "We had to go through the woods."

A shiver of fear ran up her spine as Gentry's hard eyes met hers. His gaze was sharp and accusing and if he wasn't in her employ, Lorelai was sure he would have some strong words for her. He had warned her not to travel too suddenly. From the start, he had suspected something would go awry, and she had pushed them to travel anyway and now they were miles away from her home stuck traveling in woods that were known for bandits.

She forced her breathing to steady. "You will lose your hair with all your worries, Gentry. Everything will be just fine."

He only glared at her before turning his attention back to the window, but it was as if she could hear his thoughts echoing in her head.

Who are you trying to convince?

They rode in silence. Gentry focused on the world outside and Lorelai picked at her nail beds. It was a bad habit she had picked up in childhood that she had never quite gotten over. As a child, she often chewed on the tips of her fingers, much to the ire of her father. Now, she only picked at them in times of stress.

Surely they wouldn't have to spend too much time on this forest road. They had to be close to the castle by now. They'd already been riding for hours, after all. Lorelai sighed and shook her shoulders out, releasing tension as she did. Gentry was worrying about nothing. Worrying was what he did best, after all. The chances of danger striking them were so slim they were practically nonexistent. Lorelai was confident that within the hour she would be resting in her bed at the castle, drinking warm tea and reading a new book. Everything would be just-

The carriage jerked to a halt so suddenly that she lurched forward and only Gentry's quick hand on her shoulder stopped her from crashing face first onto the bench across from her. His grip was firm, almost painful.

"Why have we stopped?" She demanded, already moving to look out the window, but Gentry's strong grasp held her back. She buckled under the weight of his hand as he pushed her sharply to the ground.

"Stay here!" He ordered, climbing over her crouched body to pull open the door of the carriage and step out.

The door slammed shut behind him, bouncing slightly before it latched closed, and Lorelai remained frozen on the ground for only a moment's time before she pulled herself up to peek out the pale pink curtains. Gentry stood just outside the carriage, his back to her and his hands on his hips, as he looked out into the woods. A gentle breeze lifted the hair by his ears, but otherwise all was still. The only sound was that of the slowly falling raindrops against the roof of the carriage.

Until an arrow whizzed through the sky, piercing through the flesh of Gentry's shoulder. The blow sent the larger man spiraling to the ground, groaning his pain, and Lorelai clutched a hand to her mouth to stop from screaming.

They came from the darkness, dressed in black with cloths tied around their necks and pulled up to hide their faces. The bandits approached with such viciousness and ferocity that their band might as well have been an army. She tried to count them, but they moved so quickly they practically blended into the night air around them.

Her coachman had climbed down from his bench to join the fray, pulling his sword before the sounds of metal clashing filled the air. Gentry stood, fighting off two of them from reaching the carriage, even with his left arm completely immobilized by his injury. Blood seeped down his shoulder, staining his ivory doublet with a crimson so dark it was practically black.

An arrow flew through the air, slicing through the glass of the window and shattering it as Lorelai ducked, just barely covering her head as the arrow flew over it. She scrambled to the other end of the carriage, ripping down the handle to push open the door and fall out of it. The skin on her palms tore as she plopped on the muddied road, catching herself on sticks and rocks. The pain was sharp, but all she could focus on was the sounds of Gentry's howls and the echoes of laughter around her.

They were going to kill him.

Years ago, she'd learned about different reactions to stressful situations. She learned some people faced danger head on by brandishing their weapons and running straight at their foes. Others let their fear carry them away from the danger. Still others remained frozen, just watching it all play out in front of them.

Lorelai's friends were the type to face the danger and fight their way out of it. Iris would slice through enemies with blades that moved faster than the eye could see. Clay would breathe fire. Rankor would smash his fists into heads and faces. Kent would simply sing everyone asleep. Even Camilla, whose powers were limited, would become a more fearsome version of herself, stabbing and maiming everyone in sight. But Lorelai wasn't like the others.

Lorelai had always been the type to run, and so that is what she did. She lifted her skirts underneath her and fled into the darkness of the woods.

She let her feet fall heavily as she moved through the forest, darting between trees and under low-hanging branches. The warm weather had made the brush thick, and it ripped at her skin and dress as she ran. Her breath came quickly, her chest pounding unhappily as her legs began to protest the exertion.

She didn't even know where she was running or to whom. She only knew she needed to get away.

After what felt like an eternity, her body finally gave out and she collapsed against the weight of an oak. Rain fell steadily around her, the trees providing little protection from it. The weather had soaked her clothes through, and they clung to her clammy skin. She pushed her dripping red hair out of her eyes with one hand while bracing herself against her knees with the other.

Only when she finally felt like she could breathe again, when the shock of what had happened settled in and the pain of her injuries suddenly registered, did a sob rip through her.

She covered her mouth, her brain telling her to stay quiet but her heart demanding a release of the pain and fear that was building inside of her. What was she going to do? Gentry was certainly dead, and her driver likely was, too. She didn't even know her way back to the main road, let alone back to the castle. Those bandits were out here, somewhere, and they would give her a fate worse than death if they found her.

A cramp pinched her side, and she rubbed at it numbly, trying to work up the confidence to keep moving. She had to keep moving.

"And who do we have here?"

An arm darted out, wrapping around her waist and pulling her back sharply against a firm chest. Instinctively, she wrapped her fingers around that meaty arm covered in coarse dark hair as she screamed, but his grip was unmovable.

"Shh," he cooed, covering her mouth under his palm. "Why don't you just calm down? There's no need to make this difficult."

Lorelai couldn't see his face, but she didn't need to. She could tell by his blood-covered fingers, worn muddy boots, and the putrid stench of ale-lined breath and body odor that he was not here to help her. Her stomach locked in an icy fear.

"Relax darlin', I won't hurt you."

Lorelai's magic sparked instantly. A shudder raced up her spine as nausea filled her stomach and her fingertips tingled.

Lie.

"You were in that carriage, weren't you?" He whispered, his hot breath sticky against her neck. "I'll help you."

Lie.

She screamed, the sound of it muffled from his hand over her mouth, and thrashed in his arms. There was nowhere for her to run now, so, as much as her instincts were pushing her to flee, she was going to have to fight. She threw her weight into him, striking out with all of her limbs.

His arms tightened against her, holding her still. The hand on her mouth disappeared for a moment and her blood-curdling shriek echoed around them, only to be silenced when he placed a blade tightly against her throat.

"Hold still," he hissed.

"Please," she whimpered. "I can pay you. I have coin-"

A gurgling sound cut her words off. Her attacker's arms released her, and she spun, desperate to both understand what had happened, and to step out of his reach.

The man was tall, with oily hair and dark eyes that were now glazed over and glassy. The knife in his hand fell to the ground as he sputtered, blood leaking from his lips.

He fell, body thumping heavily on the ground.

As he did, the woman behind him pulled her own blade out of where she had lodged it in his throat. Her ice blonde hair was folded away from her eyes in two precise plaits. Like the bandits, she wore black, but her clothes were fine, made of thick material suitable for fighting. Lorelai had spent enough time around wealthy warriors to know that clothing like that cost quite a bit.

The woman wiped her blade on the man's clothing before tucking it into a belt strapped across her waist. She turned her sparkling blue eyes, flecked with gold and ringed with the richest brown, to Lorelai.

"Men," she huffed, her voice shockingly... cheery. "The world would be better off without them."

She extended her hand and Lorelai instinctively shuffled backwards. Her dress, heavy from its dampness, and torn around her ankles, caught under her feet and she fell backward. The woman darted forward, grasping onto Lorelai's waist and holding her steady.

"Whoa there," she cautioned. "Careful."

"Who are you?" Lorelei's voice shook.

The woman grinned. "Call me Helena. I saw what happened to your coach back there. Sorry about that. I can help you get home if you want me to. I won't hurt you, I promise."

Her fingers tingled once more.

Truth.

RANKOR

A Man and His Sheep

Elaijah squealed like a small animal as the bucket of cold water washed over his sleeping body. His arms flailed wildly before his thrashing left him falling off the side of the small cot that he slept on. Rankor watched it all with his eyebrows raised high and his hands held on his hips.

"What was that for?" Elaijah demanded, shoving wet hair out of his eyes to glare up at his brother.

"The sun has been up for hours and you're still in bed."

"*And?*"

Rankor wondered if this was a common occurrence for Elaijah. Were village boys permitted to just sleep the day away? Rankor had grown accustomed to rising at the brink of dawn. When he was Elaijah's age, training in the army barracks, oversleeping often meant a verbal, and at times, physical thrashing.

And yet here was his own brother, staring up at him as if he had done something wrong by daring to wake him.

"And I do not wish to spend *my* day wondering what you're dreaming about," Rankor spit out, hating the sudden rush of emotion that filled him as he looked down at his brother.

He opened the drawer of his brother's wooden dresser and tossed him a tunic. Without another word, he left the small shack Elaijah and his mother had lived in to wait outside by where he had tied the horses to the fence post.

Elaijah would be irritable when he discovered Rankor's plan for him. That was fine. Elaijah could hate him for all he cared. He wasn't here to connect with the boy. He only needed to ensure there would be someone to care for him, and then Rankor would be on his way.

The village was alive and bustling already. People crowded the streets on their way to and fro. Their eyes constantly looked to Rankor, only to turn away when he returned the favor. Sighing, he turned his attention to grooming the large chestnut steed he had bought for himself. He couldn't blame the villagers for being suspicious of him, he supposed. He was one of them, and yet he wasn't. He was the child of a mortal woman who had spent her entire life in this single village; but he was also the child of a Descendant of Arto, and because of that, he had taken him from this place as a boy.

This was his home, and yet he would never really belong here.

He was ready to leave, anyway. Rankor had spent longer in this small village than he had ever anticipated. And after months of traveling the country, he was ready to return finally to the castle and to his friends. It had been months since he'd seen them. His plan had initially been to return to the castle in time for the Athenian Peace Celebration. Iris and Clay needed his support on that day. Now he'd be lucky to get back in time for the Peace Ball.

All because of a lanky fifteen-year-old boy who was currently stumbling out of the house with what looked like a nasty hangover.

"Drink this," Rankor commanded, shoving a canteen towards Elaijah. He'd already spent most of the morning packing as much of the boy's belongings as he could inside the saddlebags that he'd attached to their horses. The pouch strapped to his hip had plenty of dried meat and cheese for the both of them.

"Where are we going?" Elaijah asked, scanning over the horses while rubbing his temple.

Rankor didn't bother to answer him and instead focused on strapping a wide arrangement of blades and daggers onto his person. His swords, which he had named Truth and Pain, sat on the small lopsided table in the front lawn. He grabbed them both quickly, tucking one into the scabbard on his hip and the other into the strap across his back.

"Will you need all of those?" Elaijah eyed the weapons with skepticism and what looked like a bit of disdain.

Truthfully, Rankor hoped he wouldn't need them. Regardless though, when he had left the castle all those months ago to explore the edges of Athenia, he had made sure he had plenty of weapons to protect himself if he happened upon any rabid animals or worse. There weren't many of Ciclopia's beasts left in the world, but he didn't want to stumble upon one without being armed to the teeth.

No need to scare the boy, though.

"Why don't you focus more on mounting your horse and less on my weapons?"

His younger brother peered up at him with an expression of pure frustration. For a moment, Elaijah reminded him of Clay. When they were young boys, back when his mother had still been alive, Clay had been, in a word, spoiled. He was the darling prince. His every wish came true. On the rare occasions that he heard the word *no*, his rage would be insurmountable. As a Dragon, he was prone to temper, as a Prince he was prone to temper tantrums.

Elaijah's expression was quite similar to the one Clay would have shown before one of his childhood meltdowns.

"Do you need help to mount the horse?" Rankor deadpanned as the boy stood unmoving. "I can lift you. Easily."

Elaijah bared his teeth as his upper lip curled in irritation, and Rankor had to stifle his grin behind a hand. Without another word, the boy turned, stuck his foot into the stirrup and launched himself onto the smaller white horse Rankor had purchased.

"Her name is Sunbeam," Rankor told him, offering an apple slice to the horse on his open palm. "Treat her well and she'll get you where we're going."

"Which is?"

"To Uncle Clydric. He'll be looking after you from now on."

"I don't need anyone to look after me," Elaijah protested. "I'm a man and I'm perfectly capable of watching over my land and tending to my sheep."

"It's too bad I sold your sheep."

"*You sold my sheep*?!" Elaijah's voice reached a pitch that was remarkably un-manly. Rankor pulled his steed ahead so that his brother wouldn't see him chuckling, though he suspected the boy could see his shoulders quivering.

"How dare you sell my sheep! You had no right!"

"Mother asked me to make sure you are taken care of." Rankor shrugged. "Therefore, I am exactly within my rights to do what I must in order to ensure that you get settled into your new home and Uncle Clydric will need some coin to keep you. It was the logical decision."

They rode in silence for a few minutes, leaving the limits of the village without a single goodbye. Rankor didn't feel guilty about leaving without visiting Arabella one last time, they often parted ways without any formal goodbyes, but part of him wondered about Elaijah. Would he miss anyone from this small life he had led for the past fifteen years? Was there anyone he needed to exchange goodbyes with?

"Those sheep were my friends," Elaijah said softly, almost to himself.

Rankor traveled onwards and supposed he had the answer to his questions.

CAMILLA

PREMONITIONS ARE A WITCH

Camilla sat frozen at the cherry-wood dining table of her suite, staring at the box that a staff member of the palace had delivered earlier in the morning. She'd unpacked it quickly after it had arrived, not realizing who had sent it and her heart had fallen through her stomach when she recognized the things that were tossed into the box.

Her grandmother was determined to ruin her life.

A fucking fertility spell. Alina had sent her a fucking fertility spell in a box.

Did it matter that Camilla wasn't ready to be a mother? Did it matter that she didn't think she ever wanted children at all? No, obviously not.

Apparently Alina had decided that if the Prince wouldn't come willingly, they would just have to give him a reason to commit himself to Camilla. A baby was as good a reason as any.

Fine.

It wasn't like she would have to raise the damn thing. The Dragon had sent away Clay's sisters for school, after all. Camilla's child would be a royal at best and a royal bastard at worst. Either way, it would be well-provided for. Camilla could just have it shipped off and never have to acknowledge its existence.

She lifted the box and carried it into the room she'd converted into an altar room when she moved into the suite. With a match, she lit the candles that lined the walls. There were purposefully no windows in the room. Candlelight was better for the magic. Otherwise, the room was fairly bare. Greenery and plants filled the corners, and she had pushed a small wooden chest holding all of her usual spell ingredients against the far end of the wall. A likeness of her ancestor, Hypatia, hung on the wall, the Goddess's black eyes somehow tracing her movements across the room.

It was a poor excuse for an altar room. Her grandmother would hate it. Truthfully, Camilla's spells had never been all that successful, regardless of where she was casting them. Her mother had been a mortal and while Camilla had been born with just enough Godly blood to leave her with Hypatia's Mark on her ankle, it wasn't enough to make a strong Witch. Since moving out of Hypatia estate and into the castle, she hadn't much need for spell casting.

Until now, apparently.

She grasped a handful of salt and poured it into a circle on the floor before pulling out the candles needed. White for new beginnings, green for fertility and growth, pink for love. Seating herself in the center of the salt circle, she placed a candle to her left, behind her, and to her right, lighting them each in turn. The last addition to the setup was the large aquamarine crystal that she placed in front of her.

For a moment, she stared at that crystal with pure hatred. Her grandmother has always been stingy with the family crystals. They intensified spells tenfold, so Alina kept them stowed away in Hypatia manor. She only gave them out as a show of her favor, or, in this case, to be used towards her own ends. That she had sent Camilla the crystal meant she was serious about this spell being successful. She wanted Camilla married into the royal family and would stop at nothing to make it happen.

The stone was a powerful protective crystal, known for helping the Witch using it to achieve balance and clarity. Witches lucky enough to have one in their possession often used them for stress relief. When used in a fertility spell, though, they protected the baby, to help the child find safety in its new home and protect against any misfortune over the nine months it was carried.

Aquamarine would ensure the pregnancy would hold until the baby was born.

With everything set up, the only thing left to do was the actual spell. Sighing, she pulled out the last items from the box: a bowl, an egg, a fig, and a blade.

"Hypatia, hear your daughter's call."

Ever so gently, she cracked the egg, draining its contents into the bowl and setting aside the shell, careful not to further crack it.

"Delia, Goddess of Pregnancy and Children, hear this Descendants call," she intoned, drawing the blade across the fig to slice it open.

With her fingers, she gently scooped the seeds and dropped them atop the egg. She placed the rest of the fig into the eggshell, holding it until she felt the skin of the fig press into the shell.

"Let this token be the child of my womb."

Setting aside the token, she pressed the tip of the blade against her finger, wincing slightly as a bead of her blood welled against the steel. She dipped the bloodied finger into the bowl, stirring three times until her blood mixed with the seeds and egg, ensuring that she would become fertile and receptive to pregnancy.

"As these two become one by my blood," she whispered, the words falling out of her mouth even as her soul protested. "May you, Hypatia and Delia, bring life to me."

The feeling of a spell taking root was indescribable. Magic rushed over her, like a blanket thrown heavily atop her head. She felt the weight of it settle over her, foreign and still comforting, until it somehow soaked through her skin, filling her with its power and promise.

It was done.

Folding the token into the cloth of a hex bag, she carried it from the altar room, leaving the candles to burn out naturally. The sun had already begun to set and darkness was filling her suite. That was the one thing she didn't like about this suite. It was at the wrong end of the castle. It didn't matter what time of day it was, she simply never seemed to have sunlight pouring through her windows.

Camilla tucked the hex bag under the pillows atop her bed, knowing that Clay would arrive shortly and from there, it was only a matter of time until she was pregnant.

She froze suddenly, magic sparking in her gut with an uneasy premonition. Premonitions among Witches were rare, and nowhere near as clear as the visions of the Psychics of Athene, the Goddess of Wisdom. Camilla herself had only had one once before, the morning she'd gone to the Dragon's office with a certainty that he was going to hurt her.

She felt that same certainty now.

Great change was coming.

C lay didn't come to her room that night. He also didn't come to her room the night after. On the third night, she'd paced the space unhappily. The spell wouldn't last much longer. She had one night left to bed him before she would have to contact her grandmother and explain her failure.

That was a conversation she sought to avoid.

In an attempt to keep her mind from getting too anxious, she focused on preparing herself for the evening. She'd combed out her dark hair until it shined and fell softly around her in waves. She'd recently realized that Clay liked when women wore their hair loosely. In one of their brief conversations after sex, he'd mentioned that he liked her hair like that, and that he hated how all the women at court insisted on wearing their hair pinned back elaborately.

She'd massaged a smoothing cream over every inch of her skin and sprayed a perfume of vanilla over her chest and wrists. After lining her eyes in kohl and smearing a rosy hue over her lips, she'd picked a nightgown. It was the thinnest she'd owned, sheer green with tiny sparkles sprinkled throughout the fabric. It hung low over her breasts and stopped at just the tips of her thighs.

It was positively indecent.

Not a terrible choice for a woman trying to seduce someone.

Gods, she hated that thought. Camilla pulled a silk robe over herself and stared at her reflection in the mirror with disgust. She hated that she was doing this. She hated that Alina was forcing her to-

A knock at the door sounded, and she squealed softly, somehow caught terribly off guard by his presence.

This was what she had wanted.

She could do this.

One night. She just had to get through this one night.

Clay's eyes were down-turned as she opened the door and took him in. He must have had a formal engagement. He still wore his ruby encrusted crown around his golden hair. His doublet was fine, black with golden trim.

"Look at you," she grinned. "All dressed up for little old me?"

He met her eyes briefly, only to push past her into the room as he did most nights. Although, instead of immediately turning left towards the

bed as he typically did, he lingered at the dining table. Clay sighed heavily, running a hand over his jaw.

He was upset.

That was just fine. Usually, when he was upset, their engagement together was short. When he was upset, he was usually quicker in seeking what he wanted from her, which meant he was quicker in leaving her.

She went to him, reaching out with her fingertips to trace the skin along his fingers gently. It was a trick she had learned from his father, actually. The skin there could be quite sensitive when applied with just the gentlest amount of pressure.

Clay pulled his hand from hers, using it to rub out the back of his neck. "Camilla-"

"Shh," she pushed him to sit on one of the wooden chairs and began rubbing out the muscles of his shoulders.

Gods, he was tight. What in all of creation did the Prince even do with his time? At some level, she understood he likely was very busy running a kingdom, but Clay had always been so vague about how he spent his days. It had always kind of annoyed her, actually.

"You're stressed," she noted. "Let me help."

"It's not that. I actually came here to talk."

Her fingers faltered slightly. He came to *talk?* Clayton Vail never came to *talk* to her. What could he even have to talk about?

No.

No, no, no. Surely this wasn't him trying to let her down easily?

"What?" she managed to choke out through the panic that was nearly suffocating her.

This wasn't possible. It couldn't be. She couldn't let him leave her. Especially not tonight! Her grandmother would never forgive this and the potential punishment was simply too terrible to imagine.

Camilla's thought swam with rushed plans, as she tried to work out the next course of action. If she could just convince him to stay one more night, this could still work out. One more time was all she needed for the spell to take hold. Maybe she could convince him to take her right here on this table, in a last goodbye.

She could do this. She knew how to get a man succumbed to the heat in his loins. Camilla just had to trust on the skills she'd spent painful years learning.

She let her expression shift into one of a challenge. She pouted her lips, flicked her eyelashes, raised her brows. In that moment, she was a picture of seduction, and when she untied her robe and traced her fingers across her collarbone to pull aside the fabric to reveal the indecent nightgown underneath, she knew the effect her body would cause. There was victory in looking to his trousers and seeing that knowledge confirmed.

His eyes sparkled golden, the light in them shining so brightly it made her shiver. His gaze trailed her body, lingering at the crux of her thighs.

"You don't want to just talk to me," she whispered.

He didn't even bother to hide where his attention was. Clay might be a prince, but he was still just a man like any other.

"No, I don't," he admitted, before his eyes lifted to focus on her face once more. "I think it's time we end this... arrangement, though."

She wanted to scoff. Arrangement. That's the word he had given this?

Her mind was a mess, thoughts darting rapidly in one moment and entirely freezing the next. What in all of creation was happening? Why did he suddenly feel the need to end their *arrangement?* Surely this relationship was every mans dream! He got to fuck her whenever he wanted. He got to walk into her suite, bend her over, and leave without ever having to talk to her about feelings or offer her a dance at the palace balls.

Camilla damn well knew this was what men wanted.

This was all they had ever wanted from her.

"You want to stop this?" She couldn't hide the hardness in her voice.

"Camilla, I think it's for the best to end it now before things progress any further."

"Why?"

He frowned, as if the question was difficult to understand. "Why?"

Gods, did he have to be so obstinate! She fought the urge to allow all of her frustration to show on her face. She knew that wouldn't be attractive to him, but she needed to save this, and he wasn't making it easy for her. Tomorrow, after her spell had worked, she could allow him to end this *arrangement*, but tonight she needed him to be swayed to his urges. Tonight she needed him to let go of that control he always clung to so tightly.

"Why the change of heart?" She pressed. "I thought we were both having fun."

Clay looked away, heaving a sigh. "That's how you would describe this? Fun?"

"Obviously," she lied.

"Fun as it might be, we both always knew this would be temporary."

"What happened to you?" she demanded, needing to know what poison had seeped into his mind to turn him away from her.

Clay ran a hand through his hair, turning away from her quickly before facing her once more. "There was a Council meeting earlier. One in which I was very plainly reminded of the commitments and responsibilities I have as the Crown Prince. Camilla, we both always knew this would be temporary. Don't you think it's best that we return to our friendship before things get any more complicated?"

A wild laughter bubbled inside her and she swallowed it down. What friendship could ever exist between them now? This situation was already unbearably complicated, and she was running out of ideas for keeping this conversation going, for changing his mind.

In the back of her mind, she heard her grandmother's voice. She knew what Alina would tell her to do in this situation.

Whatever it takes.

Gods, when this was over and she had birthed the royal baby, she was demanding the woman gift her jewelry with the biggest diamonds this side of the world had ever seen *and* a collection of her own personal crystals.

Once more, she sought to distract his attention. She pulled the straps of her dress to the side, letting the nightgown fall off of her until she stood bare in front of him.

Camilla was not ignorant of her body. Her breasts were sizable, the kind that many women at court tried to replicate with tightened corsets and bodices stuffed with cloth. Her tan skin was smooth, unblemished. Her stomach was flat. Her hips were wide enough to catch the eye, but narrow enough to still be attractive.

No one had ever referred to her as unseemly.

Holding his eye, she pushed herself onto the wooden table. At this height, they could do it right here, while he stood. He could push her backwards, wrap his fingers around her throat, and slam into her over and over until they both came apart. He'd done it before, in fact, right here on this very table. She knew he would do it again.

"Let's talk after," she suggested, reaching out to grab his hands and pull them to her.

She placed his hands along her hips, letting him feel her bare skin under his touch before arching slightly back before him.

Clay was utterly still, jaw locked and shoulders tense, but there was an undeniable longing in his eyes.

Just give in. Just say yes.

Please.

"We're better off as friends," he finally ground out, ripping his hands away from her. "I hope we may remain that way."

Bending, he picked up her robe and passed it to her, avoiding her eyes like a fucking coward. Camilla ripped it from his grasp, folding it around herself even as she felt her heart shattering inside her.

He had no idea what punishment he'd just subjected her to.

"Get out, Clay," she muttered.

He had the graciousness to simply nod and leave before the hot tears began rolling down her cheeks.

She'd lost him.

She'd lost a second Dragon.

Her grandmother wouldn't forgive it a second time.

Camilla tore through her suite, screaming as she went. She'd left the altar room untouched after she finished the spell. The candles had burnt out, of course, but they were still in place. The salt circle was still untouched and the crystal still sat in the center, taunting her.

She kicked at the salt, scattering it on the floor around her. She swatted the candles. She tossed the bowl until the egg mixture dripped down the walls. And when there was nothing left but her grandmother's precious aquamarine crystal, a vicious roar tore through her as she threw it against the wall, feeling nothing but emptiness as it shattered into tiny shimmering pieces all around her.

A sob ripped through her as she sank to the floor, crystal shards digging into the skin of her bare legs. Camilla sat on the floor of her altar room for what felt like an eternity, crying until there was nothing left in her. Only then did she find the strength to pull herself up, open the door of her suite and demand the attention of one of the maids darting throughout the hallway.

"Yes, miss?" The girl curtsied, appearing terribly uncomfortable to have been stopped. Her hair was a dull brown, lighter than Camilla's. Her skin, too, was lighter and her eyes blue. She was unremarkable in every way.

"I seem to have made a mess in my altar room."

The girl nodded her understanding. "Of course, miss. I'll clean it up right away."

Camilla pointed towards the altar room and watched as the girl dipped her head and scurried into the suite. As she went, Camilla couldn't help but notice that there was something about the girl, perhaps the tilt of her eyes or the shape of her mouth that seemed somewhat... familiar.

IRIS

Ruby Red Danger

They'd blindfolded her first, then bound her hands together. Then they'd guided her until the sounds under her boots were less and less like those of feet against fallen branches and more and more like leather against a worn road. A musty scent caught her attention, indicating horses nearby. The arm that had been pushing at her back disappeared for a moment, and in its place, two hands firmly gripped her waist and lifted her onto a horse.

Before she knew it, a warm body was behind her, wrapping around her as the steed trotted forward, and Nikolai's voice was in her ear.

"Admittedly, I knew capturing and containing a wild bird like you wouldn't be easy," he whispered. "But I had expected to make it through our wedding night before you tried running off back to your father."

Nikolai Legum had married the Serpent's daughter!

Joliette's words traveled back to her. The girl had laughed as Iris left, swearing that she had no idea what he would do when he found her.

She hadn't been referring to her father.

Iris' mind was spinning, piecing together bits of her conversation with Joliette and the reality that was now in front of her. Nikolai and Joliette had married, and she had run away back to her father. Had she not wanted the wedding? Is that what he meant by saying he had captured her?

Fuck. Iris had gotten herself in far deeper danger than she could have possibly planned for.

She chose her words carefully, mimicking Joliette's accent. "Your expectations were wrong then."

His laughter in her ear was deep and tantalizing and his hand on her waist traced slow, lazy circles. "He will be so disappointed to hear I have taken you once more. My men tell me he has an army out searching for you."

So she was a captive then. A pawn in the war between the two of them.

And yet something about this didn't quite make sense. If Nikolai had captured the Serpent's daughter, why choose to marry her?

"Why not just kill me?" she tested.

"What's the fun in that? It will be much more rewarding when your father realizes that his only daughter is now my wife. That his legacy will be nothing more than you carrying my children."

He squeezed at her waist just as he nipped playfully at her neck, and she stiffened her back to pull away from him.

"Burn in the Underworld."

"Not just yet, bird."

Nikolai's arm around her waist pulled her back to tuck her against him again as they rode and she didn't bother fighting against him. She felt too preoccupied. Her mind was spinning, working to piece together the jagged pieces of information that had to fit into a consistent story somehow. Nikolai captured Joliette, forced her to marry him to spite her father, and then she had apparently run from him.

Which would, Iris supposed, explain why she was running *towards* the Duke's estate when the Duke had found her.

Although, the fact that she was running towards the house also implied that she knew the Serpent would be attacking it. So the attack clearly had to be well-planned far before when it actually happened.

"You're quiet," Nikolai noted, squeezing her waist once more before his fingers started idly running back and forth over her dress.

Iris wanted to cut each one off individually.

"Perhaps I am simply counting the minutes until I can get off this horse and away from you."

He laughed, the movement pressing his chest even closer to her back. "Keep counting."

They rode for what felt like hours before the horse finally slowed and Nikolai started shouting orders about watering the steeds and preparing a meal. She felt him dismount from the horse behind her before feeling him grab hold of her and pull her down, holding her close to his chest longer than was necessary.

She ripped away from him.

She had been prepared to play a role when she put on Joliette's face. She had adopted the girl's accent and mannerisms just as The Order had trained her to do. But in this, at least, she did not have to pretend. She and Joliette shared the same amount of disgust towards Nikolai Legum regardless of how breathtakingly beautiful the man may be.

He laughed at her as she stumbled back and pulled at her arm before she could ram into the horse and startle it.

"There now," his voice cajoled her, and she felt his fingers graze across her cheek. "Try not to get yourself into any more mischief."

She felt the removal of his presence, heard his steps as he walked away, and listened to him shout she should be escorted to her rooms before a tight hand grasped her arm. Instantly, she knew it wasn't Nikolai. He might have been a bastard, but so far he'd been gentle with her. With a hiss, she ripped her arm from the man's grasp.

"Do not man-handle me! I can walk just fine."

He snorted, but she felt a gentle push against her back, nonetheless. Wordlessly, she marched forward.

They left her blindfolded as they went, but it was no matter. The Order had trained her for things like this. It was forty-three steps before her boots stepped onto stone, then another twenty-two before the wind on her cheek stilled and she heard a door swing open to let her into the building. One hundred and thirty-one steps before a left turn, eighty-four before a right turn, thirty-six before a left turn and then six before a door was opened again.

The hand at her back pushed slightly, and she stumbled forward, nearly losing her footing and falling completely.

"Welcome home," the gruff voice laughed before the sound of the heavy door falling shut echoed and the lock clicked into place.

Iris pursed her lips unhappily. He could have at least bothered to untie her hands before locking her away.

No matter, the metal bangle on her wrist concealed a small razor, and she'd been subtly tugging on her wrists since the moment they were bound in order to loosen them enough that she could slide out the razor and slice through her binds.

She let the rope fall to the ground as she tugged off her blindfold and looked wildly around her. The room was surprisingly... beautiful.

Iris rarely enjoyed gothic decor, but there was something undeniably warm about the space. The ceilings were remarkably high to account for the eight-foot windows cut from elaborate arches. Intricate woodwork and carvings covered every inch of the furniture, from the enormous wardrobe to the massive bed frame to the chest at the foot of the bed. Dozens of lit candles sat scattered across the expanse of the writing desk and end tables, settling a warm glow over the room.

She trailed through the room, running her fingers against the fabric of the duvet before she stepped through a door that led to an equally impressive dressing room. Gowns and gowns and *gowns* hung around the walls. There had to be dozens of them. All the latest fashions and the finest fabrics, some even nicer than what she saw some of the wealthiest women of court wear.

Her attention turned to a large mahogany dresser and as she pulled out the top drawer, she couldn't help but grin at the sparkling jewels that laid waiting for her. Rubies, emeralds, diamonds. Who said a life of crime didn't pay well?

Iris pulled out a gleaming necklace that held five rubies the size of her knuckles, each wrapped in diamonds, and held it out to examine it.

"Well, at least he has taste," she mused to herself, not hesitating to clasp it onto herself and turn towards the vanity and looking glass on the far wall.

She nearly jumped at seeing her reflection there, still not adjusted to Joliette's face greeting her.

"Hmm."

Iris turned, returning to the bedroom once more. Part of her longed to examine the books organized on shelves above the desk, but she knew that her time alone might be limited.

She had more important things to do. Like trying to find a weapon.

To be fair, she wasn't entirely defenseless. The pins in her hair had been an invention of her own creation. They were thin enough to fold into hair easily, but thick enough and sharp enough to be wielded as miniature daggers if needed. Still, she wanted something more formidable, if possible.

The bathing room contained some perfumes and towels, nothing sharp. A second glance at the dressing room showed her nothing she hadn't already noticed, other than the drawer that contained clothing meant for a male that she wanted to rip apart. The drawers in the writing desk offered only parchment and kohl pencils, nothing that could cause any actual harm. The chest at the foot of the bed contained nothing more than winter cloaks and extra blankets. Sighing, she stood with her hands on her hips and debated her options.

The candelabra by the window, made of bronze and likely heavy, caught Iris's attention. It would do for a bash over the head if need be. Perhaps there was a belt of some sort in the dressing room that could help! Iris was nothing if not resourceful with her weaponry. She was just about to go investigate when the door opened once more and she spun to face Nikolai.

"Should I be surprised that you managed to escape your bindings?" he mused, looking over her.

It was simply wrong for a man as deplorable as Nikolai to be so hand-some. He'd changed into clean clothes and the stiff structure of his black jacket sharpened the angles of his jawline, bringing attention to the fullness of his lips, which were turned up playfully. His copper hair had been combed and tied back neatly and he smelled fresh.

"Are the rooms to your liking?" He asked, walking in and settling him-self in the armchair across from the bed.

Iris watched him cautiously as he did, not daring to relax her guard around him. Which only earned her a soft chuckle from her captor.

"After the wedding, I had wanted to bring you here, but as you know, things moved quickly."

She nodded. "So they did."

He ran a hand over his stubbled jaw. "You don't trust me."

"You're keeping me prisoner."

"You're my wife."

"I was kidnapped, forced into marriage against my will, and locked in a room. Sounds more like captivity than marriage."

His eyes danced, never leaving hers. "You seem different. When my men first captured you and brought you to me, you seemed... smaller somehow."

Iris bristled. Was it possible she had misread the fire underneath Joliette? Was she playing her role wrong? "Yes, well, perhaps being detained for a second time has only made me irritated."

Nikolai tilted his head to the side as if he were considering her words before nodding and making a move to stand. Her instincts pushed her to step away as he invaded her space, but she didn't dare give him the satisfaction. Silently, he moved closer, so close that he was only a breath away from her. So close that a single step closer would have his body pressed against hers.

He smelt of the woods on a cold winter's night when snow was just beginning to fall and he towered over her. He filled the space entirely, in fact. What had once been a beautiful and grand room seemed altogether small with him in it. Gods, was she dizzy? She took a shuddering breath in and he smiled, obviously having noticed it.

"You still didn't tell me if you like the room."

"It's dreadfully dark and depressing," she lied, hating how raspy her voice sounded.

What kind of spell was she under? Whatever it was, she needed to shake herself out of it, and fast. Iris was here for a reason and she couldn't let herself forget it simply because she got distracted by an attractive male.

Nikolai's hand grazed the skin under her collarbone, lingering there for a moment too long. The feel of his ice cold skin against hers was jarring. "You seem to at least appreciate the jewels."

She had forgotten she was wearing the necklace.

"One day." His voice was soft, as if he were speaking more to himself than he was to her. "I'd like to see you with these jewels and nothing else."

Iris moved to stomp on his foot, but he stepped aside too quickly for her to manage it.

"That day will never come," she spit out with venom.

He laughed as he pushed past her to the door. "Oh, I think it will, my darling bird. I think that day will come sooner than you're ready to admit to yourself."

Iris reached for the pillow that rested on the armchair he'd been seated in only moments earlier, content to lob it at his head. Nikolai caught it one-handed and discarded it effortlessly.

"Dress for dinner," he commanded. "I have some associates coming and you will attend."

"I will not!"

"Yes, you will," he growled, his playful expression hardening into something more akin to frustration. "Whether you like it or not, bird, you live here now. You are not a serpent any longer. You are *my* wife now. You live under my roof and under my protection. So, you will sit by my side and you will smile as you do so."

"And if I don't?"

He was in front of her in an instant, grabbing her by the chin and lifting her face to meet his gaze. Iris didn't hesitate to slide out the razor in her bracelet, her entire body poised to attack.

"This is me showing you kindness. I have gifted you a room, gowns, the jewels you did not hesitate to decorate yourself in. Do not mistake my kindness for a sign that you live without consequences here. There will be no more escape attempts. You won't be flying away from me this time."

He released her and strode to the door with firm, purposeful steps, leaving her reeling and slightly off balance.

"I'll send a maid along to help prepare you. We dine in an hour."

He left without another glance back at her and let the door slam closed heavily behind him. Iris rushed to it, but just as her fingertips grazed the doorknob, she heard the lock click into place.

"Damn it!" She screeched, kicking the pillow as she moved to throw herself onto the bed.

As she sprawled out on the mattress, she pursed her lips, one thought ringing clearly through her mind. Before this was over, she wasn't going to just kill the Serpent, she would take out Nikolai too.

Iris paced unhappily in the dressing room, torn between her own tastes that were pulling her towards the colorful fashions and gowns of every pastel imaginable, and her instincts which were warning her that Joliette wouldn't be caught dead in anything that bright.

"It's a damn shame," she muttered, running her fingers longingly against the yellow tulle that was calling to her.

Ultimately, she ended up settling on a dark black gown with a fitted bodice covered in intricate lace and puff sleeves. The skirt was full but didn't put too much weight on her hips. She'd be able to run in it if she needed to. The maid Nikolai had sent to her wasn't accustomed to styling ladies' hair, so she simply tied off Iris' corset and left her on her own to pin back pieces of Joliette's long dark hair herself.

"We must go now, madam," the maid insisted, glancing anxiously at the door.

"Very well," Iris agreed, after painting her lips red.

The maid escorted her out of her room and down the winding hallways of the home, all just as grim and gothic as her bedroom. Iris traced her steps as she went, committing each turn and doorway to memory. It wouldn't be too challenging to pick the lock on her door. Perhaps that evening, after everyone else had lulled themselves to sleep, she'd explore. Surely, there was information here The Order would find valuable!

"We're here, madam," the maid told her, pushing open a dark wooden door and stepping aside for Iris.

The dim light of candles, hung from the two chandeliers that dangled from the coffered ceiling, greeted her. Massive paintings featuring images of the Gods or lush settings covered the dark wood paneling of the walls. The sun had already set outside, so the tall windows offered nothing but more darkness to the space. In contrast to the rather dark ambiance of the home, the high-backed chairs around the dining table were upholstered in the starkest of white fabric, and at the head of the table, surrounded by men she did not know or recognize, Nikolai stared at her.

"Joliette." His voice danced over her skin and he waved his hand towards the chair at his right. "Sit."

She did as she was told, though not before glaring at him in frustration. As she settled herself into the seat, he reached for her hand, placing a kiss delicately across the knuckles, and she fought the urge to rip it from his grasp.

The waitstaff served dinner instantly, presenting a feast of glazed duck, roasted vegetables, and freshly mashed potatoes. Iris, having eaten nothing since The Order had dumped her in the woods, lost herself in the food almost immediately. She kept her attention focused on the plate, even as she discretely listened to every word of the conversation.

"Tell me of our progress with the black opal," Nikolai commanded.

Iris suppressed the urge to frown. Black opal was a rare and powerful crystal known to have several magical advantages. Witches could use them to strengthen their psychic abilities, for example. Some even argued that a Witch using black opal could see almost as far into the future as the Psychics of House Athene, though Iris doubted anyone could rival a true Psychic. Athene's line was small, but as a girl she'd once stumbled upon a Psychic on the street who took one look at her and started screaming *Order, Order, Order...* and look how that turned out.

Witches could also use black opal to create powerful amulets that suppressed fear, enhanced creativity, or aided with emotional burdens. Protection amulets of black opal were some of the most powerful in the world. The crystal was remarkably difficult to find, though, making them not only incredibly scarce but also ridiculously valuable.

A portly man with a thick belly and flushed cheeks answered from the left-hand side of the table. "We've begun mining near the Arton mountain region in the Republic of Inanis. The project is in the early stages, but I'm quite hopeful."

"Any trouble?" Nikolai asked, sipping from his crystal glass of red wine.

"The region is rather uninhabitable because of the unpredictableness of the weather. We've lost a few souls in the process, but are continuing with the work."

"And the Inani Army?"

"A few soldiers stumbled upon us. Those that could not be paid off we eliminated."

Ice raced down her spine, both at the words and the unnerving feeling of being watched. Across from where she sat, she met the hard eyes of another man who stared at her with an expression that rivaled the way her uncle sometimes looked at her. He was dressed finely, and roughly the same age as Nikolai. Given his seat at Nikolais left, he was obviously important.

"That's good," Nikolai murmured. "Keep me updated. I have a buyer lined up already. She's somewhat of a crystal collector."

"Of course, sir."

The portly man bowed his head and turned his attention back to his plate, stuffing bits of duck into his mouth with an impressive amount of vigor. Iris watched him for a moment before turning to return her attention to her own plate, only to cross gazes with the man across from her once more. She quickly averted her eyes.

"Have we any updates on the Serpent's plans?" Nikolai asked.

An awkward hush settled over the table. The clatter of cutlery on plates stilled as all eyes seem to rest on her before quickly turning away. The man across from her cleared his throat, finally turning away from her to look at Nikolai.

"Perhaps that is a topic to discuss at a later time, Nik."

So they were on a nickname basis?

Nikolai smiled, the kind of eager, sinister smile that almost invited someone to challenge his authority. Slowly, purposefully, he reached across the table to take hold of Iris' hand. This time, she didn't pull away from him. Nikolai has promised she was under his protection. It was time to see just how far that protection extended.

"And why's that, Jace?" Nikolai asked, aimlessly tracing circles across her knuckles. She absently wondered if he intended for his touch to leave her feeling slightly unsteady or if that was just an unfortunate byproduct.

Fury rolled off of Jace in waves, clear to anyone with eyes. He turned his body to Nikolai, cemented his gaze on *Nik*. And while he seemingly ignored her completely, she still tightened her grasp on her dinner knife. She would be ready if he made a move for her.

"Why don't we ask the Serpent girl about her father's motivations?"

Nikolai stilled. "You mean my wife?"

"Nik, you must see reason. I care little for what whore you stick your cock in, but she is the *daughter of the serpent!* She cannot be trusted. Hasn't she already proven that to you?"

Silence fell. Nikolai's right hand remained in hers while his left traced circles around the rim of a water glass in front of him. His lips pursed as if he were considering Jace's words and Iris steeled her stomach, preparing herself to fight her way out of this room if necessary.

From the way he was holding her hand, it would be easy to grasp onto it and twist with just enough pressure that the bone would snap. Her dinner knife wasn't as good as a dagger or sword, but a quick swipe to the carotid was all she needed to -

Jace choked.

Softly, at first, then again, and again, and once more. His cheeks reddened. He grasped at his throat. He leaned forward, opened his mouth... and water poured forth into puddles on the table before them.

Iris shot to her feet, brandishing her knife as she watched Jace drown in front of her eyes. And yet... no one else moved. No one else reacted.

No one but Nikolai, who shot forward and grasped onto the hair at the back of Jace's head and pulled until he held the man trapped as he struggled to breathe.

"Do you know how much water the human body contains?" Nikolai asked, his voice menacing. "It's enough to drown in. And without all that water inside you? Cells die, tissues become damaged, organs shut down, even your blood stops pumping. Without water, you're nothing but a corpse."

He loosened his grip on Jace and the man fell forward, face flopping onto his plate and splattering potatoes and water around the room. Iris stumbled back, brushing the potatoes off her dress and then immediately feeling disgusted at herself for worrying about a dress when she'd just watched Nikolai murder a man.

And there was no doubt in her mind that Nikolai had done that.

Nikolai Legum was a Descendant. She knew with certainty that if she scoured his body, she would find the same Mark that her friend Kent wore on his body. Only Nikolai wasn't a Siren with the ability to read and manipulate emotions. Nikolai was a Water Elemental, and apparently an extremely skilled one at that.

He looked at her, hazel eyes scanning over her and lingering on the knife she clutched in her hand. Wordlessly, he held out his hand to her and, with shaking fingers, she placed it into his palm. It went against her every instinct to give away one of her only weapons just when the danger she was in had increased tenfold, but at this point, what choice did she have?

Nikolai placed the knife down onto the fabric of the tablecloth next to his and then nodded to her chair with an impatient expression. Iris sat and returned her hand to where his now waited for her.

"My bird?"

"Yes?"

His attention on her was absolute. "Do you care to share why your father was raiding the Duke of Eagirton's estate?"

Her stomach flopped uneasily, adrenaline coursing through her system. It nearly overwhelmed her ability to think clearly, to make a plan that would get her safely out of this situation. "I don't know. He never told me his plans."

Nikolai made a soft, inquisitive sound. "Anyone else have questions for my wife?"

There was a chorus of 'No sir' and 'None at all' before silence fell over the room. Nikolai nodded and took a slow sip of his wine and though Iris knew better than to lose her wits while on a mission, she couldn't help but pull her own glass close and drink deeply.

"I want a report of everything we know about the Serpent's plans written on my desk before the end of the night."

With that, Nikolai effectively ended the conversation. Waitstaff came to remove Jace's body from the room before bringing out plates of dessert for them and they ate in silence, though most just picked at the apple crumble absently. Iris, for one, didn't have the stomach for it. There's just something about watching a man drown that can really kill your appetite.

When Nikolai finally stood and announced that he was retiring, the others were quick to do the same. He instructed one of the staff to walk her back to her room and turned away.

She didn't hesitate to swipe the knife off the table and hide it in her sleeve when he turned his back.

KENT

YOU CAN ALWAYS COME HOME

Kent arrived at his family's home just as the sun was setting. The three days of riding had been grueling, and he was ready for a warm bed and the embrace of his loved ones. There hadn't been time to send word in advance that he would be coming due to how swiftly he had left the castle, so when he opened the wooden door to the house, he was greeted by the shrill sounds of Kressida's screaming.

"Dear Gods!" she cried, reaching over to smack him. "You nearly sent me to the Underworld!"

His twin sisters had seen just about twelve summers and were of the age where they had started trying to seem older and wiser than their years. Ultimately, they just came off as a bit dramatic.

"That's an overstatement." He greeted her with a hug, looking around the house for his mother and other sister, Kreyana.

"They're upstairs," Kressida whispered. "But I wouldn't go up to greet them quite yet. Kreyana has her bleeds for the first time, and she's being terribly melodramatic about the whole thing."

"Kressida!" Kent smacked a hand over his face and suppressed the urge to shudder. Hearing about his baby sister's *bleeds* was not the welcome home he had wanted or expected.

Kressida only giggled and motioned towards the kitchen. He followed her, leaning against the worn countertop as she set about preparing some tea. She must have learned it from their mother. The elder woman was insistent that tea was the only proper way to welcome guests into the home, and Kent supposed that's what he was. He hadn't lived in this house since he was Kressida's age. It was as unfamiliar to him as it would be to any other guest.

"You're here for the wedding?" Kressida guessed.

Kent nodded, taking the mug she stretched towards him and sipping on it gently. The amber liquid was bitter and still filled with crusted leaves that invaded his mouth, but Kressida watched him eagerly, so he smiled and nodded at her. While she may try to emulate their mother's hospitality, it would seem she hadn't quite mastered the art of actually making quality tea.

"I was invited. It's only proper to attend."

Kressida's eyebrows darted up accusingly. How could a twelve-year-old girl look so disappointed in her much older brother?

"Sure," she drug out the word sarcastically and Kent had to turn from the room before she could say anything further.

It's not that he wanted to stop the wedding. Not necessarily, at least. All he wanted was for Seralyn to be happy. If he saw her and she was, indeed, as happy as a blushing bride should be, then he would wish her well and celebrate her union.

If she wasn't, though, well, there was no harm in letting her know he could support her taking an extended visit to the castle to clear her head and consider her options.

Their family home looked the same as it always had, he noted as he walked into the living space. Worn chairs and settees sat in a circle around the fireplace, where the flames were dwindling. Blankets and quilts that his mother had expertly sewn together were tossed over the backs of the seating. The wallpaper was still the atrocious puke green pattern that he had hated growing up, though it was fraying around the corners.

The family could certainly afford to refurbish the home and stock it with higher-quality items, but Kent's mother insisted on leaving the home how it has always been. He suspected it's because she found comfort in being surrounded by the items she and his father had picked out together. As if some part of him still lived in this home they had built together.

He supposed he couldn't fault her for that.

"Kentoni?" She called, and he turned to the stairs.

"Kent!" Kreyana rushed past their mother, who stood motionless on the stairs, a hand pressed to her chest.

Kreyana crashed into him, squeezing him with surprisingly impressive strength. Unlike Kressida, who wore her dark hair in thick curls, Kreyana had arranged hers into intricate braids. Otherwise, they were as identical as always. Same oversized eyes and thick lashes, same narrow frames and moderate height.

Kressida peeled her twin off of him so that their mother could step forward and rest her hand on his cheek.

"You've waited too long before visiting, Kentoni."

His mother was the only one who ever used his full name. He'd grown up hating it and convinced it was a mouthful, but she never adopted the nickname that everyone else used with him. She insisted that was the name she gave him and so that is how she would refer to him.

Nowadays, he towered over her. Her head barely reached his shoulders, but she never failed to treat him like a boy when he visited. Her complexion was just a touch lighter than that of his and his sisters. And though she looked older since he had last been home, with laughter lines now surrounding her eyes, she was just as beautiful as ever.

"Hello, mother."

Her hug was tight, as if she were trying to make up for every lost minute with this one embrace, but Kent didn't dare complain. He could feel her shoulders trembling. From the corner of his vision, he saw Kreyana and Kressida clasp hands, both uncomfortable with their mother's tears.

These were good tears, though.

These were the happy tears that were shed when a family reunited after too many years apart.

"I'm glad you're here," she whispered, still holding on to him too tightly.

He rested his head on her shoulder, feeling like a child once more instead of a man who had lived through far more battle than he should have at barely twenty-three summers. "I'm glad to be home."

In just under an hour, their mother prepared a dinner of roasted beef with boiled potatoes, vegetable casserole, and freshly baked bread. Kent had been spoiled in his years of friendship with Clay - dining with the prince often meant indulging in dishes created by the finest chefs in the kingdom - but the flavors of his mother's cooking evoked a sense of home. It was food prepared with love, which made it the best thing he'd tasted in years.

Kreyana and Kressida took turns telling stories of the random mischief they found themselves in, and Kent was sure to laugh at all their jokes and express outrage at any potential slight they had experienced. The girls dripped in personality. Kreyana was the more reserved of the two, though not by much. While Kressida often interrupted her sisters' stories to make them seem all the more grander, Kreyana listened to Kressida speak with a gentle smile and reassuring nod.

Even though they were older than when Kent had last seen them, their bond with each other was, thankfully, still as strong as ever. The girls had lost their father and had a brother that rarely visited. At least they could always rely on each other.

Kent's mother was quiet throughout their dinner, listening intently and asking Kent about his life at court whenever there were pauses in the conversation. He felt her eyes on him constantly, scanning over him and assessing him. Every so often, she would reach over and pile more food onto his plate, as if she still felt the need to care for him and ensure he was well fed. He didn't complain.

Eventually, they moved to the sitting room and Kent built up the fire once more while telling stories of places he'd visited recently and answering questions about how his friends were doing.

"Iris was leaving the castle on her first mission for The Order when I left."

His mother perched a brow. "Nasty business for a sweet girl like her. It will change her."

"I think it's cool!" Kressida declared. "I wish I knew how to fight like an Order member."

Kreyana smacked her sister. "You cry after nothing more than a pinch."

Kent smiled at the girls and continued talking with his mother. After some time, the twins curled up together on the settee and began dozing off, and his mother returned to the kitchen briefly to bring him a chilled glass of whiskey. When she sat, she looked at him expectantly and he realized the time for surface level conversation had passed.

His mother had always seen right into the very soul of him.

"Shall we discuss it, then?" She suggested.

He sighed, running a tired hand over his face, the questions he wanted to ask burning his lips.

"Is she... happy?" He finally asked, his voice timid.

His mother looked away, staring at the fire for so long his nerves almost pushed him directly out of his seat and down the dirt road to Seralyn's cottage. Finally, she set her dark eyes on his once more.

"Seralyn is not the girl you once knew."

"How so?"

She shrugged. "As a child, you could always tell exactly what she was thinking or feeling. It was always written so plainly on her face. With maturity, she has grown to be more reserved.

Kent shifted his weight, leaning forward to rest his elbows on his knees while he spun the glass in circles in his hands. He thought of Seralyn, the girl who he had always known to be so vivacious and tried to imagine her as quiet and demure as all the ladies he knew at court. He didn't much like the thought.

"Over the past few months, she's been even more difficult to read." His mother smiled ruefully. "Especially for those of us without the magical ability to understand others so intimately."

Kent was the only Descendant in his family. It had been a genetic fluke, really. It had been generations since magic had run in his family's veins. They had long since assumed their bloodline was diluted enough that they were permanently a family of mortals. Then, Kent had been born with a Descendants Mark stamped behind his ear, marking him as slightly different from everyone else he loved.

Despite his fear of leaving home as a boy, it had been nice to finally be surrounded by others with magic. It had been nice to find brotherhood with Clay and Rankor as they too learned to manage their Godly gifts.

"And Jaxon," Kent drew out the words, hating to realize how painful they were to say. "Is he a good man?"

His mother's eyes were sharp, all-seeing. She scanned over her son with an intimate awareness of every emotion that was raging inside him. She may not be a Siren herself, but mothers didn't need magic to know what their children were going through. A mother's intuition was the strongest magic in the kingdom.

She stood and took the glass from his hand, squeezing his shoulder reassuringly.

"He's new to the village, only arrived a few months back after inheriting some land from his uncle. He seems lovely from what I can tell, but my interactions have been brief."

Kent stood, stretching his tight muscles. "It's late, mother. You need your rest."

He motioned towards the staircase, pushing her gently towards it. His old room was still waiting for him. She always left it ready for him to come home to whenever he needed to be here. She was always waiting for him.

"Kentoni," she stopped him, fingers tight on his hand. "What will you do?"

Her words dripped in intensity and truthfully, he wasn't sure of the answer to her question. What was he going to do? Why had he even decided to come to this damn wedding in the first place? What kind of masochist was he to subject himself to this kind of pain?

He'd come so far in life. And yet...

"I just have to know she's happy. I have to see that."

"Kentoni, she's not yours to protect."

He knew that. Gods, it killed him, but he knew that.

IRIS

A Plan in Motion

For the first hour after dinner, she had paced the room, thinking through her strategy. Eventually, though, after she'd turned over every course of action three times, she found herself terribly... bored.

She wandered into the dressing room again, pulling out every gown, shoe, and necklace to examine them all. Then she'd traveled to the bathing room, smelling every luxurious soap and perfume that had been left for her. Soon enough, maids came by with buckets of warm bath water for her and had filled the tub with bubbles and steaming liquid that made the entire room smell like a garden, but Iris only stared at it, unwilling to get in.

Ultimately, she'd returned to pacing.

The Order had sent her on this mission to find the Duke of Eagirton's wife, discover the Serpent's plans, and eliminate him as a threat to the security of Athenia. Now she was locked in Nikolai Legum's house with no idea how many people she was up against, where the Serpent was, or how to get to him. She was going to go down as the least successful member of The Order in history.

Although she had discovered that Nikolai was a Water Elemental, so if she did make it out of this house and back to the castle alive, at least she could provide that new information.

That was at least some consolation.

And perhaps there was more to learn here. She was still planning on breaking out of the room tonight. Maybe she'd be able to find something useful while poking around. Maybe this mission wasn't a complete failure yet.

Iris jumped at the sound of her door opening and spun, jamming her elbow instinctively at whoever had caught her unaware. Nikolai only caught her arm in his strong hand and slowly lowered it, locking his eyes on hers as he did.

"It's only me."

She scoffed. "As if that is supposed to make me feel better."

"Considering I'm one of the few people in this house who doesn't want you dead, it should."

He stalked past her, seating himself on the edge of her bed and beginning to unlace his boots, not bothering to offer any explanation for why he had suddenly arrived in her suite.

Iris rested her hands on her hips and stared at him with wide eyes. "What do you think you're doing?"

His eyebrows lifted. "Preparing to bathe after a long day."

"Don't you have your own room to do that in?"

"Yes."

He returned his attention to his shoes, apparently unbothered by her obvious frustration, and she suppressed the urge to stamp her foot. Nikolai made quick work of his laces and sat his boots neatly on the floor by the bed before pulling out his ivory tunic from where it had been tucked into his trousers.

What purpose could he have for bathing here? The hour was late, far too late for common discussions. Was he planning to sleep here?

Oh, Gods, what if he was planning to consummate their marriage? She had not prepared herself for that possibility when she embarked on this mission. Iris was committed to The Order, of course, but she couldn't bring herself to do *that*. Not with him!

She'd have to kill him. Without knowing any information about where she was or how many other people were in this house, she was going to have to just kill him first and figure the rest out after.

"What are you thinking?" He asked suddenly, pulling her attention out of her thoughts.

"What?"

"You get a crease between your brows when you're lost in thought. Were you thinking of dinner?"

"No," she answered honestly. "I was considering killing you."

She wasn't sure how she had expected him to respond to that, but she certainly hadn't expected him to throw back his head and laugh at her. She had just threatened to kill him and he *laughed*.

"You are welcome to try, little bird. You have an impressive elbow strike, I'll admit that, but I believe I've already proven I can be deadlier than that."

"Hmph." If only he knew he was talking to one of the deadliest assassins in the world.

Nikolai stood and pulled his shirt off the top of his head, walking towards the bathing chamber as he did.

"You cannot bathe here!" She cried, following him. "This is *my* room."

"It is *a* room in *my* house. I can bathe wherever I please. I'm choosing to bathe where I will be sleeping."

No. "You cannot sleep here!"

He turned to her with a playful expression as he unlaced his trousers. "Why would I sleep anywhere else than next to my wife?"

"You cannot because... because -" Iris sputtered, voice trailing as he finished the last lace on his trousers. Was he about to completely undress himself in front of her? He turned, and his pants fell, exposing an ass so perfectly tan and round that it-

"Did you get distracted, my bird?"

His voice was light and taunting as he glanced at her from over his shoulder and Iris practically screamed as she turned and closed her eyes, heat covering every inch of her body.

It's not like she hadn't seen a naked body before. Iris had seen plenty, in fact. She'd always believed in seeking your pleasure wherever you may find it. So it was only with an objective honesty that she could note that Nikolai was remarkably sculpted.

Not that it mattered.

Not that it ever could.

The weight settling low in her belly was simply a reflection of a natural inclination to appreciate beautiful things.

Damn it!

She shook her head to clear it and stomped out of the bathing room before throwing herself face first onto the mattress.

This entire process would be much easier if she didn't feel so physically attracted to the man she had to kill.

It didn't matter, though. Iris *would* kill him. She would move past it, get her job done, and go back home where she could sleep with literally anyone else she wanted to help relieve this burning tension within her.

Nikolai returned from the bathing room some time later, his hair hanging in damp waves, wearing nothing but loose-fitting trousers that hung low enough she could see the musculature on his abdomen forming two perfect dips that drew your eyes right to -

No! She mentally chastised herself.

He busied himself removing pillows from the bedding and stacking them neatly on the writing desk while Iris watched him with silent interest. He was, admittedly, quite the paradox. In some ways, he was just the villain she had imagined him to be - a criminal who killed without a second thought. And yet, he had been, so far, kind to her despite the fact she was the daughter of his enemy. It made little sense. Nothing about him made sense to her.

"You have the wrinkle between your eyes again," he noted, not even bothering to look away from his task.

She crossed her arms over her chest. "What you did... at dinner-"

"Was necessary."

Iris had no right to be upset with him over it. It was rather hypocritical considering that she herself was a trained spy and assassin here with the intent of eventually killing him. But still...

"You didn't even seem remorseful."

Finally he looked at her, hazel eyes burning as he walked to her. "I am not remorseful. I feel no regret over making a statement that was both needed and effective."

"And what statement is that?"

Another step closer.

Then another.

He was so close now that she could reach out and touch him. So close now, she could smell his soap and his woodsy scent buried underneath it. His eyes trailed over her before he reached out and smoothed her hair back over her shoulder.

"That you are mine," he whispered. "You are mine alone to criticize or punish if you jeopardize the work I'm doing, but until then, you are under my protection."

"And why would you do that?"

He grinned, a quick upturn of the lips that distracted her so much she didn't even have time to react before his arm snaked around her waist and pulled her flush against him. She gasped at the sensation of him, firm against her hips and chest and his honey crested green eyes never left hers as his hand traced down her hip to lift her thigh against him.

She should stop him. She could. She was fully capable of stopping this. And yet…

"I can't tell you all my secrets just yet, little bird." His hand continued its deadly path until he had lifted her skirt. The cold sensation of his touch against her ankle sent shivers down her spine. Unable to stop herself, she pressed against him harder. Until that hand darted into her boot, pulled out the knife she had stashed from dinner, and held it like a prize between them. "Not when you still keep so many from me."

Nikolai was gone in an instant, leaving Iris to steady her breathing as he tossed the blade out the window before sealing it shut once more. With gentle precision, he blew out the many candles on the writing desk.

"Go change into a nightgown, bird. It's time for us to sleep."

With that, he pulled back the duvet, slipped into the bed, and turned away from her. Momentarily frozen, she watched him. She watched his chest steadily rise and fall before finally stomping into the dressing room to do as he had instructed.

Three things had become abundantly clear.

Nikolai Legum was far more dangerous than anyone had originally thought.

Nikolai Legum was far more clever than anyone had originally thought.

And if Nikolai Legum didn't kill her before this was over, then Walric certainly would, because she was absolutely failing at her first mission. A mistake that The Order would not forgive.

There was, at least, one thing about Nikolai that was undesirable and it was his God's damned snoring. Not that Iris would have slept peacefully sharing a bed with him anyway, but that atrocious sound had seemed to echo throughout the space all night long. She'd spent most of the night seated in the armchair across from the bed, watching him, twirling a hairpin between her fingers, and debating her next move.

Since his presence had prevented her from exploring the home under the cloak of darkness, she'd have to find a way to snoop during the day. It wasn't ideal, but it also wasn't impossible.

What was going to be more challenging was getting Nikolai to fully trust her.

It had been late in the evening, well past the time her *husband* had fallen asleep, that she realized her flaw in thinking thus far.

Iris wanted to know what the Serpent was planning and what had drawn him to the Duke of Eagirton's estate. Nikolai, too, was searching for those answers. She had misguided herself by being so focused on killing Nikolai and escaping this house. The far better plan was to *use* Nikolai to gain the information she wanted on the Serpent. Enemy of my enemy and all that.

Which meant she was going to need to convince him she was loyal to him and only him, and he was going to need to trust her enough to be honest with her about anything he learned.

And if there was one thing she had learned from her friend Camilla, it was that you could often bend men to your will when you dangled the right prize in front of them.

She went to dress before he woke, choosing another dark dress, this one with shimmering red fabric under the black lace of the billowing sleeves. The neckline hung low, giving an ample view of her breasts, which she called attention to with a chain necklace that boasted a single droplet cut ruby that rested right at the tip of her cleavage. She pinned her hair out of her face but let it fall in easy waves down her waist before taking her time smearing kohl on her eyes to angle them seductively.

"You're awake early," he noted when she returned to the bedroom just as the sun was rising.

"I often am."

He laid on his back, an arm tucked behind his head in a way that made the muscle bulge. The duvet was pushed to his waist, exposing his entire bare torso to the eyes. She suspected he had done that on purpose.

"Interesting choice of gown."

"Is that a complaint?"

His eyes lingered exactly where she wanted them to. "Not at all."

Silence fell between them as she walked to the window to look out at the rolling fields beyond the glass. There was no identifiable landmark to help her figure out where she was.

"You have something on your mind?"

She turned to him. "I would like something."

He chuckled softly. "Have I not provided you with enough jewels and gowns?"

"I don't want more finery." She stepped forward, resting an arm against the post of the bed and angling herself so that the neckline of her gown slipped slightly lower. Nikolai pushed himself up on the bed, lifting a knee and propping his elbow against it.

"Whatever it is you want, Joliette, just name it and it will be yours."

Alarm bells sounded in her head that perhaps he'd seen through her little game. It was so rare that he called her by her name. Still, she persisted.

"I want a weapon."

Nikolai threw off the blanket with a frown. An icy chill passed in the air as he brushed by her to relieve himself in the bathing room. Iris followed him, lingering in the hallway even as he went to dress himself.

"You cannot have a weapon."

"And just why not?"

The look he sent her over his shoulder could have withered flowers. "Do you think me an idiot?"

She sighed dramatically, some of her own personality leaking out, even though she still wore Joliette's face. "And if I swear I won't use it to harm anyone?"

He stalked past her again, shrugging on his jacket as he did. "Says the woman who fled from my presence two days ago."

Well... that was a very fair point. But that had been the *real* Joliette.

"I want you to trust me."

Nikolai glared at her suspiciously as he fumbled with his buttons. With a small grin, she went to him, stilling his fingers, and beginning to button his jacket for him. He was stiff at first, but relaxed eventually.

"Why should I?" He asked, but his voice only seemed inquisitive as if he was only trying to understand her motivations rather than cast doubt on them.

She peered up at him through her lashes. "I'm your wife."

"A fact you haven't seemed too happy about."

"I'm not," she admitted, patting his chest as she finished the last button and letting her hand linger there between him. "But you've made it very clear I won't be escaping a second time. And besides, it's not like I'd even have anywhere to go."

His eyes narrowed slightly, almost unnoticeably, and she begged any God listening that he would fall for the trap she had just set.

"And why's that?"

Yes.

"My father is the Serpent. He's the most renowned criminal on this side of the Sea of Palaemon. Surely you didn't mistake him for a kind man?"

His head inclined ever so slightly as he took her in, searching for any trace of dishonesty on her face. "It is well known that your father doted on you, Joliette. Loved you."

She chuckled darkly. "Is that what you would call it? You do not trust me, a defenseless girl standing right here in front of you because of a pretty lie you've heard from your spies? You know only what he wanted you to. I know what I lived and I have no desire to return to it."

Nikolai lifted a hand to her shoulder once more, brushing back the hair there and letting his touch linger on the skin of her throat. The touch was just as sensual as it was threatening. Slowly, he leaned forward, letting his breath whisper against her ear. "Then where were you running to?"

She shrugged. "Away from what I thought was just another monster."

"And you do not think me a monster now? Even after what you saw last night?"

Iris was quiet, calculating what the best response would be, but when she opened her mouth to speak it wasn't the words of fake Joliette that settled between them - it was her own truth.

"I do think you're a monster, Nikolai, but right now we're both two wretched creatures that need each other."

"Tell me why I should trust you, bird."

His lips lingered across her chin and she lifted her neck to the side, giving him more access to the most vulnerable part of her, all while ignoring the way his deep baritone voice was sending shockwaves through her system. Iris wet her lips and pressed herself tighter to him, content to beat him at his own game.

"Because," she whispered, allowing her voice to become breathy and needy. "One day, I'm going to help you kill him."

Nikolai stilled, and Iris wasn't sure what she expected him to do next. Would he pull out a stashed weapon and gut her right there, or would he finally press his lips to hers and push her back against the bed that was only mere feet away from where they were standing now?

In the end, he only kissed her softly, almost diplomatically, in the delicate area at the base of her neck before stepping away and heading to the door.

"Despite all that beautiful anger inside you, I don't believe you're capable of murder, my sweet bird."

An uncomfortable pit fell in his stomach. She was quite capable of murder. He just didn't know that yet.

"I'll need to attend to business outside of the home today," he told her. "I shall see you for dinner this evening."

She threw her arms up in frustration. "And what am I supposed to do locked in this room all day?"

He smirked at her over his shoulder as he pulled the door open, the *unlocked* door. He hadn't locked it when he came in last night! Nikolai had been so confident that she wouldn't dare step out of line that he hadn't even bothered with the lock.

She wasn't sure if she should feel offended or grateful that he was underestimating her.

"Write me love letters," he taunted with a suggestive waggle of his brows.

Iris reached for the pillow on the armchair with remarkable speed, but by the time she launched it at his head, it only hit the wood of the closed door.

The lock clicked into place moments later.

RANKOR

MIRROR IMAGES

Elaijah was a remarkably terrible travel companion. He complained about hunger after they'd been riding for little more than half an hour, he chattered endlessly about the most useless topics, and he flopped so unsteadily on his horse that Rankor doubted anyone had ever given the boy a proper riding lesson.

How in all of creation did he get assigned with this task?

"I'll take another cheese cube!" Elaijah exclaimed with a joyful grin.

Rankor forced himself to breathe through his frustration, grinding his teeth together forcefully. "You will not. You've eaten far too much already, and I doubt you'll be any help with finding dinner."

"We won't be eating at a tavern?"

"We won't be stopping in a town."

Puzzlement crossed Elijah's face. "I didn't think it was common for inns to be stationed outside of towns and villages."

Gods, was he naturally this obtuse or is it something he had to work towards?

Rankor's horse snorted suddenly, as if even he too felt surprised by the boy's inability to grasp their situation. With a deep, calming breath, he turned to face his brother. Based on Elaijah's responding flinch, though, Rankor's smile was likely more cruel than it was reassuring.

"We won't be stopping in a town. Not to eat. Not to sleep. And before you ask, no, it's not up for discussion. You will do what I tell you when I tell you and you will, for the love of the Gods, spend the next hour in silence."

Elaijah's face fell and Rankor wasn't sure if that was because of his harsh words or because the boy was realizing they would sleep on the ground. He didn't particularly care one way or the other.

He shook his head as if to clear his thoughts. Rankor didn't usually find himself this irritable. When training the new recruits at the palace, he was usually patient and encouraging. Something about his mortal brother brought out a different side of him, though. Maybe it was the differences between their lives. Rankor believed deep down that he was living the life he was meant for, but maybe if fate had played out differently, he would have been the son who stayed in the village.

Perhaps he would have married Arabella and had children of his own. Perhaps he would have had the opportunity to grow close to the mother Elaijah now grieved.

Instead, he was the hardened brother. He was the brother who knew how to kill better than he knew how to tend to sheep. He was the brother who felt nothing for the woman who birthed him and everything for the father who gave his life for his country.

"You know what I think," Elaijah said softly, his voice darker than it ever had been before.

Rankor didn't bother to turn to his brother. "I believe I asked for silence."

"I think you're a terrible excuse for family. You're mean and lack any sense of empathy. And while you may count the minutes until we can part ways, rest assured that you are not the only one. After you leave me at Uncle Clydric's house, don't bother planning any additional visits."

He dug his heels into his horse and trotted ahead, leaving Rankor staring after him and nursing an unexpectedly overwhelming sense of guilt.

When the sun had finally set and Elaijah's stomach was growling loudly enough to scare away any of the game they might hope to catch for dinner, Rankor decided it was past time for them to set up camp for the night. He found a small clearing within a patch of trees on the side of the main road they were traveling. He tasked the young boy with gathering wood for the fire while he killed some rabbits for their meals.

"Where did you learn how to do this?" Elaijah asked as he watched Rankor prepare to cook the rabbit over their growing fire.

"During the Great War, I spent many nights camped out in woods. Hunting and preparing our own food was the only option we had, so we all learned quickly."

Elaijah nodded, contemplating his brother's words. After a moment, he picked up the second rabbit that laid on the ground, snatched a blade from where Rankor had left his weapons, and began copying his older brother's movements. Rankor watched silently for a few moments before reaching over to adjust his brother's blade.

"Hold it like this," he explained, moving Elaijah's hands into the right position. "You're less likely to cut yourself."

Elaijah nodded and took the criticism easily, adjusting his stance. In no time, he had skinned the rabbit completely and was preparing to roast it. Rankor nodded approvingly, somewhat impressed by how quickly the boy had learned. Perhaps he wasn't a total failure after all.

"Was it difficult being in the war?" Elaijah asked softly.

His words brought flashes of memories to Rankor's mind. Battlefields that lay strewn with bodies of both friends and strangers. Moments when his own sword had slashed through an enemy and sent them to the Underworld. Dark corners where he had allowed himself the briefest of moments to cry over his loved ones.

"The war is not a time I like to think back on," Rankor admitted. "It was the most brutal display of humanity I have ever witnessed. Some of that death will haunt me for the rest of my days."

"I'm sorry for that," Elaijah told him. "You saved our country, though. You should be proud."

"I am."

Rankor handed him a bit of the cooked meat and together they ate in silence, staring out at the darkness of the woods around them and listening to the sounds of nature. Eventually, after they had both sated themselves, they unfolded their bedrolls and laid next to each other.

"Do you think you will see battle again?" Elaijah asked.

Rankor thought of his words. The war was over. If they were lucky, it would be decades before war tainted this land again. Still, Rankor knew he was bred for battle. The battlefield was a place he hated more than anything else, but it was also the place he felt most alive and something in him told him he hadn't fought his last battle quite yet.

"I do not know. I hope not for some time."

"Were you at the battle Papa died at?" Elaijah's voice was soft and boy-like again.

A dawn of realization settled over Rankor as he stared up at the sky above them. Elaijah was just as confused about Rankor and their father as Rankor was about Elaijah and their mother. He didn't know how to mourn the man who had created him, who had loved him, but who had not been there for him. Just as Rankor did not know how to mourn their mother.

"I was not. It is said that he fought bravely though. He was a good man. Strong, compassionate, dutiful."

"Were you two close?"

"Were you close with our mother?"

Silence.

Elaijah and Rankor both shifted uncomfortably.

"Now there's only us," Elaijah mused, staring up at the sky.

Rankor looked at him, suddenly noticing for the first time that the boy's nose had the same hitch as their father. Rankor's nose turned up that same way too. They were mirror images of each other and entirely opposite all at the same time.

"Now there's only us," Rankor agreed.

They laid together quietly, staring up at the star-filled sky, and Rankor was somewhat surprised by the level of companionship he felt sitting with his brother. It was the kind of peaceful togetherness he had felt with too few people in his life. Eventually, he closed his eyes, content to drift off before what would be another long day of traveling when he woke.

"Did you hear that?" Elaijah suddenly whispered. "I think there's something in the woods."

Rankor sleepily grunted.

"I'm serious!" Elaijah hissed.

"It's nothing," Rankor assured him. "It's not uncommon to be on edge during your first night sleeping out like this. It's just your mind, Elaijah. Try to relax and get some rest."

Elaijah hung his head in the air for a moment, looking like he might want to protest farther, but eventually he tucked his elbows under him, settled onto his bedroll and closed his eyes. Rankor stayed awake long enough to hear his brothers breathing steady into deep, long inhales before finally allowing himself to sleep.

Lorelai

The Oddest Job

Helena rifled through the pockets of the body at her feet, pulling out gold and trinkets and stuffing them into the coin purse strapped to her waist.

Lorelai only watched, a hand pressed to her stomach as she tried to regain her breathing. She was alone. She was alone in Gods knew where and had just watched a man be slain right in front of her eyes. How was she possibly going to get back to the castle safely? She could run, she supposed, but would she be faster than the woman lingering before her? It was only a matter of time before Helena took a second glance at her and realized the jewels on her neck and dangling from ears were genuine diamonds and emeralds.

She had to get out of here.

Slowly, she began inching away from the woman, praying that she wouldn't step on a branch and alert Helena to her escape. The woman stood suddenly though, brushing off her hands on the thighs of her pants and beginning to walk in the opposite direction. Lorelai's breath caught in her throat.

She was just… leaving?

Helena turned to glance at Lorelai over her shoulder, a white-blonde braid flopping over her shoulder. "Well?"

Lorelai sputtered.

"Are you coming?"

Lorelai's mouth gaped, opening and closing as she struggled to find words to say. "You wish for me to come with you?"

Helena's lips twitched, and she raised her arms awkwardly as if to say *obviously.*

"You're not going to rob me?"

Helena threw her head back, laughing deeply. "I told you I wouldn't hurt you. Now, if you want to stay out here in the rain, be my guest. I'm going to go bathe and get a hot meal. You're welcome to come."

She stalked off without a second glance back, her boots squishing heavily on the damp ground. Lorelai stood frozen for only a moment longer before running after her.

"And where are you going?"

"Home."

Lorelai huffed in frustration. "Which is?"

"Charlington."

"Charlington!"

The port city was known for being overrun by criminals and those of improper professions. It was hardly the place for a lady like herself. She quickly unhooked the jewels from around her neck and stuffed them away under the neckline of her soggy gown. Helena watched her from the corner of her eye and chuckled softly under her breath as she pushed a low-hanging branch out of their way.

"That is where I live, yes."

Lorelai sighed heavily. "And what is it that you do there?"

Helena shrugged. "Oh, odd jobs here and there."

"Well, that's vague."

"Why would I tell you my secrets when I don't even know your name?"

She chewed on her lip, remembering that she hadn't yet introduced herself yet. Could she trust this woman with her true identity? Or was admitting that she was a lady of the court just asking for more trouble? Lorelai didn't think she could handle anymore stress than she'd already experienced.

"Melanie," Lorelai finally lied, feeling the improperness of it in her core. It was entirely antithetical for a Truthseeker to lie. "I work for a lady of the Athenian court. I was traveling from my mistress's estate to deliver dresses to her when the bandits attacked our carriage."

Helena raised a brow at her in an expression that betrayed she didn't quite believe Lorelai's story. "Very well, Melanie. We're a good way off from the city of Alepolis right now, and I suspect you don't quite know the way back on your own?"

Embarrassment colored her cheeks red. "Your assumption would be correct."

"Then congratulations, you're my new odd job. I'm sure your lady will pay me handsomely for returning you home safely."

They breached the cover of the trees onto a dirt road. In the distance, Lorelai could see the outline of the city buildings ahead of them. Helena walked forward without hesitation and without waiting to see if Lorelai would follow her.

For a moment, Lorelai paused, debating what she should do next, if she *should* follow the woman.

As much as she hated to admit it, Helena was right. She didn't know how to get back to the castle on her own. She didn't really have another option but to trust the woman, and when they returned to the castle she would, indeed, have to pay her handsomely for her efforts.

She could only imagine how irritated her father would be with her when he heard this story.

They walked through the city streets quickly, avoiding wayward carriages and running children as they went. Many people hollered out to Helena from windows and alleys as they walked by and she greeted them all with winks and nods. Her gait was effortless and confident. She was utterly at ease in a place that left Lorelai feeling terribly off balance.

Finally, they turned down a side street that led to a tall stone building and Helena ducked under an awning that led to a stairwell.

"It's just up this way," she called over her shoulder.

Lorelai quickly scurried after her, awkwardly sidestepping an elderly man, who was sleeping soundly on the ground at their feet.

"That's Carle," Helena explained. "He lives below me but gets so piss drunk he often can't find his way home before passing out."

Helena laughed as they climbed the stairs and Lorelai wondered to herself when passing out drunk had become something that one might consider... endearing. They came upon a landing where the staircase met a door, but Helena only turned and continued climbing further up. As they went, the most atrocious acidic smell overtook her senses, and she grimaced.

"Is that-"

"Piss," Helena confirmed. "I'd watch your feet."

She pointed at the puddle Lorelai was about to step in, and she screeched unhappily. She was wearing fine fabric and nearly dipped it into some unknown person's *urine*? Oh, the Gods above certainly hated her!

Not that this dress would ever get worn again. It was already stained with mud, blood and sweat, and hung heavily around her from being soaked through.

Finally, they reached a second landing and Helena pulled out a key from her belt to unlock the door. She held it ajar and beckoned Lorelai inside, sighing with irritation when she didn't step into the place fast enough.

Though Lorelai doubted there were many people that would happily step into a place like this without hesitation.

Cobwebs and dirt lingered in the corners of the dim space. A single worn orange sofa, patched in areas with various fabrics, sat against the wall, the seat on the right side sinking in, and an oversized armoire across from it with one door hanging halfway off the hinges. To her right was what she assumed constituted as the kitchen of the home. In truth, it was little more than a single countertop covered with pans stacked atop one another next to a wooden table with a single chair. She didn't step closer to look at the pans, her instincts were telling her they likely were not clean.

She folded her hands into one another in front of her waist as she heard Helena close the door behind her.

"You have a lovely - Oh!" Lorelai jumped backwards, heart racing and hand flying to her throat, as a rat scurried from under the armoire to the couch.

"Oh, damn those rodents!" Helena grumbled, chasing after the creature that fled through a tiny hole in the wall. "They keep chewing holes through my couch!"

Lorelai scraped her hands against her damp skirts, desperately trying to calm her heart rate and stop herself from having a complete and total meltdown. She had to be dreaming. This had to be some terrible nightmare, and she was going to wake up in her bed at her manor and her Spring Soiree would proceed with no problems.

She pinched her arm as if she could just will herself into waking. No such luck.

Helena pulled some clothes from the armoire and tossed them to her before pointing to a dark hallway in front of them. "Washrooms through there. I think I'm out of soap, but you can use whatever you like in there and then change out of those wet clothes."

Who in all of creation runs out of soap!

She made a move towards the washroom, desperate to rinse away the mud that lingered on her ankles only to pause when she examined the bundle of fabric in her arms.

"I can't wear these!" Lorelai protested.

Helena shifted, her brows lowering in confusion. "And just why not?"

"These are trousers!" Lorelai held up the offensive garment in the air between them. "Surely you must have a dress I could wear."

"Do I look like the kind of person who own's a dress?"

Lorelai bit down on the inside of her cheek, so hard that she tasted the tang of salty blood. Of course, Helena wasn't the kind of person to own a dress. She apparently wasn't even the kind of person who owned soap!

"Go wash up. I'll fetch us some dinner for the evening while you do."

Lorelai wanted to grumble and complain more, but she knew when she was fighting a losing battle. So, she pulled the trousers back towards her and stepped down the hallway to the washroom, eager to at least be out of her sopping gown.

The washroom was small, with piles of dust shoved into the corners of the tiled floor. A single pale of freezing cold water waited for her, along with a small rag that smelt... questionable. Helplessly, she looked around as if desperate to find some small thing that might be familiar enough to bring her comfort.

Ultimately, she just found herself staring at her own reflection in the looking glass. Not even that seemed recognizable now.

IRIS

How to Build an Empire

She waited for an hour or two to be sure he was out of the house before making her move. After seating herself at the writing desk, she pulled out several scraps of parchment and began scribbling random notes on them before folding them neatly. Then she let her magic fall, let Joliette's face fade out of existence, until her own eyes and tawny skin greeted her in the looking glass.

Iris allowed herself a single minute to feel at home in her own skin before she shifted once more, this time taking on the appearance of the maid who had escorted her to dinner the night before. It took her a few moments to get comfortable in the way this new body moved, but she wasted no more time than was necessary before bending by the door and pressing her ear against the small crack.

Silence.

Then footsteps.

Moving from her left to her right.

Then silence again.

She waited another moment to be sure that whoever was walking past was gone before she fitted her two hair pins into the lock and began pushing and pulling them together, sliding them where she wanted until she felt the mechanism click and the door unlock.

Damn. That had been quick. Maybe even a new personal record. She'd have to tell Walric about it when she got home.

She pulled open the door and fell into character, instantly grumbling about messy bedsheets and splattered water. The hallway was empty, but she could hear voices in the distance alerting her to the fact that regardless of Nikolai's absence, there were still eyes all around her. She needed to be quick and careful.

She wasn't quite sure where best to go, so she followed the path she had taken to dinner the night before. Turned out luck was on her side, because it just so happened that directly across the hall from the dining chamber was an open door and inside was another maid tidying an office.

Based on the grandeur of the massively large desk with expertly carved wooden paneling and the shelves filled with rare crystals, weapons, and what she suspected were magic-infused goods, it had to be Nikolai's. It just had to be.

"Mr. Legum instructed me to leave these for him," she said to the other woman, a girl barely older than seventeen, as she held the parchment up between them. "Why don't you let me finish this up and you can take a break? You look positively exhausted."

The maid glanced up at her from where she had been dusting the baseboards on her hands and knees. "Oh, that's unnecessary."

Iris wrapped her arms affectionally around the girl and pulled her to her feet. "Nonsense, girl. Didn't anyone ever teach you not to turn down a gift when it's offered?"

"Well, if you're sure..."

"I am, go now."

Thankfully, the girl did look fairly tired, and it didn't take too much coaxing to get her to leave. Iris watched her retreat down the hallway before gently pushing closed the door, locking it, and launching herself upon the desk, rifling through papers as she did.

She wasn't sure what exactly she was looking for, but at this point, practically anything would be helpful.

There were contracts, billing statements, letters requesting Nikolai's services in procuring some rare artifact. Nothing that would help her learn more about the Serpent and his plans. Hadn't Nikolai demanded that information be delivered to him last night? It had to be around here somewhere.

She pulled out the drawer on the right-hand side of the desk, disappointed to find nothing but a few blades and some quills and ink. The drawer beneath it was filled with more contracts. The drawer on the left was...

Locked.

"Well, would you look at that."

She set to work picking the lock, careful to keep her attention on the door and any sounds that might linger outside of it. When she finally got the drawer open, she stifled a grin as she pulled out the tiny notebook bound in brown leather and marked with Nikolai's initials.

Greedily, she flipped through the pages, soaking in as much information as she could from his personal journal. This little book detailed all of his enterprises. If The Order got their hands on this, they could make some actual progress in eliminating criminal activity in Athenia!

Then she stumbled upon a single page that made the rhythm of her heart stutter.

He's gone too far this time. Attacking a Duke's home invites too much attention. It's only a matter of time before the King's assassins get involved. I've no doubt they have methods for infiltrating the Serpent's ranks and from there it's only a matter of time before the bastards are on my doorstep.

She would worry later about how Nikolai was already suspicious of The Order. For now, the only question ringing through her mind was what could have motivated the Serpent to risk that. Surely he would have also realized the scrutiny that this kind of attack would bring. So what in all of creation could make that worthwhile?

It seemed Nikolai had the same question.

Our intel suggests the Serpent has men posted outside the Duke of Eagirton's estate. The Duke hasn't yet returned from the castle, so is it possible they're waiting for him? But for what purpose? To kill him and, if so, why?

Nikolai must not have known that the Serpent had the Duke's wife, because that piece of information changed the entire nature of this situation. You wouldn't kidnap a wife just to kill the husband. No, you kidnap a wife for leverage.

You kidnap a wife to blackmail a Duke.

Which then begged the question... what information did the Duke of Eagirton have that the Serpent wanted?

Iris tucked away the journal and hurried down the halls back towards her suite, not wanting to linger outside of her rooms any longer than necessary. She'd gotten the information she needed and nothing else would be worth risking being caught.

But once she had reset the lock and shut herself away, there was nothing left for her to do but return to her pacing and scheming while she waited for Nikolai's return.

After staying on guard and awake all night watching Nikolai, she couldn't stop herself from dozing off in the hours she spent alone in that room. She must have slept for some time, because when she woke to the sensation of Nikolai brushing her hair out of her face, the crisp golden light of the setting sun was drifting in through the windows.

"I brought you something to eat," he told her softly.

She lifted her arms above her head, stretching out her stiff muscles, and his eyes lingered at where her chest lifted softly. "No fancy meals with all your associates?"

"I thought tonight we might dine alone."

Nikolai stood and went to the armchair by the door, where he'd left a tray piled with roasted meat and steamed vegetables. Wordlessly, he placed it before her and sat down at the foot of the bed.

"You wish to eat in bed?" Iris frowned.

Nikolai shrugged at first, only to glance up at her with an expression that might have been classified as alarm. "Would you prefer to dine with more finery?"

"No!" she assured him. Iris quite preferred this in fact. Still, it wasn't quite what she had expected from him. "I suppose you just surprise me."

Nikolai chuckled softly, grabbing a carrot between his fingers and plopping it into his mouth. "I suppose I do."

For a few moments, they sat together quietly, each eating and focused on their own thoughts, but Iris couldn't help but to simply observe him. Like this, in the privacy of her - *their* - room, Nikolai differed greatly from the version of him she had seen at dinner the night before. Now his shoulders slumped slightly, and the dark circles under his eyes seemed more prominent.

"What are you thinking?" he asked, not looking up from the plate of food.

"You seem tired," she noted. "Long day?"

He was quiet for some time until he finally lifted his head and his hazel eyes met hers. He carried so much in those eyes, so many emotions that were painted so clearly within them. Anger, conflict, exhaustion, pain. So much pain.

And though Iris knew she shouldn't, that she wasn't here for the purpose of understanding Nikolai Legum, she couldn't help herself from wanting to peel back his layers and understand what it was that could have caused such heartache for him.

"Two of my men, friends, were found dead this morning. I spent the day retrieving their bodies and delivering them to their families."

Whatever Iris had been expecting him to say, it hadn't been that.

"How?"

He turned away from her, jaw working. "We found puncture wounds in each of their necks."

The Serpent. It was his calling card, of sorts. Puncture wounds to resemble that of a snake bite, left behind in each of his victims.

She shivered.

"I'm sorry, Nikolai."

He stood suddenly, nearly tipping the tray of food over in his rush if it hadn't been for Iris' quick reflexes, pushing her to grasp hold of it. He paced the room, his movements sharp and rushed as he ran a hand down his face.

"The man is a bastard!" Nikolai hissed. "I've lost too many men, *good* men, to his childish games."

She let him go for some time, allowing him to rant until his movements slowed, and he threw his head back to look towards the ceiling as if he was waiting for the Gods themselves to give him some peace of mind.

"How did this start?" she asked softly. "Your rivalry with him?"

He turned towards her suddenly, eyes narrowed. "You don't remember?"

Her heart skipped a beat. Shit, had she just exposed herself as an imposter?

"I'm not surprised," he continued after a moment, returning to sit across from her once more. "We were young. I think you stayed with your mother more in those days."

"That was often the case."

"I was eight when his men raided my house and killed my parents. They brought me to him as a present. For the first few years I worked around the home, doing the scut work no one else wanted. Cleaning chamber pots and the like. Until one day I'd finally had enough, when one of his men went to backhand me for not being quick enough to bring his ale, I grabbed the knife off the table and jammed it into his throat right in front of your father."

"What did he do?"

"He was proud," Nikolai laughed darkly. "That night he requested that I be moved from the servant's quarters to an actual room within the manor, and I officially became his apprentice."

Iris listened with bated breath, understanding that she was hearing a story that no one else in the kingdom had ever quite come to know. She committed each word to memory, sure that Walric would want to hear every little detail when she returned home.

"Eventually, by the time I was fifteen, he had molded me into his own personal hitman. He would send me out daily to eliminate those he considered a threat, but each day, his targets became stranger and stranger. It went from being sent after another crime lord to being sent after a new mother who claimed to have never even heard who the Serpent was. I tried to reason with him, but he wouldn't listen. He was too paranoid to listen. So I left. I started my own empire, and he hated me for it."

"He speaks of you very poorly, but didn't share this with me."

Nikolai chuckled, leaning back slightly on his hands and his long copper hair fell softly over his shoulder. "He likely doesn't want to admit the role he had in shaping his own enemy."

"Why marry me then?" she finally asked, still not understanding how this arrangement between him and Joliette came to be. "If you want revenge on my father, why not just kill me?"

He looked at her for a long moment, gaze trailing over her eyes, lips, breasts, and back up again. And yet, he didn't gaze upon her with longing or lust. Rather, his eyes continued to tell stories of pain and regret.

"I don't wish for vengeance, Joliette. I'm just smart enough to know what was coming next on the horizon, and a war with your father would only lead to too many casualties on both sides."

Understanding dawned on her as he lifted the tray and mumbled about returning later in the evening. When the bedroom door closed behind him and she was alone once more, she lifted her hand to her mouth, pulling at her bottom lip as she thought over their conversation.

Nikolai Legum had married Joliette in order to join their two rival gangs, not because he wanted control over the Serpent's empire but simply because he wanted to avoid the unnecessary bloodshed that resulted in them being at odds with each other.

Which, on the surface, seemed almost admirable.

CAMILLA
GOLDEN CAGES

Camilla woke in a cold sweat in the middle of the night, jerked into consciousness by the feeling of someone else's magic falling over her. Her nightgown and sheets were soaked through, but she hardly even had time to notice them before her feet were throwing themselves off the bed, compelled by the summoning spell that had been cast on her.

She wasn't entirely surprised that her grandmother was summoning her. She suspected it would happen the moment she had to confess that Clay had rejected her, in fact. Summoning spells were just another way that Alina liked to torture her. It wasn't enough to demand that Camilla return to Hypatia manor, she would force her to come at the most inconvenient times possible without even giving her the autonomy to clean or dress herself.

Her legs were already carrying her to the door, and she was utterly helpless to fight against the magic. She just barely slipped her feet into some hard-soled slippers and grabbed a cloak from where she had hung it next to the door before she was stepping out of her suite. She tossed it over herself and pulled up the hood high to hide herself as she traveled through the castle and stepped out into the chilled night air.

The stable hand had retired to his home long ago, leaving the horses unattended, so it was easy to simply grab hold of one and throw herself upon it. Camilla was an expert rider. Horses had been one of the few things her grandmother had allowed her to love as a girl. Still, no amount of experience would make riding bareback through the night comfortable, but the magic pulling her home was insistent and didn't allow her the time it would take to properly saddle and prepare the horse.

"I'm sorry for this," she whispered to the white steed. "You have as little choice in this as I do."

She kicked her heel into the horse's side, bringing it to a gallop, and her hood fell as the wind pushed through her dark hair. They were off, and they wouldn't stop until she reached her grandmother. Camilla let herself try to relax against the familiar feeling of riding. She didn't even need to worry about directing the horse, her magically controlled body would do it for her, so she stared off into the distance, marveling at a small white butterfly that miraculously seemed to flutter by her side throughout the entire journey.

Her cousin Erilea was waiting for her as she arrived, leaning against the banister of the decaying wooden porch that wrapped around the otherwise shabby house known as Hypatia manor. Erilea was two years her younger, and had been a pain in her side ever since her parents had sent her to live at Hypatia manor permanently with Alina and Camilla. They had decided it would be the perfect opportunity for Erilea to learn the craft. Erilea had decided it would be the perfect opportunity to join their grandmother in tormenting Camilla.

Erilea was a short and stout little thing, the kind of woman who never quite lost the childish chubbiness around her cheeks. Her brown hair was stringy and never looked completely clean and the proportions of her face were ever so slightly misaligned, drawing attention to the small crook in her nose. It didn't help that she perpetually had a scowl pasted across her face. Perhaps if she smiled in joy, she might be pretty, but Erilea only ever smiled with venom.

Her cousin lifted her eyes from where she had been examining her nail beds and gave Camilla that very smile. "Took your time, didn't you?"

Camilla's exhaustion was absolute, both from being awoken in the night to having had to ride for several hours. Her thighs, core, and lower back ached more than they ever had and she was sure she would have bruises on her sit bones. Without having been given the time to don proper riding pants, she'd left her bare skin against the horse, which had left her severely chaffed and uncomfortable.

"Bite me." She sneered at her cousin.

Erilea snapped her jaw towards Camilla playfully before snapping her fingers and releasing Camilla from the summoning spell.

"Grandmother let me summon you this time," she bragged. "She said my powers have gotten more impressive than yours ever were."

"You should throw a party," Camilla suggested sarcastically as she pushed past Erilea and into the house.

It looked the same as it ever did. The floorboards had scuffs and scratches, the horrid yellow wallpaper was fraying in the corners of the wall, and boxes and boxes of useless artifacts and junk filled every inch of the floor. Camilla had to step over a crate of what looked like decaying rabbits' feet to even step into the place. The stench of the home was positively revolting, as was the unbearable heat of it. The season hadn't even gotten to its warmest point yet, but Hypatia manor always seemed to swelter. It was truly how she imagined the darkest parts of the Underworld to feel.

"So lovely to come home and see how well you've maintained the place," Camilla remarked, even while hating herself for referencing this place as her home. It wasn't, and it never had been.

She climbed the steps to the upper floor, well-acquainted with the routine of being summoned here. Her grandmother would allow her a few minutes to change and clean herself before she would expect her in the sitting room to hear whatever lecture her grandmother had planned for her.

The wooden stairs creaked under her steps as she climbed the three stories to the room that had always been reserved for her on the top floor. As she opened the doorway, a plume of dust blew into her face and she batted her arm through it, coughing uncomfortably as she took in the tiny space she had grown up in.

The bed was as measly as she remembered it, barely small enough for a child and resting on a rusting bronze frame with nothing more than a small crocheted blanked atop it. Camilla didn't even know how many winter nights she had spent shivering in this room. Across from her bed was the small armoire that carried the few gowns that she had left here before she moved to the castle. Nothing terribly remarkable. A small desk, which sat crooked because of the leg that was falling off, contained what few items her grandmother had allowed her to personally keep for spell crafting. Alina had always insisted on only allowing Camilla to *borrow* ingredients for spells that she approved of.

And to Camilla's left was the cage.

She took her time in turning to look at it, swallowing down the bile that rose in her throat as she stared at the glass awning in her room. On the outside, it simply looked like a small three-sided window alcove made of beautiful stained glass. From inside the room, Camilla could see if for what it was... a coffin, complete with a metal gate.

Alina reserved the cage for times when she was truly disappointed in Camilla. The first time she'd used it had been shortly after Camilla's father had died, when she first came to live at Hypatia Manor. She'd been only seven years old at the time and in an attempt to climb the kitchen counters to access the place where Alina had hidden the sweets, her foot had knocked over a carnelian crystal and Alina had dragged her by her hair to the cage.

"And you deserved it," her grandmother taunted from behind her.

Camilla spun on her heels, surprised by the old woman's sudden presence, but as she faced the door she had come from, Alina was nowhere to be found. No one stood in her doorway. Frowning, Camilla took a few steps out of her room and peered down the winding staircase. She could just make out the image of Alina's grey hair on the first floor as the elder woman walked through the parlor towards the sitting room to wait for Camilla.

She must have imagined it. Odd.

Being in this house was already putting her on edge. She sighed heavily and pulled out a worn grey gown from the armoire. It was a size too small. The sleeves barely covered her forearms, and the skirts stopped above her ankles. But it would have to do. It's not like she would impress anyone in this house, anyway.

Camilla rubbed a soothing powder onto her chaffed thighs and took one quick glance at herself in the mirror before closing the bedroom door behind her to go downstairs. She just had to get this over with. Her grandmother would yell for sometime and then she would dismiss her back to the castle and her life could go back to normal.

With a deep breath, she steeled herself as she stepped into the parlor. Silently, she climbed over the discarded belongings as she made her way to where Erilea and Alina waited for her.

Just be quiet and get through it, she coached herself. *This will all be over soon.*

"Camilla," her grandmother greeted her from the couch. Alina's age was showing in her gray hair and wrinkled skin, but she still held herself as tall and capable as ever.

"You summoned?"

"Sit," her grandmother demanded. "I believe we have some things to discuss.

KENT

CAN'T FOOL A SIREN

Kent woke with the sun the next morning, his muscles sore from the ride and demanding to be stretched out. So, he left the home quietly to complete his morning exercises outside in the spring air. His routine was simple, a dance of various stretches and movements to activate the muscles and prepare him for the day. It was a practice he had picked up in the army, a way to calm himself before grueling days of battle, but even now, in these times of peace, it still brought him comfort.

And the Gods knew he needed it today.

He would have to see her today. He needed to. There were only a few days before the wedding. He needed to check in on her now so that there was enough time to help her if she needed him. Best to do that now before she was draped in her wedding gown.

As he ended his stretches, he was acutely aware of eyes on him, a sensation he'd honed during his time in the barracks. Without alerting them to the fact that he could sense them, he let his magic reach out, falling over the twins and creating a connection between him and them.

Kressida's emotions were a pleasant rush of amusement and joy, whereas her twin was feeling an overwhelming burst of embarrassment, sadness, and anxiety. He frowned as he took in her feelings and hummed a low pitch, forwarded a magical rush of happiness to her through his voice. From over his shoulder, he felt her sigh in contentment.

"Come," his mother called to him, her nervousness adding to the mix of foreign emotions in his system.

He took a final deep breath out and shut down the channel that connected him to his family members. The magic splintered in a tight crack, flying back towards him sharply. It had taken him some time to hone the ability to sever connections between himself and others. For many years, he simply lived day to day intimately, understanding how others around him were feeling before he gained the ability to offer them a level of privacy. Severing the connection between himself and others around him was painful, admittedly, like an elastic snapping back after being stretched too far, but a moment of pain for him was worth it to make others around him more comfortable.

Breakfast was simple, nothing more than a fresh porridge with berries the twins had picked from the bush behind the home, but Kent appreciated it nonetheless. He ate quietly, content to let his sisters carry the conversation while his mind continued spinning around thoughts of Seralyn.

"There will be a celebration today," his mother said to him, pulling him from his thoughts. "It's a time to bring gifts to the new couple to wish them well on their upcoming lives together. I made some quilts to give them, one for them and one for a child in the future."

Kent's fists clenched at the mention of a child. His heart hadn't allowed him to consider the potential of that yet.

"Will you be attending with us?" His mother asked.

Kent nodded, not trusting his voice. His sister Kressida snickered next to him and he glared at her with narrowed eyes. She stifled her grin behind a bite of her porridge while Kreyana sighed heavily next to her.

"What?" He snapped.

Kreyana's mouth opened and closed, as if she were weighing her words carefully. "Well, it's just... you should probably bathe before you go."

He frowned as he looked down at his sweat-soaked shirt. A subtle sniff of his underarm was all he needed to know his younger sisters were right. Their eyes followed him wryly as he dropped his spoon heavily in his bowl, porridge splattering onto the wooden table as he did, and stood to leave the room.

In a small town like this one, there weren't many reasons to celebrate, so the entire village had gathered in the square to greet the young couple. Kreyana had spent nearly half an hour debating which outfit she wanted to wear while Kressida poked fun at her, so Kent's family was one of the last groups to arrive.

The town center was circular, surrounded by small shops and bakeries. In the middle rested the fountain that had been the pride and joy of the people. A large bronze salmon spewing water from its mouth, a tribute to the many people who made their living here as fishermen. Based on the way the crowd pressed together, pushing towards it, Kent suspected he would find Seralyn and her new betrothed near said fountain.

He had come to one of these celebrations as a boy and remembered a little of it. If his memory served him right, everyone would approach the couple individually to offer gifts and congratulations, before the traditional wedding song would begin and they would all join the couple in a celebratory dance, followed by an evening feast. It signified the official start of the wedding festivities.

As his family arrived, Kreyana and Kressida darted off almost immediately, finding some other girls of their age and sprinting towards them. Kent watched them with a sensation of longing. He missed his own friends. Although, admittedly, if Rankor knew he was here doing this right now, he would probably receive a swift slap over the head and a demand to head away from this party and towards the nearest tavern.

"Does that happen often?" He asked, nodding to where his sisters showed off their matching blue dresses to their friends.

"More and more these days." His mother sighed and shifted the weight of the quilts in her hands. "They're of that age when friends are more fun to be around than their old mother."

Kent took the weight of the blankets from her. "You're not old."

"Kent?"

A heavy hand clapped him on the shoulder and he turned to the burly grunt of a man behind him. He looked to have come straight from the docks. His hands were still slick with the grease of freshly caught fish and his trousers were damp from the knees down. His face, covered in the mask of a thick black beard, sparked an inkling of familiarity in Kent that lingered in the corners of his mind, ever so slightly out of reach.

"Good Gods boy, you've shot up like a weed. I hardly recognized you."

Kent's mother folded her arm into his. "Grant, it is good to see you. How is Elora?"

Ah, Grant. An old fishing buddy of his father's.

Grant smiled. "She is well. We're expecting our fourth any day now."

"How lovely. I shall have to bring by a casserole after the baby comes and sit with her."

"She would love that." Grant turned, his attention lingering over the crowd. His height gave him the advantage of being able to see over the many heads around them. "I imagine Seralyn will be happy to see you Kent, you two were always thick as thieves. A decade ago, I might have placed my bets that it would have been you up there with her."

Kent's jaw locked as he ground his teeth together hard enough that he was sure they might crack. Were the Gods determined to make this day that much harder on him? He felt his mother's fingers gently knead on his arm in comfort as she smiled at Grant.

"Yes, well, the Gods put us all on our paths, do they not?"

Grant bowed his head. "Thank Zion for that."

What path were the Gods placing him on exactly? One directed towards impending heartbreak?

"If you'll excuse us, Grant, my son and I should make our way to deliver our gifts."

Kent didn't hesitate to push away from him and lead his mother away through the masses, forcing himself closer and closer to where Seralyn waited for him. His mother was quiet as they made their way, but he felt her attention on him. He felt the weight of her concern, heavy as a woolen blanket over his shoulders, and shuddered. He'd let his magic slip without meaning to, as it so often did when he was feeling powerful emotions himself.

And his emotions were ragged right now.

He was a mess of anticipation, nervousness, excitement, dread.

She was calling to him. Every step forward was bringing him closer to Seralyn and he could *feel* her presence, calling to him like the beacon she had always been.

Finally, the crowd seemed to part for him. The fountain became visible, its water trickling down in a steady rhythm. And the world around him seemed to fade as he finally saw her again.

Gods, she was beautiful.

She was just as he remembered, and yet so much more. She still wore her auburn hair long and thick, but she'd decorated it for the celebration, folding it back into twists and braids. A gentle blush colored her freckled cheeks as her soft pink lips opened wide for her to smile at the small child she was talking to. Her almond eyes, smeared in kohl, were entirely focused on the boy, and sparkling with joy. She wore white, as tradition dictated. The bodice of her gown cinched so tightly that her waist was impossibly narrow and her breasts difficult to ignore. Delicate olive-hued lace danced over her bosom, her family's color. She took a bouquet from the boy with a gentle thank you and passed it to her mother, who stood behind her organizing the gifts.

She was turning her attention back to the crowd, seeking the next offering to attend to, when her impossibly large eyes locked onto Kent's.

Her breath hitched as her hand gently fell to her bodice. "Kent?"

Her voice echoed through him, shaking his body - his soul. They both stood frozen, staring at each other, neither daring to breathe and risk this moment being nothing more than an illusion that would fade away at the slightest movement.

But then, all too suddenly, she was laughing as her eyes welled with tears and he was stepping towards her. And then she was in his arms again, her arms wrapped around his neck and the scent of her lily soap invading his nose.

"You came! I wasn't sure you would be able to."

"I wouldn't have missed it for the world, Sera."

A masculine throat cleared, and she stiffened, backing out of his arms suddenly and turning towards the man at her left. She placed a hand on his arm familiarly and stepped backwards, out of Kent's space and into that of her... betrothed.

"My Gods, my apologies, Kent. This is my betrothed, Jaxon Tried. Jaxon, you remember me mentioning my childhood acquaintance, Kentoni?"

For a moment, Kent bristled at being called an *acquaintance*. As if the pull that existed between them could be dismissed as nothing more than a passing childhood ally. Still, if his time in the Athenian court had taught him anything, it was how to recover his composure.

Jaxon was his opposite in every way. Where Kent was tall, lean and dark-skinned, Jaxon was a foot shorter, with arms that were disproportionately thick, and skin that was so ivory his veins were visible blue lines across his body. He wore his hair long, tied back at the nape of his neck, and had donned a simple navy vest over cream trousers that were tucked into muddied knee-high leather boots.

He extended his hand to Kent with a measured smile. "All the way from the castle? That's quite a distance to travel."

Kent shook Jaxon's hand, noting the way the other man tightened his grip as he spoke. "Yes, well, I had been planning a trip home for some time. The timing aligned well," he lied.

Jaxon nodded, brown eyes narrowed. Without changing his expression, Kent let his powers melt out of him. A decade ago, it would have been impossible for him to function in a crowd like this, with so many thoughts and feelings vying for his attention.

But he was no longer a boy.

He felt the connection between him and Jaxon switch into place instantly, and the man's feelings flowed into him quickly. They were easy to identify. Suspicion, directed towards Kent, the oily satisfaction that spoke to some sense of arrogance and vanity, and an overwhelming sense of... superiority. Kent severed the connection before he lost control of himself and let his lip curl up in disgust.

"Well, we are certainly grateful you could attend Kent." Seralyn grinned at him, and his heart sputtered. It was a grin he had seen a million times. A grin that had so often been reserved only for him. "It is so good to see you again."

Kent's mother stepped forward, offering her quilts to the couple and extending her congratulations. Seralyn focused in on the older woman, smiling and offering polite thanks, but her eyes often flashed to Kent's as they spoke.

He was aware of the crowd pressing in on him. His mother's words slowed, their conversation beginning to end. Jaxon had already turned away, talking to someone new. Kent had only a moment left to do what he had come here for.

He let his magic out once more, connecting to Seralyn and letting her emotions flow into him.

"Come," his mother commanded, taking hold of his arm once more and pulling them away. Her dark eyes bounced from left to right, seeking where his two sisters had run off to.

Some part of him was aware his mother was speaking to him, but he couldn't quite grasp the words she was saying. The connection between him and Seralyn was still open, though it weakened with every step he took away from her. Even as it faded, though, her emotions still weighed on him.

Joy.

Excitement.

Relief.

And underneath it all... fear.

IRIS

The Dance of Death

I ris paced the room uneasily. It had been some time since Nikolai had left and there had been no sign at all of when, or if, she should expect him to return. And with each moment that passed, she felt more and more anxious that she'd pushed him too far or said too much. Nikolai's journal had already exposed the fact that he suspected The Order would become involved in his business. Had he somehow already figured out who she was?

She needed to be on guard. The Order had taught her to always be prepared for the unexpected, and that was exactly what she would do. If Nikolai was going to make a move against her, she would have to be prepared for it.

Iris was so lost in her planning that she almost didn't hear the door quietly sliding open, too quietly, as if whoever was approaching didn't want her to know they were there. This was it, she realized suddenly, the moment where everything fell apart and she would have to kill Nikolai and fight her way out of this house.

By the time she had turned, though, hands reaching for the razor sharp pins in her hair, she had only a split second to realize that it wasn't Nikolai's golden-ringed eyes that met hers before the pommel of a sword was brought down on her head and darkness fell over her as pain exploded through her skull.

S he awoke to a pounding in her left temple and the sensation of blood dripping slowly down her brow and cheek. At least she could be grateful that the bastards hadn't even hit her in the right spot. A blow two inches to the left, where the skull was the thinnest, might have killed her. All they did was give her a temporary headache. Idiots.

They had pinned her hands tightly behind her back and it took a few minutes for her eyes to adjust to the darkness she was in, but as they did, she could make out stone walls and a dirt floor underneath her. There was a sound of a consistent dripping from the ceiling onto a small puddle where her feet rested, leaving the bottom of her skirt damp and muddied.

They'd thrown her in some kind of underground prison cell, not entirely unlike The Order's own dungeon.

She had no way of knowing who had taken her or why. There was, of course, the possibility that they had discovered she wasn't who she said she was. Although, it hadn't been Nikolai's steps in her room. He could always have ordered someone else to attack her, of course, but she suspected if he was involved, he would have been present. He would have made a show of confronting her.

So maybe this had nothing to do with Iris and everything to do with Joliette.

The binds on her wrist were tight, tight enough that to get out of them she was likely going to need to dislocate her thumb. It wouldn't be pleasant, but unfortunately, it also wouldn't be her first time. The Orders training methods were rather comprehensive.

Gritting her teeth together, she maneuvered her wrists so that she could grasp onto the thumb on her left hand and force the finger backward. The pain was immediate, as was the sickening sound of the pop as the joint gave way. She bit down on her bottom lip to stop from screaming as nausea flooded her in a rush. Her hand slid out easily. Iris worked to steady her breathing, keeping her hands behind her back.

That left hand would be useless until she got to a healer, but at least now her right was free.

The sound of approaching footsteps echoed, and she jerked into alertness, pain forgotten as two figures approached.

She recognized one as the portly man from the night before. His skin was pale and his eyes bounced nervously around him, lingering in every dark shadow as if he were waiting for danger to jump out at him.

Next to him was a man not much older than herself, with dark hair and a thin, pointed nose. His jaw firmly set, he looked at her with an expression that lacked any warmth. It wasn't necessarily the look of pure disdain on his face that gave her pause, though. It was the *shape* of this face. That perfect oval shape that was so familiar to her.

And it was familiar because she'd gotten quite used to seeing it in the mirror lately.

"Hello cousin," he greeted her, voice filled with malice.

Well, wasn't this interesting...

Joliette's cousin was working with Nikolai's associate to kidnap her.

"Have you come to take me home?" She asked, decorating her voice with an air of naïve hopefulness.

He laughed darkly. "There's no need to pretend with me, Joliette. I know exactly who you are."

Unable to make sense of his words, Iris mentally prepared herself to fight.

"We should do this quickly," Nikolai's associate practically whined, his eyes still flitting about. "It would be better to be done with this before anyone notices she's missing."

Joliette's cousin bared his teeth at him with such ferocity that the other man took a few steps back, bowing his head.

"This isn't personal," Joliette's cousin said, lowering in front of her and grasping hold of her chin to twist her face back and forth while he inspected her. "But the Serpent's need a clear leader right now."

"What does that have to do with me?"

He titled his head, expression filled with disappointment. "You're a smart girl, Joliette. Surely you knew this was coming."

She chose her words carefully. "I suppose."

"Your father is still hoping you'll kill Nikolai," he mused, twirling one of the many rings on his fingers. "But if you kill Nikolai, I lose my chance to show everyone that *I'm* the best choice to succeed your father."

Like pieces of a puzzle, the information began melding itself together in her mind. "So you kill me, blame Nikolai, and demand to avenge my death?"

Her cousin grinned, one cheek dimpling slightly. "You always were more clever than I gave you credit for. That's why it has to be this way."

Iris took stock of the weapons in the room. Joliette's cousin had a sword strapped across his back and a dagger tucked into his belt. The rings adorning his fist could also be dangerous if he hit her. Nikolai's man, practically cowering in the corner, appeared to be free of any weapons, but that didn't mean he didn't have them tucked away out of sight.

After days locked away with Nikolai, muscles tense and demanding to be exercised, it was finally time for her to put some of her training to use.

"It's only fair." Iris sighed, looking up at them through her lashes. "That I offer you the chance to run before I decide to kill you."

Joliette's cousin threw his head back in a hearty laugh. His eyes were still dancing in amusement when he pulled the sword from his back and leveled it at her.

"I will see you in the Underworld, Joliette."

She waited until the blade was mere inches from her heart before she struck.

Iris threw out her legs, kicking out his ankles. His body surged forward just as she ducked to her left, reaching out with her good hand to grasp at the skin on his wrist and apply pressure to the delicate tendons there. His hand released, dropping the sword to the ground as he roared in anger.

Nikolai's man ran, sprinting heavily down whatever dark corner he had come from as Iris rushed to her feet. There was a brief moment when she met eyes with Joliette's cousin before they both were diving for the sword.

In the end, Iris was faster.

She grasped the sword, swinging it to loosen up her wrist as Joliette's cousin stared at her wide eyed. Quickly, his attention darted to her left hand, where her thumb still hung at an odd angle.

"I see Nikolai has taught you a few things," he noted.

"Not quite." Iris grinned, walking to her right in an attempt to back him into the wall. He fell for it. It would appear that his anger lacked the true skill to back it up. "Surely you had to have known that kidnapping a duchess wouldn't go unnoticed by the Dragon."

She gave him a moment to let the realization settle over him and thoroughly enjoyed watching his eyes shift from confusion to understanding as her words made sense.

"*You're a bitch from The Order,*" he hissed.

Iris bowed, twirling her hand in an elaborate flourish. "Guilty as charged. To be fair, I offered you the chance to run."

He attacked, grasping onto the dagger on his hip and charging for her, all fury and speed and no technique. Fighting had come naturally to her. As a fairy, she was lighter on her feet than most and Iris had spent much of her girlhood obsessed with the dancers who often came to perform for the Dragon and the Queen. She would sneak into the dressing rooms and beg them to teach her the most complicated steps.

Fighting was a lot like dancing.

That was the thing that men like this didn't understand. They hid behind the brute strength of their arms instead of learning how valuable their feet were.

Iris danced to the left, leading him there, only to spin behind herself and jam her elbow into the back of his head. He let out a vicious curse and twisted the blade in his fingers, rotating the tip towards her and jabbing it backwards. Moving swiftly, she darted out of the way, just barely avoiding it, and made a mental note to remember that move for later.

"Joliette!" a deep baritone voice echoed down the chamber.

Nikolai.

Shit. Her cousin's eyes darted towards the voice and for a moment it was as if she could see his mind at work as he weighed out the options of having to face Nikolai's wrath or hers. Panic railed through her as he opened his mouth, decision made.

"She's not-"

Iris plunged the sword through deep into his gut just as Nikolai came running down the hall, dozens of men trailing behind him.

The man sputtered, blood leaking from his lips in a steady stream as he turned towards Nikolai, desperately still trying to release the secret into the world. "Joliette-"

Iris jammed the sword in deeper.

He fell to the ground, and she stumbled backwards. Adrenaline coursed through her system, leaving her head feeling weightless and somewhat detached from her body. As she turned to face Nikolai, she couldn't quite understand his expression.

He furrowed his brows, pinching them together in what seemed like confusion. Until suddenly, his eyes widened as they trailed down her body. Frowning, Iris looked down at herself, gasping as she saw the hilt of a dagger protruding from her belly.

"Ouch," she moaned, pain slowly leaking into her awareness.

Nikolai stepped forward, concern clear in the set of his jaw and the tightness of his shoulders. He reached for her and she moved to step forward, but that simple motion was all it took for the adrenaline to fade and the agony of her injuries to come rushing over her. Her head throbbed, her thumb ached, and everything below her waist felt as if it were suddenly burning.

He caught her as she stumbled forward, hauling her into his arms easily.

"Get me a healer!" he barked, and the men with him stepped aside, clearing a path for him to carry her out.

LORELAI

An Unlikely Alliance

She had *never* in her life bathed in cold water.

Her shivering increased with every brush of the frigid rag across the skin and she swore to herself that she would never subject herself to this form of torture again.

When she finally finished scrubbing her skin raw, she still didn't even feel clean. The blood and muck were gone from her pale skin, but it was as if she could still feel it on her. She stared at herself for a long time in the looking glass, debating if she could really allow herself to stay in this cesspool of impending infection.

She had no choice.

Maybe when she finally got back to the castle, she would insist on Kent teaching her navigation skills. Maybe she could use the stars to guide herself home if she ever found herself in the situation again.

But oh Gods, she hoped she never found herself in this situation again.

She slid the trousers and tunic on before padding back out to the living space. Helena sat on the floor, one leg kicked up and the other spread wide as she gnawed on a bone. Like an animal.

"Got turkey legs for dinner." Her words were garbled by chewing as she gestured to the hunk of meat that sat on a cracking porcelain plate on the floor.

"Have you ever considered that eating at a table might be more sanitary than the floor?"

Lorelai couldn't shake the image of the rat running across the room from her mind's eye.

Helena only shrugged, picked up another turkey leg, and shoved it at Lorelai. "Eat first, complain second."

Lorelai couldn't help it when her lips finally turned down as she took the bone between her thumb and pointer finger. It was heavier than she expected and fell upside down until it hung awkwardly between them. Helena rolled her eyes, grasped hold of Lorelai's wrist and pushed the food closer towards her.

"What? They don't eat this at the fancy castle?"

Lorelai almost laughed at the idea of her friends eating meat off the bones. Rankor would love it. In fact, she suspected that he would choose it as his preferred meal. Clay, on the other hand, would insist that it be taken back to the kitchen and served to him correctly. Iris - well, Iris would try anything at least once.

"Just try it for the Gods' sake!" Helena insisted, sighing heavily, and pushing the food to her once more.

Lorelai acquiesced, bringing it to her mouth slowly and biting into the smallest bite she could.

It was surprisingly... tender meat.

The crispy exterior gave way to a pleasantly juicy texture. Despite the smoky smell, the flavors were hearty and savory, incorporating a wide blend of spices and herbs.

Helena watched her eat, a small grin growing across her cheeks. "Told ya. No one has ever disliked Mort's turkey legs, not even prissy ladies like yourself."

Lorelai coughed softly, covering her mouth with the back of her hand. "These were made by a man named *Mort?*"

"No," Helena drew out the word before biting deeply on another turkey leg and sucking a large hunk of meat into her mouth. "They were made by a very lovely woman named Mort."

They were both quiet for a moment, testing out the others' reaction, before they slowly began to chuckle together.

"I am not prissy, by the way."

"Says the woman who's offended by the fact she has to wear pants."

"It's simply not proper!"

Helena raised a brow in an expression that seemed to say *See?*

Lorelai only narrowed her eyes at the girl ruefully. Perhaps she was a bit... uptight. That was how she had been raised, though. It was all she had ever known. Could anyone really blame her?

They finished their meal in silence, the only interaction between them being when Helena passed her a jug of water to wash down her food with. When she finished eating, the odd woman simply wiped off her hands on the leg of her pants before standing to clean up the mess. With no other washcloth in sight, Lorelai resigned herself to doing the same.

She stood awkwardly, tucking her hands behind her back, unsure of what to do next. What was it that one did to relax in a place like Charling-ton? Helena didn't appear to have any books or playing tables and with how offputting the girl was, she doubted highly that Helena had many friends.

Gods, this place was already making her so mean.

The silence became overwhelming as Helena watched Lorelai scan over the room. The girl stood leaning against the wall, leg kicked up and arms crossed, watching Lorelai with an unflinching, calculating gaze, as if she was

trying to look through Lorelai and see all of her secrets. It was somewhat...
unnerving.

"Should we rest now?" Lorelai asked uncomfortably.

Helena chuckled, the sound little more than a breath of air escaping her.
"Are you tired?"

Lorelai's gaze flickered to the windows, where sunlight still danced
through into the tiny space. No, she wasn't tired at all, but she wasn't sure
she could handle another second of quietly sharing this space with the girl
with no form of conversation or entertainment.

Ultimately, she shrugged.

Helena nodded and, without explanation, walked to where Lorelai had
left her muddied boots by the door. She tossed them to her and Lorelai
hinged at the waist after them, barely catching one while the other fell
heavily towards the floor.

"What was that for?" she demanded.

Helena, infuriatingly, merely shrugged and opened the door, holding it
open in a silent invitation. When Lorelai hesitated, she huffed in annoy-
ance.

"Look, if you want to sleep, be my guest. It just seems like this is the
first time in your life you've actually left the security of your fancy castle
and country estates and I thought you might like to see how the rest of
the country lives. It's possible that I was incorrect, though. Maybe you're
perfectly happy with your small, delicate life. Maybe you're perfectly content to feel nothing more than the slightest fluctuations in emotion while
you move from one tea party to the next. *Me?* I like to spend my life living,
feeling every incredible high and every awful low. So that's what I'm going
to go do right now. Are you coming or not?"

Helena didn't bother to wait and hear the answer before marching out
the door into the world outside. For a moment, Lorelai stood frozen,
unable to do anything more than simply watch the girl walk away.

Eventually, though, she pulled on her boots and followed, wondering if perhaps Helena actually *had* been able to see inside her and know her on a deeper level than she maybe even knew herself.

CAMILLA

A New Punishment

Alina prattled on, her voice a grating symphony of disappointment and insults. It was nothing Camilla hadn't heard a million times before. Erilea sat next to their grandmother, absently petting the fur of her orange tabby, Muffin, while Camilla pretended to pay attention to the lecture she was receiving. She nodded when she needed to, apologized when she needed to, even cried when she knew that's what Alina wanted. She had long since gotten accustomed to giving Alina the performance the elder woman longed for.

And yet they had long since passed the point when her grandmother's rants usually would have ended.

Which was... suspicious.

"It is time you start contributing to the well-being of this family, Camilla!" Alina insisted.

She bit back the biting remark that flew to her tongue. Had she not been contributing to the well-being of this family when Alina demanded she spread her legs and entrap a prince?

Had she not been contributing to the well-being of this family for years now?

She looked around herself. The sitting room that they currently sat in was the most commonly used space in the home. It was filled with fine furniture. In fact, it was the only room in the home with fine furniture, thick-stylish curtains, and beautiful paintings on the wall. Camilla had bought all of them with coins the Dragon had given her. Coins that Alina had demanded be used for the *upkeep of Hypatia manor.*

The very furniture her grandmother sat on was just another example of the ways Camilla had contributed to the well-being of the family.

Now in the few occasions that company would come to call on Alina, she would bring them into this room, seat them so that they could look out at the view of the Great Lake of Athenia, and bring in cups of tea in an attempt to seem more refined than she truly was.

"Yes, grandmother," Camilla intoned.

Alina had been going for a little over an hour at this point. If this went on for much longer, Camilla's hunger was going to become audibly clear, which would only cause her grandmother to get that much more frustrated with her. It wasn't just her stomach and sore muscles leaving her uncomfortable, though. Sweat was beading across her hairline and down her lower back as she sat in the velveteen chair next to the fireplace.

Only Alina would have a fire roaring at the start of spring.

It seemed fitting that the old woman was somehow always impossibly cold. Her soul was positively frigid, after all.

"I have tried to educate you, girl." Alina sighed, smoothing her hair from where she had tied it into a delicate bun at the nape of her neck. "Yet, you continue to be a complete disappointment to me, to your dead father, and to the Goddess who bore you."

Camilla absently wondered what Hypatia actually thought of all this. Was she able to look down on her from the Upperworld? Was she truly as disappointed as Alina claimed her to be? Did becoming the matriarch of the family somehow give Alina more insight into the Goddess' thoughts than the rest of them had?

"Get out of my sight." Alina dismissed her with nothing more than a wave of her palm.

And that was it. There was no more room for conversation. No room for Camilla to express her own thoughts, feelings, or opinions. Alina had summoned her to this house just so that she could speak at her and then dismiss her without even a goodbye.

Camilla stood from her chair, eager to get out of the heat, and began making her way to the door. She didn't care how sore she was from the ride here. She wasn't wasting another second before heading back to the castle.

"Where do you think you're going?" Alina's voice was icy, filled with distaste and an undertone of mockery.

Camilla turned just as Erilea covered her laugh with a cough. Their grandmother glared at the girl before turning her heated stare back to Camilla.

"You won't be leaving quite yet, dear," she told her. "I believe it's best if you spent some time back home, learning how to bring respect to the family name."

Camilla's heart pounded heavily in her chest. She could hear the echo of its beating roaring through her head. She... couldn't stay here. She just couldn't. How long did Alina even want her to stay here? What levels of torment would her grandmother and cousin subject her to during that time?

"How would you like me to do that?" She asked.

Alina smiled and waved her arms, gesturing to the mess around them. "You may leave when Hypatia manor has been cleaned."

"That will take days! If not weeks."

No. Camilla couldn't stay here that long. She'd lose her mind if she had to stay locked away in here with Alina and Erilea, sentenced to clean this impossible filth while her grandmother and cousin mocked and tortured her.

"I suppose you'd better get started soon," Erilea suggested, twirling a thread of her oily hair around her finger.

"This manor has been a mess for years," Camilla protested. "Why the sudden need to clean it?"

Alina's eyes darkened, and the old woman stood slowly. She didn't bother to rush towards Camilla; Alina knew Camilla wouldn't run away from her. She'd learned a long time ago it was better to just accept what was coming from her grandmother than to accept double the punishment for running.

The slap was sharp and stinging, and Alina's long, pointed nails ever so slightly grazed Camilla's cheek. She bit down hard on her lip to stop from crying out, but allowed herself the briefest of moments to feel the pain before raising her eyes back to her grandmother's gaze.

"You know better than to talk back."

"Yes, grandmother."

Erilea snickered in the corner. "Perhaps you could start by tidying my room for me?"

Camilla was quite positive that Erilea was entirely capable of cleaning her own mess. She was also quite positive that upon learning that Alina was going to be summoning Camilla home, Erilea had likely destroyed the room to prepare for just this moment.

Alina looked at Erilea and nodded in agreement. "Yes, you may start there and don't waste time. I want you prepared to serve our morning tea before Erilea's lessons."

With that, Alina turned away to sit on the couch next to Erilea and the two began whispering to each other. Her dismissal was clear and Camilla practically ran from the room and up the steps to the room Alina had given Erilea when she moved into the manor. It was three times the size of Camilla's, with a plush seating area, an enormous bed with a goose-feathered mattress, and a fully filled closet of gowns that did nothing to hide how truly ugly her cousin was.

Erilea and Alina had bonded immediately. Perhaps the ugly in one recognized the hideousness of the other.

Her cousin had most definitely destroyed the room in an effort to upset Camilla. She'd thrown clothes about the room, food on the floor, and had sat her muddied boots atop the vanity. It was disgusting. It was as disgusting as she was and as disgusting as this entire house was.

And everything about this place and her life was positively *awful*.

Camilla kicked the stack of books that sat by the foot of her cousin's bed, not minding the way her toes stung. At least if she could focus on the pain in her foot, she would be less likely to let the lump in her throat turn into tears that she wouldn't be able to stop from flowing.

Camilla wasn't typically one to cry. Too many years of too many tragedies had hardened her against it. And yet, for the first time in many years, the wretchedness of her life suddenly seemed to overtake her.

RANKOR

THE SHARP SIDE OF THE BLADE

"Rankor, wake up!" Elaijah's hushed voice was tense and his grip firm as he grasped onto his brother's arm and shook intensely.

Rankor was alert instantly, having been woken on the eve of impending battles too many times before. His skin was crawling with awareness as he listened to the sounds of heavy panting coming from the surrounding forest. They were heavily drawn puffs of rhythmic air. Louder than any human could make.

"Fuck," he grunted under his breath.

"I *told you* there was something out there!"

He refrained from his urge to smack his brother upside the head.

Beasts weren't common in this part of the woods. The chances of stumbling upon one were so miniscule it was nearly an impossibility. And yet here they were, in the dark of night with one of Ciclopia's beasts lurking in the shadows.

For months he had traveled this country without so much as a drunkard getting in his way. And yet now that he had an untrained fifteen-year-old boy with him, he'd managed to stumble into a beast's den.

He blamed his bad luck on Elaijah.

The boy was wide eyed and nearly trembling with fear. He moved to shuffle back away from the sound, and Rankor grabbed his wrist quickly, holding him in place. He hoped his gaze was reassuring.

"Don't move."

Based on Elaijah's flinch, Rankor's gaze was not as reassuring as he had hoped. Still, Elaijah nodded and stilled.

"What is it?" Elaijah whispered.

The sound of a shrieking, animalistic cry suddenly filled the air, and Elaijah yelped. Rankor moved as quickly as was possible to cover the boy's mouth, but he could only pray to the Gods that whatever beast stalked them hadn't heard his brother. The creature that lingered in the darkness had clearly found their horses. The animal cries were followed by a gurgling that filled his stomach with dread and left a memory flooding his vision.

Blood.

It was everywhere. It stained his face, his hands, his arm. He was in a field of pure crimson. Was this what the Underworld looked like?

Someone shouted his name, and he turned just in time to duck out of the way of an impending sword. Had he been a second later, his own blood would have flooded this field. He reached out, grasping the top of the Promissan soldier's head and squeezed, pulling on the inhuman strength from his Godly ancestor. It didn't take more than a moment before the bone crushed under his grasp.

His head burst like a berry held too tightly between his fingers.

Gods, there was more blood dripping down his arm.

He heard Kent's roar, and he turned wildly. Kent needed to be okay. Rankor would not get through this battle if Kent didn't make it. He ducked under swords, blocked flying arrows with his shield, and pushed through the field, hunting for familiar faces.

"No!"

Rankor whirled, drawn to that voice like a child to its mother. Darius stood behind him, and a spear that must have been aimed at his own back pierced through his friend's gut. Rankor reached for him, catching him as he fell.

"Darius," he gasped, pressing onto the wound.

"It's been an honor, brother."

"No!" Rankor protested, unwilling to hear the customary last words of the Athenian army from another friend's lips. "You will not die here."

Darius opened his mouth, but the gurgling sounds of his choking on his own blood swallowed his words.

Blood.

It was everywhere.

"Rankor!" Elaijah's voice pulled him back to the present.

The horse had gone quiet, finally dead from whatever had attacked him. That heavy panting was even closer now. Too close.

"Do you have *any* experience with a blade?" Rankor whispered in an urgent rush.

Elaijah's eyes widened so much that Rankor had the answer to his question. He had gone to sleep with his weapons at his side, something he'd been taught to do when he was younger than Elaijah. He grasped onto his daggers and thrust them at Elaijah.

"If it comes for you, point the sharp side towards it."

"What is *it?*"

The wind rustled and the sound of a high-pitched growl settled around them. Fallen leaves crinkled under a heavy weight and then, under the silver moonlight, the beast stepped out from the trees and locked its white eyes onto the two of them.

"I'm going to shit myself," Elaijah whispered, almost sounding surprised by this realization.

Adrenaline was already coursing through Rankor's body as he prepared himself for what could easily be a fight to the death. Still, he couldn't help but laugh as he shoved the boy behind him and stood to greet the beast.

Rankor had never seen a Chrimprani in person before. He'd studied all the beasts of the realm during his education, but seeing one in front of him was an otherworldly experience.

The beast had the head of a jackal with long, pointed ears. Fur mutated into heavy brown feathers down its chest and two front legs, which resembled those of a hawk. His backside and hind legs were that of a lion, complete with a long tail that flicked agitatedly from side to side. Quickly, he jerked his head from one side to another, white eyes locked on Rankor, and then, slowly, a growl sounded as the beast bared its teeth.

There was only a single moment for Rankor to compose himself before the Chrimprani spread its giant wings and leaped into the air.

"Move!" He yelled, grabbing onto Elaijah and pushing him out of the way as the Chrimprani dove towards them.

Rankor readied his swords, Truth and Pain, rolling them through the air as the Chrimprani began its descent. When the creature was no more than six feet above his head, Rankor bent at the knees and jumped, using his Godly strength to gain height. Holding his blades downward, he aimed for the fleshy area between the beast's wings.

The Chrimprani roared and threw its weight to the left, rolling easily in the air out of Rankor's path. Rankor fell heavily to the ground, only just missing the sharp end of his own blades. The Chrimprani landed across from it, steam billowing from its nose as it stamped its front talon down onto the ground with anger.

It ran for him.

Rankor twisted, spinning and shoving his foot into the beast's front talon so that it stumbled and crashed into the ground.

"Stab it!" Elaijah yelled from his left.

Rankor and the Chrimprani both looked towards the boy. Idiot.

The Chrimprani, having identified Elaijah as the easier kill, stretched its wings once more and lifted high into the air. Its white eyes locked on Elaijah from the sky and it let out a shrieking battle cry as it readied itself to dive. From across the clearing, Elaijah muttered a curse under his breath and lifted the blade Rankor had given him, holding it in front of his body with shaking hands.

"Good Gods," Rankor sighed, throwing his weight into a sprint towards his brother.

"What do I do?" Elaijah squeaked as the creature began its dive.

"Duck!"

Rankor leaped just as his brother ducked, landing in a crouched position before him. He lifted Truth and Pain into the air at a cross and stood to meet the Chrimprani, slicing two clean cuts across its breast. The beast raged, throwing out its talons and grasping onto Rankor's shoulders. He roared as its claws pierced through his flesh.

"It's going to take you!" Elaijah screamed.

While Elaijah may not have learned how to wield steel in the village, at least he had a decent education, Rankor thought absently. Chrimprani's were known to carry their meals back to the nests they created high above mountain tops.

Rankor had no intention of being anyone's dinner, though.

"My sword!" He called, fighting through the burning pain in his shoulders as he reached up to grab the beast on either side of his wings.

Then he pulled.

The Chrimprani fought, flapping its wings wildly. It took all of his magical strength to keep the creature from flying off into the air and taking him with it. Elaijah rushed to his side, picking up Truth from where it laid on the grass that was now scarlet with Rankor's blood.

"Gods, this is heavy!"

If Rankor wasn't already going dizzy from his wounds, he might have yelled at the boy. Of course it was heavy! It was a broadsword, made of the strongest steel of Athenia. He'd even had weight added to it so that it wouldn't feel too light in his hands when he was using his power to bolster his own strength.

"Just prop it up, sword towards the sky, and release it when I say now."

Elaijah looked skeptical, as if he was unsure of his ability to do such a thing and truthfully, Rankor doubted he could, but there was no room right now for either of them to consider the possibility that he couldn't lift the sword. If Elaijah didn't do as he was told, they were both going to die.

The beast cried out, its call strained and angry as it squeezed its talons into Rankor's shoulders more tightly and it beat its wings madly. The force of its flapping sent the grass and fallen leaves flying into the night air around them. Rankor's power was already fading. He wouldn't be able to hold the beast for much longer.

Elaijah wrapped his arms around the hilt of the blade and pulled. He pulled until he felt as if his arms would break apart and his knees would give out, and yet the blade did not move. Blood soaked the ground under his feet from Rankor's injuries as the larger man wavered on his feet. They were running out of time and options, and Elaijah realized all too suddenly that lifting from the weighted hilt would not give him the leverage he needed.

So he released the sword, ignored his brother's grunt of rage, and wrapped his hands around the top of the blade, biting into his cheek as the blade sliced into his palms. Grunting, he bent at the knees and pushed with all his might until his own roar of anger met the sound of the beast's cries. Impossibly, the blade lifted, and he held it into the air.

"Now!" Rankor yelled.

Elaijah released the sword just as Rankor tucked at the side and threw the beast onto the blade. Its howl was bone-shaking, and it released Rankor, only to slice down his chest as it thrashed helplessly, fighting off the visage of death that was slowly coming for it.

Rankor quickly slid away from the beast on his hands and knees before collapsing onto the ground. His head spun as darkness began covering patches of his vision. One hoarse grunt was all he released before consciousness slipped away.

The dead beast sat on Elaijah's right and his unconscious brother on his left. The air was finally quiet again and a fear stronger than any Elaijah had ever felt before chilled his bones.

IRIS

Trust in the Afterglow

"It's almost over," Nikolai assured her, pulling her hair back off her neck as beads of sweat dribbled down her skin.

The healer had worked on her stab wound at first and the feeling of her skin magically sewing itself back together had been almost as painful as receiving the wound had been in the first place. When the woman turned towards her head, the sensation of healing whatever damage had been done to her brain upset Iris' stomach so much that they had to pause the process for her to get sick into a wastebasket. All the while, Nikolai held back her hair and rubbed gentle circles on her back.

Now, she sat in her bed, leaning back against his broad chest as they prepared to restore her thumb into its socket.

"This will hurt," the healer warned her.

"Because everything has been so pleasant thus far," Iris snapped, irritable from the exhaustion and pain.

Nikolai chuckled from behind her, and his chest shook gently underneath her.

"Hush, my bird," he commanded, and he grasped onto her good arm with one hand as he wrapped his other arm around her chest.

Holding her like this was incredibly intimate, and the feeling of his arms wrapped around her, holding her close to him, sent a warm shiver down her spine even as the healer grasped onto her injured hand and pulled it into her lap, fingers probing gently. Iris hissed air through her lips at the sharp sting and Nikolai lowered his head, brushing the stubble of hair on his jaw against her throat. She leaned into him without intending to, too delerious with pain to stop herself from slightly arching her neck to give him better access, and he rewarded her efforts by trailing his lips down the line of her neck.

"What are you doing?" She whispered to him.

"Shh."

He reached the most delicate spot and although they were very much not alone and he was very much her enemy, she couldn't stop a small breathy sound from escaping. She felt his lips pull into a smile against her before they pressed down in a gentle kiss. His tongue darted out, hot against her skin, sending shockwaves of awareness and anticipation through her. His arm pulled her tighter against him even as his teeth began scraping against her skin and-

The healer popped the joint back into place and Iris screamed, railing back against him while he whispered soothing words in her ear.

As her cries softened and her shaking slowed, the healer looked up at Nikolai with a bored expression.

"Will there be anything else, sir?"

He shook his head. "See that a hot meal and fresh bath water are brought to my wife immediately."

She nodded, wiping her hands on her apron as she stood and exited the room, leaving Nikolai and Iris alone, still tangled together in the bed. She inhaled a shaky breath, suddenly painfully aware of everywhere he was touching her. Goosebumps peppered her skin as he removed his arm from her chest, trailing his fingers across her skin as he did.

"How are you feeling?"

"Like I was bashed over the head, held in a dirty tomb of a cell, and the worst part of it all was a healer putting me back together."

He laughed as he put his hands on her waist, lifting her slightly so he could remove himself from behind her and carry the wastebasket from earlier outside of the room. Wordlessly, he sat it down in the hall and closed the door beside him.

"That man," she started, trying to choose her words carefully despite how her head was still swimming from the rush of the fight and the equally heady rush of him being pressed against her. "The man who works with you-"

"For me," he corrected shortly.

She fought the urge to grin. "There was a man there who works for you."

"We found him outside when we arrived. He's been taken care of."

"Dead?"

Nikolai nodded as he stood by the door and folded his arms across his chest. The purposeful amount of space that he kept between them was obvious, and she wasn't sure why it bothered her so much. The logical explanation was that she needed to worry that he was now suspicious of her.

The real reason was that it had been... nice to have someone supporting her while the healer patched her back together.

One of her first lessons in The Order had been how to withstand severe pain. She had been cut, bruised, and bloodied over and over, with no one to show her an ounce of sympathy or support. Eventually, she learned to numb herself to it and get through. Still, she couldn't deny that she had enjoyed his tenderness, that she had relished his distraction, that she had appreciated him being there with her - for her.

"You can fight," he finally said, after the silence between them grew unbearable.

Iris folded her legs underneath her and nodded. "I've been taught a few things over the years." Then, for good measure, added, "I told you growing up with my father wasn't as idyllic as you believed. I had to learn to defend myself."

His eyes were unflinching as he looked at her, seeming more emerald than usual. He pursed his lips as he considered her words, considered her.

"Did he say anything to you?"

"Only that if my father thought you killed me, then he would declare war."

"He was trying to use you as a pawn in this game between us?"

Iris wanted to laugh at the venom in his voice. "Isn't that exactly what you did?"

Nikolai opened his mouth to say something, only to pause, reconsider, and tilt his head to the side softly in acknowledgement of her words. "I suppose you're right. I suppose I have been using you and almost got you killed because of it."

"It wasn't your fault."

"You're just a girl, bird. You shouldn't have to be spending your days living in fear. Not in your father's home, and certainly not in mine."

His voice differed from how she had ever heard it before. There was no taunting, no grins. Only cold detachment. Indifference.

"What are you saying?"

"I'll instruct my staff to ensure you're kept company when you wish and that you're to be allowed to roam the manner. Word of our marriage has already spread, so the safest place for you is here, but for now, I shall allow you your privacy. I'll remove my belongings from the room and sleep elsewhere."

She was watching his guard go up. His face was cementing, his expression closing itself off to her as he began to turn and leave the room. His voice was still echoing around her, saying something along the lines of this being in her best interest, but she couldn't focus on his words, not when all of her instincts were screaming at her to *stop him.*

The relationship that was building between them was new and tenuous, built on nothing but lies and sexual tension, but Iris knew without any doubt that if she allowed him to walk out of this door, then whatever existed between them would die and she couldn't allow that. She didn't need him to distance himself from her. What she needed was for him to trust her, to include her in his plans, to tell her his secrets.

And yet, when she stood, crossed the room, and grabbed his face between her palms, she knew that the good of the mission wasn't the only reason she was willing to cross this line. It wasn't the only thing that was drawing her to him.

"What if that's not what I want?" She whispered, letting the tips of her fingers brush against the silkiness of his hair.

He didn't move. He hardly seemed to breathe, but his eyes lingered on her lips. "What if it's what's best for you?"

Iris smiled. "I'm not a girl and I'm not a delicate little bird. I can decide what's best for me."

Finally, he budged. Finally, he shifted, bringing his hands to rest on her waist and giving a gentle squeeze, while she took another step forward until they were pressed together. Until their lips were only inches apart. Slowly, taking her time so that he could stop her if he wanted, she lifted onto her toes and pressed her mouth to his.

The kiss was slow at first, tentative, both of them seeming to test out the boundaries of the other until all at once, like an elastic that had been pulled far too tight, everything seemed to snap into place. The *rightness* of it seemed to snap into place. Her arms tightened around his neck, pulling him closer as his slid up her back. His chest vibrated against hers with a soft growl.

"I thought you smarter than to think that any part of me was in your best interest."

His voice fell over her skin like the kiss of warm sunlight on the first day of summer, and she felt like she might melt into a puddle. He separated his lips from hers for only a moment before gripping her by the back of the neck and pulling her to him once more. He was desperate in his need, and she opened for him, feeling an electric rush as his tongue danced over hers and his teeth nipped at her bottom lip. Iris grasped onto his tunic, stained and stiff from where her blood had leaked onto it, and pulled, leading him backwards to the bed.

He went willingly, and when he pulled back to look at her, there was nothing but pure lust in his eyes. He bent slightly, gripping her waist and practically throwing her backward on the bed. Not that she particularly minded the roughness. Her core was molten lava, hungry and desperate for the release that they had been dancing around since the moment he'd found her in the woods.

Without breaking eye contact, he reached over his shoulder and pulled off his tunic, allowing her a moment to gaze upon the expanse of his lean, muscular torso. It wasn't the first time she had seen him half-dressed, of course, but it was the first time she allowed herself the permission to appreciate him. His body was a map of life. Pale pink scars dancing across his shoulders and stomach served as permanent reminders of a life spent locked in battle. She imagined that her own bare body, her true bare body, the one she never fully allowed anyone to see, looked much the same.

He crawled over her slowly, letting his hands and mouth linger. When he reached her chest, he kissed along the neckline of her dress and she felt her breasts swelling, her nipples hardening under the hands that grasped them. Nikolai took one into his mouth, sucking and teasing so intensely that even though the now damp fabric of her dress separated them, she was practically writhing.

"So needy," he teased. "You must be patient."

"I don't want to be patient."

"Ah, but I truly want to take my time with you. I want to touch every inch of you, *taste* every inch of you. I want you to leave this room with no doubt of who you belong to."

So much talking.

In a sense, talking was good. Talking was how she got information out of him.

But, if she were honest with herself, this had stopped being about the mission the minute she kissed him and right now, talking to him was the last thing she wanted to do.

"Nikolai," she whimpered, pitching her hips up against him and loving the sensation of feeling his hardness firm and ready for her.

"Shh. Tell me what you want, love."

She wanted everything. She wanted to cry and scream and laugh all at once. She was burning alive, and he was the only one who could stop it.

"Touch me."

He dragged a finger across her lips as his other hand dipped to her dress, pulling up the hem so that he could run his touch against the bare skin of her leg. The sensation sent shivers racing down her spine.

"Didn't anyone teach you manners, little bird? What do you say when you want something?"

His hand was climbing higher, so high she could hardly think. His fingers grazed against the thin lace of her undergarments, circling that sensitive bud for just a single, tantalizing second before pulling away so fast that she practically growled in frustration.

"What do you say?" He asked, his lips spread in a smug smile.

"Please," she begged. "Please touch me."

He laughed, kissing her with a ferocity that made her head spin and her blood dance, all the while that hand kept pressing against her over the fabric of her undergarment. She rocked her hips against him, desperate for more friction, but she couldn't find the release she needed. It wasn't enough. She needed to feel his skin on hers.

Nikolai pulled away, staring at her as he lowered himself.

"What are you doing?"

"I told you," he smirked as he undid the laces of her boots, pulled them off, and then reached up to pull her undergarments off as well. She lifted her hips as he did to help. "I want to taste you everywhere."

She didn't even have time to react before he planted himself between her thighs and feasted on her.

"Oh," she cried, voice high.

His tongue raced against her, teasing as he sucked and played with her. Pleasure rolled over her in a steady rhythm, and she lost herself in it, until all she could think about was him, the way his tongue moved on her, and the sounds of approval he was making.

Just when she thought she couldn't take any more, his hand reached between her legs and two fingers parted her flesh, sliding into her slickness while he continued that maddening swirl against her. Her eyes snapped closed as the pleasure erupted inside her, leaving her body shaking in aftershocks.

The world came back into focus slowly.

But then he was standing, unlacing his trousers, and it was so clear that they weren't done. That she didn't *want* to be done.

He let his pants fall to the floor around him and she had only a moment to marvel at the impressive length of him before he was atop of her once more, ripping her dress higher and pulling a thigh up high against his hip.

With no more warning than a grin, he centered himself at her entrance and began pushing in.

The fullness was overwhelming, borderline painful, and she gasped, fingernails leaving small-half moons in his skin as she gripped onto him.

"Relax, you can take me," he coached her, voice surprisingly gentle despite the passion on his face.

So she did. She relaxed against him and, with one more sudden thrust, he seated himself fully inside her. She cried out and he let her adjust to the size of him until he moved again, thrusting in a steady rhythm that had her stomach tightening in tension once more.

Before she knew it, she was rocking against him, chasing that wave of pleasure once more, only this time she kept her eyes open. She kept her eyes locked on his as her thighs trembled and her core tightened.

"That's it," he coaxed. "Sing for me, my beautiful bird."

And when her climax hit her for a second time, impossibly stronger than the first, she did. She screamed his name and the sound only egged him on further. He lost himself in her, pounding into her at a pace she couldn't possibly match until he let loose a guttural roar and buried himself in her to the hilt.

When it was over, they could only look at each other, sharing each other's breath and relishing the joy of the afterglow together.

Iris laid draped across Nikolai's chest, absently tracing circles on his skin as he ran his fingers through her hair.

Joliette's hair.

Because she was in Joliette's body.

Once the absolute ecstasy of their joining had worn off, all she could think about was the fact that nothing about that moment had been genuine. He hadn't been losing himself in her. He had been losing himself in the illusion of Joliette.

And even though Iris knew that was her job, that it was her duty to convince him to love her and reveal his secrets, it upset her more than she liked to admit.

Because the truth of the matter was that what she was feeling for him might be extending past physical attraction.

"You're quiet," he noted. "Are you well?"

She looked up at him. "Very well."

Nikolai sighed heavily, his chest lifting and falling under her, as he leaned down to kiss the top of her head. "I am sorry, bird, for the way you're going to be put in the middle of this."

Iris shifted, pulling back to rest her weight on her elbows and look at him more fully. "What do you mean?"

"What your father did by attacking the Duke of Eagirton has brought suspicion from the crown to the province and my business can't afford for the Dragon to gain a sudden interest in what we're doing here."

"You're going to war with the Serpent?"

Nikolai took a piece of her hair in his fingertips, twisting the delicate lock before tucking it affectionately behind her ear. "I don't have a choice now."

Here it was, the moment that she had been waiting for.

Iris met his eyes, marveling at the honey ring around his otherwise remarkably green eyes.

"Take me with you," she asked.

"It's not safe, bird."

"I can take care of myself."

"And I don't need your help," he countered, shifting out from under her to stand from the bed and begin pulling on his trousers.

Nikolai left for the washroom and every second he spent away from her felt like an eternity. Anxiously, she chewed at her lip. She needed to convince him to take her. He was right, though. He didn't need her help. Nikolai had an army in his employ. To convince him to bring her, she needed to prove her value.

She stood in a rush, pulling the sheets around her body to follow him as he made his way to gather a clean shirt from the dressing room.

"I know where he'll be."

Nikolai stilled, hands on the scarlet tunic he had been about to throw over his head. After a moment, he turned to her, face hard and voice measured. "What do you mean?"

"That day, he didn't just rob the house. He also took the Duke's wife, which leads me to suspect that his business with the Duke isn't finished."

"And how would you know that?"

"My cousin mentioned it when he kidnapped me," she lied.

He pulled his shirt over his head before walking slowly towards her. With a slow breath, his hand wrapped around her chin, harshly pulling her face up to look at him.

"The Duke escaped my father the last time he attacked the manor," she reasoned with him. "He won't allow that same mistake again. He'll have dozens with him, if not hundreds. You won't get anywhere close to him."

"But you will?"

"I could," she told him. "If you bring me with you."

He stared down at her and all the while, her stomach railed against her with nervous energy. His grip on her face was firm, almost painful, and for a second, she considered releasing the razor hidden in her bangle.

But then he was leaning down. He brushed his lips against hers, the touch so gentle that she might not have even felt it at all.

"Can I trust you?" He whispered, voice airy with genuine cautiousness.

"Yes," she lied.

KENT

EMOTIONAL MESSES

Wedding celebrations had always annoyed him for how long and drawn out they were. He didn't necessarily understand the need for it all. At the end of the day, a marriage was about two people in love. The ceremony should be intimate, meant only for the two people pledging their lives and souls to one another.

Apparently, the rest of the world felt a bit different, though.

He'd been to his fair share of wedding celebrations over the years, all ranging in grandeur. When the Dragon married Queen Valentina, the celebrations had lasted nearly a month. Even in this small little fishing town where residents had only as much gold as they needed, they worked hard to make everything special.

For tonight's wedding feast, tables were arranged outside in the court-yard with small bouquets of flowers sat atop each. Candles were spread along the ground and hung delicately from the trees, leaving the air around them slightly warm and glowing. Each family brought a special dish to share with the others and dressed in their finest evening wear.

Seralyn had changed into an ivory gown that hung low across her back and cuffed at her wrists, but otherwise fell neatly in satin waves towards her feet. Her hair was still in its intricate array from earlier, but the day in the sun had left her cheeks even more rosy. It suited her.

Truthfully, Kent couldn't take his eyes off her.

He sat at his family's table, where his sisters ate quickly and gossiped among each other. Throughout the entirety of his meal, though, his attention remained on the small rectangular table in the center of the courtyard where the bride and groom were eating their dinner. In surprising contrast, Jaxon's attention seemed to be on anything but his beautiful bride-to-be. His eyes darted around the room as he scratched at his beard, one arm thrown carelessly over the back of her chair.

"You're staring," Kent's mother whispered to him.

He sighed, but didn't bother to look over at her. That would require looking away from Seralyn, something he couldn't quite manage. "It's the night before his wedding. He could at least pretend to be enjoying himself."

"He's probably just as bored as I am!" Kreyana whined, which earned her a sharp smack on the wrist from their mother. She pouted for a moment before turning back to her sister.

"It is not our place to judge, Kentoni," their mother reminded him.

Still, as he watched Seralyn lean over to say something to her betrothed only for him to look at her from the side of his eye and turn away without responding to her at all, he couldn't help himself. He judged. A few minutes of watching their interactions had been all Kent needed to know that this marriage wasn't right for Seralyn. Jaxon would not respect and care for her, not the way she deserved.

Not the way he could love her if she gave him that chance.

Seralyn's mother approached their table, saying something to them before the couple nodded and stood. Jaxon took Seralyn's arm, and they began circling the courtyard, stopping at each of the tables to greet their guests and thank them for their attendance.

Kent watched them through it all, noticing the way Seralyn's face lit up in kindness every time she spoke while Jaxon kept a firm grip on her arm without ever saying more than a few words at a time.

And then suddenly, the couple was approaching his table and Seralyn's back stiffened as her eyes quickly darted between Kent and her betrothed.

"Thank you so much for coming." She smiled as they came to stand near Kent's mother. "We're so grateful to have you here to celebrate with us."

Kent suddenly noticed what his mother had meant about Seralyn seeming more difficult to read than when they were kids. Her expressions were as animated as they had ever been, and yet there was something infinitely more guarded about the way she held herself. It was as if the smile on her face was more defensive than truly joyful.

"How are you girls enjoying the feast?" Serayln asked his sisters.

They each gave her a thumbs up, their mouths too full to respond to her, which earned them a chuckle from her. Kent's mother only sighed in embarrassment.

"I apologize," she said. "They have not yet gotten to the age where they appreciate proper manners."

The girls whined their protests briefly before pivoting their attention back to each other and communicating in that odd way they only did with one another. As they did, an awkwardness settled over the table as Seralyn finally turned to him.

"And how long will you be visiting for?" she asked, her gentle bell-like voice sending shockwaves down his spine.

For a moment, his throat felt too clogged with emotion for him to utter a response.

"Just until the festivities are over," he finally grumbled out.

She nodded, a momentary flicker of disappointment flashing over her features, before the same calm smile took over once more. "I see. Well, we do appreciate you making the journey. I'm sure your family is greatly enjoying having you home again."

Jaxon began tugging at her arm, signaling that it was time for them to make their way to the next table, and Kent nearly burst from his seat, desperate to keep her with him if only for a moment longer. The words were out of his mouth before he could stop them.

"And you?"

His mother kicked him under the table, her eyes wide as she glanced at him in surprise and all too suddenly, he realized what he'd asked her.

"I mean, and you two?" Kent stumbled over his words, stuttering in a way he hadn't since he was a boy. "How did you two meet?"

He could have buried a blade in his own gut right then and there and it still wouldn't feel as bad as the raging embarrassment that settled heavily in his stomach as Seralyn and Jaxon turned back to him, Seralyn the picture of confusion and Jaxon frowning in obvious irritation.

"Seralyn was acquainted with my younger brother, actually," Jaxon explained, his deep voice terse.

Her cheeks flushed a deep shade of crimson. "My family purchased a mare from Jaxon's brother last autumn. I met Jaxon shortly thereafter."

"Oh, how sweet!" Kent's mother praised. "Jaxon, where is your family seated this evening?"

Jaxon's eyes darkened, and he turned away slightly, pulling his arm from Seralyn's grip. She quickly tucked her hands behind her back, but there was no mistaking the nervous flinch when he stepped to the side.

"My family couldn't attend this evening, but they send their regards. If you'll excuse us, we must greet our other guests."

Kent watched them as they left. He watched them as they began talking to another table. He watched them as they continued traveling the room without ever joining hands again. He watched their every move until he couldn't bear the anger building in him for a second longer. And though he knew he shouldn't, though he knew it was an invasion of privacy, he let his magic connect with them once more.

Seralyn's emotions were jumbled, a mess of multiple feelings all tangled together. There was a rush of anxiety and fear, but also a glimmer of joy, and even beyond that, a feeling of anticipation.

Jaxon's emotions were more simplistic. He felt nothing more than pure rage.

"There's something very wrong with them," he whispered under his breath to his mother.

She followed his gaze to the couple and sighed, reaching over to pat his hand reassuringly. "She's a grown woman. Allow her the freedom to make her own choices."

"Sometimes people make bad choices. Choices that put them in danger."

"Do you rely so heavily on your magic that you do not think yourself capable of being swayed by your own emotions?" His mother snapped at him sharply. He pulled his hand out from under hers.

"What do you mean by that?"

"I mean, you're in love with the girl Kentoni. You're looking for a problem because you don't want to watch her marry someone else, but *you* made the choice to stay at the castle after the war. You had served your time and easily could have come home. You didn't. So you have no right to come here after years away and begrudge her for moving on with her life in your absence."

He wanted to protest, to explain how clearly wrong she was. His magic wasn't something that was swayed by his own feelings or desires. It was pure power from the Gods that gave him insight into others' true emotions. What he may or may not feel for Seralyn wasn't relevant.

The only thing that mattered was that she was clearly afraid to be marrying this man.

And someone had to do something about that.

CAMILLA

THE BUTTERFLY AND THE BEAST

The amount of dust that littered every surface of every piece of furniture in Hypatia manor was like a slow-moving poison through Camilla's system. She'd spent most of the morning with a pounding headache and fighting off countless sneezes. It had been two days since she'd started her task and so far she had cleaned Erilea's room, cleaned three of the guest bedrooms, cleaned the kitchen and re-cleaned Erilea's room after the wretched girl *accidentally* spilled a tube of paints onto her bed.

She'd stood by and laughed as Camilla had to hand-wash the fabrics three times to get the stain out.

All the while, Alina had her serving tea in the morning and the afternoon, aiding the kitchen cook in preparing meals, and assisting in Erilea's spell-casting lessons.

Camilla hated to admit it, but the girl had some natural talent in spell-casting, and her potion brewing had always been excellent. Truthfully, that was probably the reason Alina had taken Erilea under her wing instead of Camilla. Alina valued power, always had, and Camilla's magic had always been terribly weak thanks to her mortal mother.

"Camilla!" Erilea's piercing holler called to her from the bottom of the stairs.

Sighing, she stood from where she'd been organizing different spell-casting candles and brushed her dusty hands on the apron she had tied around her waist. Erilea waited for her on the main floor, her hand extended with a wicker basket swinging from her fingers.

"Grandmother and I are making a healing potion for a sick boy in town," she said by way of explanation. "Go and fetch us some Chaga mushroom."

"And how much are you earning for saving a boy's life?" Camilla knew her grandmother well enough to know that none of her potions or spells were given for free, no matter how dire the circumstances were.

Erilea rolled her eyes and flicked her braid over her shoulder. "Just go."

With that, she slinked back to the kitchen to, presumably, continue working on whatever else the townsfolk had commissioned her and Alina for. For a moment, Camilla just had to stand on the bottom of the staircase to center her breathing. Everything they did was so ridiculously manipulative. Alina had forbid her from leaving until the house was clean, and yet this was the third errand she'd sent her on this morning. At this rate, it would be a full fortnight before she could escape this place.

As she stepped into the spring air and made her way to the edge of the scattered patch of wood on the edge of the property, she pulled the skirt of her dress into a knot at her knees to prevent it from tangling in the weeds and began marching forward. At least the mushroom shouldn't be too hard to find, unlike the hawthorn berries she'd spent hours looking for in the early morning as the sun had risen around her. Chagas were the most commonly used mushrooms in healing potions, given how abundant they grew around birch trees, so hopefully she'd be able to find one quickly and get back to finishing the room she had been working on.

The forest floor was soft under her feet, thick with ferns and moss. Every so often she would have to step over fallen branches or duck underneath low hanging leaves as she searched for the -

Ah, there!

Camilla walked to the singular birch tree where Chaga mushrooms grew in various sizes and shapes along the trunk. Curling her lip in distaste, she bent to her knees and began pulling the crusty black mushrooms and piling them into her basket, stopping only when a butterfly landed on her finger as she reached to grab her last prize.

It flittered its wings quickly before stilling, settling on her.

Camilla sighed. "I sure hope you're having a better day than I am."

A crack sounded behind her suddenly and Camilla jumped to her feet, dropping the basket of mushrooms to the ground as she turned her head wildly from side to side, looking for the source of the sound.

No one ever came to these woods.

The world was still around her, spare the gentle breeze that rustled the olive and golden yellow leaves around her. Not even a chipmunk rushed across the ground.

"I must be imagining things." She ran a tired hand over her eyes. Since coming to this house, Camilla hadn't been sleeping well.

With a heavy sigh, she bent to pick up the basket and begin the trek back to the house. Clearly, she just needed to finish here as soon as possible so that she could get back to her room at the castle and actually get a proper meal and a full night's sleep.

Although, admittedly, she wasn't sure what her role looked like now at court. Both the Dragon and Clay had cast her off now. How could she and Clay ever be the same around each other as they were before they got intimate? Rankor would tease them endlessly about it, and Iris would obviously shun her in favor of Clay. Where Iris went, Lorelai was sure to follow, too. Kent was likely the only one who would even bother to check in on her.

What life did she even have to go back to?

Crack.

Camilla spun again, this time in the opposite direction, absolutely sure that she had *not* been imagining that sound.

"Hello?" she called stupidly.

Crack.

She spun to the left.

Crack.

She spun to the right.

"Who are you?" She screamed, struggling to catch her breath. What kind of beast could move so quickly to jump from her left to her right without being seen?

And what did they want with her?

"Boo!"

Camilla screamed.

RANKOR

FEEL IT

Rankor fought to stay conscious as the sun began rising in the east. He looked to the fragments of tangerine light over his left shoulder before turning to his brother.

"The sun rises to the east. You'll need to travel north to the next town."

"*We* will travel north," his brother replied curtly, not even bothering to look up from where he was slicing several of his shirts against Rankor's blade. "I will not leave you here."

Rankor wanted to laugh. The boy was barely more than fifteen. He would be lucky if he managed to get himself out of these woods and back onto the road into town. There was no way he would be able to support Rankor through that journey.

Rankor had seen enough deadly injuries to know what one looked like.

The beast had ripped through the muscle and tendon on both of his shoulders, nearly ripping off both of his arms entirely. When its talons had sliced down his chest, he hadn't even felt the wound. By that time, the sensation of icy coldness had already become the only thing he could focus on.

That and keeping his brother alive.

He'd promised his mother that he would take care of Elaijah, make sure he was safely looked after once she passed. He hated himself for not keeping that promise to the woman who had birthed him, but at least his last action would be saving the boy from the Chrimprani.

"You will not die!" Elaijah insisted. "Now stop mumbling to yourself so I can focus."

He set about wrapping Rankor's wounds in tight knots of fabric, ignoring when the larger man roared in pain. Eventually, though, after he had tied off both shoulder wounds and set about trying to gently clean the sliced flesh of his chest, Rankor quieted.

By the time Elaijah frantically looked up to his face, he had already passed out.

"Fuck," Elaijah muttered under his breath, reaching for Rankor's wrist.

His pulse was slow, his fingertips already turning blue. They didn't have much time before his body started shutting down entirely. With how filthy the Chrimprani's claws were, it was also only a matter of time before the infection set in.

And then Rankor would only have hours.

"You will not die," Elaijah whispered once more, even though he knew his brother couldn't hear him now.

Rankor blinked awake, feeling a bit dazed as he stared up at the blue sky above him. Tendrils of puffy white clouds floated slowly in the air and the movement of it was almost... peaceful. He felt at peace now. There was no more pain.

He turned his head to the left, searching for Elaijah.

"Elaijah?" He called, his voice hoarse and throat aching.

He heard no answer. There were only the sounds of the wind pushing through the leaves of the trees and insects and forest creatures scattering around the grass.

He could feel them all.

"I feel it," Cristoff mused, his wide eyes staring up aimlessly above them. Rankor pushed at the skin above his brow to examine his eyes. His pupils were dilated, one obviously moreso than the other.

"What do you feel?" He asked, trying to keep the soldier talking and aware until a healer could reach them on the edges of the battlefield.

"Life. I feel the life all around me. I'm part of it, Rankor. We all are."

He wasn't making any sense. And the more he spoke, the more difficult to understand he became as his words melted into each other.

"That sounds great, buddy."

"You don't have to be afraid of the Underworld," he mused. "I understand it now. It's all life."

Rankor pressed his hand against the wound. "I need a healer!"

Cristoff gasped suddenly and Rankor cursed, cupping the boy's cheek to look into his eyes again. By the time he did, in the single second it had taken him to focus on his face, the light in his amber eyes had faded. Rankor felt the dampness on his fingers, leaking from Cristoff's ears, and knew it was too late.

"No!" Rankor fought the urge to shake the boy, to force him to come back from the Underworld to live a few more days in the Mortal Realm.

It was no use, though. The blow to his head had been too much for him to survive until a healer got here. He was gone. Just seventeen years old, and already another victim of the war.

"I know what you mean now, Cristoff. I feel it too."

Rankor closed his eyes, oddly comforted by the fact that Elaijah had left him. It was good that the boy had gone off to find safety. That meant that Rankor's job was complete. He was free to become part of the life around him.

Just as Cristoff and Darius did. Just like all of his friends in the war had.

It had all been leading to this. Rankor knew he should have gone out with his friends, honorably in battle. At least now he would finally be able to see them again.

"Rankor!"

The desperate, shrieking voice was just beginning to pull him back to consciousness when he felt the sudden sting of a slap against his cheek.

"Wake up right now, you giant lug of meat!" Elaijah's voice was frantic, thick with emotion.

"What did you just call me?"

"Oh, thank the Gods!"

Rankor blinked into awareness, unable to fully process what was happening around him. Elaijah sat hunched over him, filthy in muck and scratches as if he had run through the woods with no regard for the branches which might tear through his skin. Over his brother's shoulder, he could just make out two broad men, sitting down a cot between them.

"What's happening?" Rankor groaned.

"These men are going to help you," Elaijah explained. "I've brought some medicine for your wounds and they're going to carry you through the woods into town, where a healer should be waiting for us by now. They had to send for her from the next town over."

Rankor glanced at the two older men Elaijah had brought with him suspiciously. Rankor knew better than to trust that any men would do favors like this out of the kindness of their hearts.

"Your brother here was a hard man to say no to," one of them explained, sensing his hesitancy. "Came into our bar downright demanding help. Says he's an expert shepherd and would lead all of our livestock out of town if we didn't come."

Rankor wanted to laugh, but the motion sent waves of pain through him. Perhaps the medicine Elaijah had smeared over his wounds while he was unconscious was worth something if he could feel pain again.

"No," Rankor protested, struggling to find his voice and weakly using his injured arms to push away his brother. "Leave me be."

"I will not!" Elaijah insisted, fingers twitching like he wanted to slap his brother once more.

"I can be with my brothers now. Let me be! I can be part of the afterlife with them. I belong with them." He was speaking to Elaijah, and he also wasn't. His eyes saw the concerned face of his younger brother, but his mind saw the dozens of friends he had lost in battle.

Cristoff.

Darius.

Monte.

Gregory.

Bryce.

Kalcum.

And so many more. Their names haunted his every thought. He saw their faces every time he closed his eyes. Didn't Elaijah understand? This was finally *his* time to join them.

Elaijah gripped onto Rankor's hand suddenly and fiercely, applying enough pressure to bring Rankor back to the present time.

"Listen to me," Elaijah whispered fiercely. "I won't pretend to know who you lost or what you went through in that war, but I'm your brother, too. I'm your family too. And I *need* you, Rankor. You're all I have left and I'm all you have left. I may not be the kind of brother you want, but I'm the one you got, and I'll be damned if I let you die in these woods. So snap out of it and be the warrior I know you can be. The warrior our mother and father *always* knew you were."

Rankor stared at his younger brother, and for a moment, the faces of his dead brothers morphed into visages of his own mother and father. He saw the features that had passed from each of them onto Elaijah. Their father's nose. Their mother's eyes. Their father's dimples. Their mother's eyebrows.

He looked to Elaijah and saw another version of himself.

No, Elaijah wasn't skilled with a sword or as precautious and strong as Rankor was because he'd never had to be. When it counted, though, at the moment Rankor had needed him, Elaijah had come back. Elaijah possessed an innate strength that couldn't be taught.

He had the strength that made you overcome any obstacle when your family needed you.

Rankor squeezed his brother's hand, realizing something terribly important. This *wasn't* his time to join his brothers because he still had one more brother in this realm who still needed him.

He had made a promise to care for Elaijah, and by the Gods he was going to keep it.

"Okay," he whispered. "Let's get me patched up."

KENT

FOREVERMORE

As the meal wound down, people stood to walk around and mingle. The sun had long since set, bringing a slight chill to the air, so the twins quickly began complaining about being cold. It was clear their mother wanted to stay for longer, but many of the townspeople with younglings were beginning to take their leave, eager to tuck tired children into bed.

"Come now," their mother finally announced, standing and brushing off her hands. "You two need to rest."

The twins burst up from their seats, Kreyana thanking her and Kressida protesting that she was *not* tired. As they began to gather their belongings and prepare to make their way home, Kent remained still, his unblinking attention still focused on Seralyn, who danced with some girls she had been friends with during their childhood days.

"Kentoni," his mother called to him sharply. "We should leave."

Seralyn, caught in a fit of laughter, excused herself to walk to the table filled with pitchers of water and lemonade. It was the first time all evening that she seemed to be separated from Jaxon. The first time that everyone's attention seemed to be elsewhere.

"I'll be home shortly, mother. You should put the twins to bed."

"Kentoni," she hissed. "Staying here longer will bring no good."

The twins watched their exchange with nervous apprehension. Their mother was a firm woman who accepted no talking back or disrespect. When she said it was time to leave, she meant it. But Kent was a man, and he had lived on his own for several years. He wasn't about to start following guidelines from his mother.

"I shall see you at home, mother," he told her again firmly, standing.

She glared at him for a moment longer, disappointment evident in her eyes, before she finally turned and hurried the girls along, one hand on each of their backs. He watched them go, watched their figures disappear into the shadows of the night before he went to Seralyn, careful to ensure that no eyes were watching them as he approached.

"Kent!" She jumped slightly as he took hold of her hand. "You scared me."

"Come with me." He pulled her slightly, bringing her away from the crowd and into a darkened alley where no one would see them. Rats scurried quickly by their feet as they moved and she jumped slightly, gripping onto his hand tighter. The feeling felt so natural and right that it nearly distracted him from the purpose of this getaway.

Still, he directed her towards the darkest corner of the alley, the corner which was somewhat hidden by a long hanging garden that, in the daylight, was actually remarkably beautiful. This far away, caught in the shadows of the flowers, no one passing by would be able to see who they were, or what they were doing.

"Kent, what are you doing?" Her head turned nervously back in the direction of the party.

"We should talk."

"We have talked," she reminded him, voice shaking slightly.

He inclined his head at her, as if she had obviously missed his point.

Seralyn sighed heavily and leaned back against the wall, dropping the fake mask of joy that she'd been wearing all night and finally looking like the girl he had grown up with. "We have nothing to talk about, Kent."

"What are you doing with him, Seralyn? You're obviously not in love with each other."

She began toying with a piece of her auburn hair and he fought the familiar urge to tug it out of her fingers and begin playing with it himself.

"We're very happy with one another, Kent."

"Then why are you so damn afraid?"

Her eyes flashed in irritation, and she pushed off the wall. "Are you reading my emotions?"

Seralyn had been the first person to teach him how invasive his power felt to others. When he was learning to control it, they would get in vicious arguments because she hated feeling like she couldn't *feel* anything without him prying into her privacy. Once he'd finally gained some control, he'd sworn to her he would never use his powers on her without her permission and he'd sworn to himself that he'd only use them in situations that were emergencies or when he felt it was in another person's best interest.

That was the predicament here, though. By keeping his promise to himself of using his powers to help others, he'd broken his promise to her.

"You swore to me you wouldn't do that!"

She levied an accusatory finger at him and he pushed it down with his hand, entwining his fingers with hers instead. Mercifully, she didn't fight him.

This was right. Them, hand in hand. This was what had always been meant to happen.

"I had to know you were happy, Sera."

"Why do you care?" She demanded, turning away from him so that he couldn't see the way her eyes had misted over. "You left Kent, and you never came back!"

He felt a rush of irritation, but his fingers kept tight on hers even when she tried to pull away from him. "And you stopped writing to me."

"Why should I have continued?" She threw her free hand up in the air. "What was the point of being in love with a man who would never come home to me?"

Time seemed to stop.

His heart froze, unmoving in his chest, as he tried to process what she had just spat at him.

"You love me?" The words were quiet, said both like a prayer and a plea.

Seralyn sighed softly, the exhale carrying a slight hum that hung in the air around them, and he didn't need to read her emotions to see the sadness that was painted plainly across her face.

"*Loved*, Kent," she reached up, caressing his cheek with her hand. "I couldn't stay in love with a man who became nothing more than a letter."

"I'm here now."

"And I'm betrothed now."

Why didn't she see what was so obvious to him? Why couldn't she feel this spark between them, as alive and hungry as it had always been? He and Seralyn were two halves to the same whole. They always had been and if she just let him in again, they could stay that way forevermore.

He rested his free hand on her waist while his thumb stroked circles over her wrist. He felt the moment her pulse jumped as he stepped closer to her. When she whispered his name once more, this time sounding somewhat less like a warning and somewhat more like a plea, he felt his cock thicken in his trousers for her.

"Tell me he knows you better than I do. Tell me he makes you feel as seen and complete as I can."

"He does."

"You're lying."

Her breath caught as he reached up to smooth her hair back over her shoulders. Kent let his fingers linger, delicately trailing a line against her collarbone, and when she turned her face away with an irritated huff, he knew she was just as affected by him as he was by her.

"It doesn't matter," she sighed. "It doesn't matter who I *want* to be with. I must marry Jaxon."

"Seralyn, all that matters is you getting everything you want from this life. Don't you see how much you deserve that?"

She released a small whimper as she faced him, and he reached up to wipe a tear away from her cheek. He felt oddly at war with himself as he looked at her. The Seralyn he had known had always been so open about her every thought and feeling. This version of her was so guarded, even from him. Her words and her body language were so misaligned that he couldn't get a single grasp on what she was actually thinking. And he *needed* to know what she was thinking. He needed to know if she really felt nothing for him at all.

So once more, he broke his vow to her and he let his magic connect them. The sensation of her emotions bleeding into his was instantaneous, like a sea crashing against the shore in the most terrible of storms. She was feeling so much and feeling all of it with an impossible intensity.

Fear, anger, sadness, regret.

And unabashed longing.

Her love for him was so obvious.

Unable to hold himself back from her for a second longer, Kent stepped forward rapidly and pressed his mouth to hers.

She was still for a moment, surprised, before her arms wrapped around his neck and held him to her. Even after all these years, her taste was still as sweet and her touch just as gentle as ever. Her softness fit perfectly against his hardness as if she had been created by the Gods specifically for him. She was perfect in every way.

Everything she did, everything she said, was beyond reproach. And by the Gods, he did not understand how any man could have this beautiful woman on his arm and feel anything but complete and utter gratitude that she had chosen him to be there.

Jaxon was entirely undeserving of her.

"Serayln!"

They flew apart from each other as the sound of another person in the alley crashed down upon them and ruined their brief moment of happiness. Jaxon's jaw worked as he stood, arms crossed, and took in the two of them.

Fuck.

Kent had been so sure that no one could see them from this far away, and so desperate to finally speak to her alone that he hadn't quite factored in the fact that her betrothed might actually come looking for her.

"Jaxon!" she breathed. "We were just-"

"I think it's quite obvious what you were just doing."

Kent sighed and began to mentally ready himself for the inevitable fight. When he, Rankor, and Clay were nothing more than teenage boys fucking their way through every town and village their army squad moved through, Rankor had once learned an important lesson that he repeated back to his friends as often as he could.

If you're going to screw around with another man's woman, you should be prepared to get hit.

Kent wiped his mouth with the back of his hand and began rolling out his wrists.

"Come, Seralyn," Jaxon commanded, not even deigning to look in Kent's direction. "Your mother would like to say goodnight for the evening."

Seralyn, working hard to get her breathing under control once more, nodded and went to him, taking hold of his outstretched hand. The two of them retreated from the alleyway and back to the celebration, as if nothing untoward had happened at all, as if Jaxon hadn't just watched his bride-to-be in the arms of her former lover on the eve of their wedding.

He watched them go, frozen, and trying to figure out what in all of creation had just happened.

IRIS

DOUBLE LIVES NEVER END WELL

They rode to the Duke's estate in silence, every member of their party focused on the task at hand. The plan was simple: get in, kill everyone as quietly as possible, and get out.

None of Nikolai's men questioned her presence there, but she felt their suspicious eyes on her, nonetheless. They didn't trust her, and, admittedly, they shouldn't.

Iris couldn't help but let her own eyes linger on Nikolai's back from where he rode in front of her. She never should have lain with him. Now her thoughts were flooded with memories of the way they had fit together so perfectly and her stomach fluttered every time he glanced back at her with a soft, reassuring smile.

Her feelings for him didn't matter, though.

This mission of hers was rapidly coming to an end and by the time she walked out of the Duke's estate, both the Serpent and Nikolai would be dead.

The sun had started to set some time ago, so only fragments of light remained around them. Shadows were emerging from the surrounding trees, joining them on their journey. She drew in a shaky breath as she took in the spiked towers of the Duke of Eagirton's estate ahead. The night was quiet, the only sound that of the wildlife around them, and the silence only put Iris further on edge.

On the hill ahead of them, she could just make out dark shapes patrolling the grounds. The Serpent and his army of supporters were already here.

Nikolai commanded their group to gather with a single flick of his wrist.

"We go in quickly and quietly," he told them, voice low and eyes deadly serious.

Gone was the version of him who had stroked her skin and promised to protect her. He was now every bit the dangerous criminal she knew him to be. Good. That would make her job easier.

"Artie, Jackyl, and Maxwell, you take out those posted on the east wing. Luther and Silas, you do the West. When you've cleared the exterior, send the signal before entering the premises. Joliette and I will follow after. We all clear?"

There were sounds of nods and agreement before Nikolai surveyed his group and sighed heavily, breaking away from his authoritative stance to meet each person's eyes with the sincerest of concern.

"I expect to see all of you back home unharmed. Don't disappoint me."

With that they dismounted from their horses, tied the beasts off to some nearby trees and took off towards the house, hiding in overgrown brush and brandishing their weapons while Nikolai and Iris hung back, waiting for their cue.

She avoided his gaze as he came to her and helped her down from her horse. She ignored the way his touch sent a rush of energy through her, all while she fought against the overwhelming feeling of guilt for what she was about to do.

Nikolai gripped her chin and brought her gaze to his. "Are you all right? You seem pale."

"Just nervous."

He brushed her hair back away from her shoulders, eyes lingering on the skin at the base of her neck. "You don't have to do this."

If only it was that simple. If only she could say okay, go back to his house, and continue living this lie with him.

"I do have to do this," she sighed unhappily.

After a moment he nodded before bowing to press his lips briefly to her forehead. "Very well then."

He pressed something cold and hard into her fingertips and she looked down to see a dagger between them. Its hilt was wrapped in leather, with a large round ruby placed in its center. The blade itself was slender, tapered to a point. Well-balanced. Recently sharpened. It was impressive.

For more than just its deadliness.

"Is this-"

He gave her a lopsided grin. "One of the twelve daggers Arto had fashioned for his favorite children. Very rare and very expensive. It was one of the first magical artifacts I ever got my hands on, and now it's yours."

She drug her eyes away from the artifact in her hands to his face. "Why would you give this to me?"

Iris wasn't ignorant of the significance of a blade created by the God of Violence. It was said that weapons created by his touch were the deadliest in the realm, able to strengthen the user and increase their pain tolerance. Arto had left very few in the Mortal Realm before the Gods raised the Veil. The blade in her hand was worth enough coin to buy a small island if he wanted.

Nikolai rested his hands on either side of her face and pulled her to him, kissing her so fiercely her head spun.

"I know you haven't given me all of your secrets, bird," he whispered against her mouth as he rested his forehead on hers. "But as reckless and stupid as it might make me, I actually trust you won't betray me. And either way, I need to know that you make it out of this alive."

His words were like slices directly through her heart and she struggled to find the words to say to him.

In the end she didn't have to, because Artie gave the whistle and before she knew it he was grabbing her hand and pulling her towards the house. It was time.

Their steps were silent as they walked through the house, each looking suspiciously down every dark hallway. She knew his men were somewhere close, also inspecting the property, but for now it all seemed... empty.

Which seemed wrong.

"Where is the Duke?" Iris asked Nikolai in a hushed whisper. "Or his children?"

His brow furrowed, and he brought a finger to his lips, instructing her to listen.

She struggled to hear anything in the overwhelming silence of the house until...

There!

It was a soft sound, the kind that a body releases when it's taken too much pain, a whimper that's entirely uncontrollable. She should know. She's made that sound before, and she's evoked it in plenty of others.

Nikolai nodded, indicating he had heard it too, and pointed to the staircase to their left. He took the lead, pushing Iris slightly behind him, two swords balanced in each of his hands, poised and at the ready as they began the slow descent down the carpeted stairway.

The stairs opened into a smoking room, outfitted with bar carts and cabinets filled with cigars. A table sat in the center of the room with cards scattered across it, as if someone had left the space in the middle of the game. A few nearly burnt out candles splattered light across the room.

And down the hall, the whimper was turning to a scream.

"You!"

The voice that greeted them filled with such hatred that it made Iris' blood turn icy. Her adrenaline spiked as she turned just in time to push Nikolai back from where a broadsword was swinging through the air. He spared her a momentary glance of appreciation before turning to meet the next blow with his own blade.

He was quick to disarm his attacker and end the fight with a quick slice across the throat, but by then, the damage had already been done. The sounds of the blades slapping together had echoed through the small space and brought five new men to them.

The battle was upon them.

And yet, it wasn't.

Because these men weren't *her* enemies.

These men worked for Joliette's *father*. When they saw her, they simply gave her a momentary look of confusion before focusing solely on Nikolai. No one raised a single weapon against her. Even when she began pulling them away from him, even when she slammed her blade through the back of the man who was aiming a club at Nikolai's head, no one bothered to pay her any attention.

Nikolai looked at her, grinning even as blood dripped from his split lip. "Go!"

Her body moved before her brain could stop it. She fell backwards a few steps before freezing, overpowered by a sickening realization.

He was going to die if she left him here. Nikolai was a skilled fighter and a powerful Descendant, but not even he could win a fight that was five against one. If she left him, he wouldn't survive.

And wouldn't that make her life easier?

This way, at least she wouldn't have to be the one watching the life slip from him and feeling her heart shatter while it does.

Iris had been trained to kill, she hadn't been trained to watch someone she loved die.

"Go bird, I can handle this."

She was at war with herself, knowing she needed to leave, but hating herself for even considering it.

Ultimately, her decision boiled down to one fact: Iris wasn't Joliette.

Iris wasn't married to Nikolai.

Iris wasn't the one he affectionately called his bird.

Iris had been sent here for one purpose, and she couldn't let herself forget that no matter how badly it hurt.

So she turned, and she ran down the hall, pushing herself farther and faster from him. The sounds of screaming grew in intensity, stemming from the dark wooden door at the end of the hallway. She pushed towards it, throwing it open just as the pained shouts became silent and as she did, Iris finally met the gaze of the Serpent.

"Joliette!" He cried in surprise as she closed the door behind her.

The Serpent was an older man, still lean and strong, but covered in wrinkles and gray hair. A scar sliced across his right brow and his white clothes were stained and dripping with blood. Blood that likely came from what remained of the Duke, who sat strapped to a desk chair in the center of the office, hunched over and bleeding from every inch of his body. A large gash covered his swollen brow and two of his fingers were missing. He looked disgusting, and he smelt worse. The metallic stench of it was as familiar as it was repulsive.

The Serpent rushed to her and pulled her close, wrapping her in an embrace that smeared the scarlet stickiness across her ivory gown, painting her with her future sins.

"Have you done it? Have you finally killed him?" He asked, looking over her for any signs of harm.

"Not yet," she answered, not moving her eyes from the Duke's labored breathing.

The Serpent nodded, the motion too sudden and intense. "Soon. I know you'll do it soon. But it's good you're here now. This was your idea. You should finish it."

Iris frowned, trying to follow his line of thought. This had been *Joliette's* idea?

"You were right all along, dear. My smart daughter seducing the Duke's son. He knows something, Joliette. I know he does."

The Serpent rushed and slurred his words, making it nearly impossible to distinguish one sound from the next. He paced the room rapidly, jerking his head every which way.

He was positively mad.

Surely, this wasn't the mastermind behind one of the biggest criminal enterprises in the country.

The Duke finally lifted his head and as his gaze fell on her his body erupted into trembles.

"No!" He cried. "Please, I'll tell you. I'll tell you!"

All this time, The Order had been mistaken, she realized sharply.

It wasn't the Serpent himself who was such a danger to the Crown. It wasn't the Serpent who had made the call to attack the Duke. It wasn't the Serpent who was Nikolai's true enemy.

All along, it had been Joliette.

"You were right," the Duke huffed, his breathing labored. "Someone is planning a coup."

The drafty office room suddenly felt colder. Iris tightened her grip on the blade between her fingers as the Serpent rushed towards her, grabbing her shoulders and jumping excitedly. "Do you know how much this information will be worth to us?"

Yes. Yes, she did.

The Serpent swung around, leveling his gaze on the Duke. "Tell us! Tell us right now."

Iris' heart pounded heavily in her chest as her adrenaline soared.

She had to stop this right now.

She rushed forward, blade at the ready, but no amount of speed could have brought her to the Duke's side before he opened his mouth and released the information she had been holding close to her heart for nearly two years.

"Clayton Vail," he sighed, shoulders sinking heavily in defeat. "The Prince was getting too close to figuring out my business arrangements with the Alchemist. I hired spies who found out his plans."

The Duke met her eyes with an expression of simple resignation. He knew what was coming next. Either by her hand or someone else's. The Duke's death warrant had been signed the second he had learned of Clay's plans.

It didn't matter that The Order wanted him alive.

It didn't matter that killing a Duke was high treason.

All that mattered now was that if that information ever got back to the Dragon, he would kill Clay and name one of Clay's sisters as the new heir. Iris couldn't let that happen. She had to protect her cousin, no matter the cost.

"Thank you for your honesty," she said to the Duke, stalking forward to him as the Serpent watched her with proud, hungry eyes. "Where are the spies who told you of this?"

"Dead," he confessed. "I didn't want the information spread until I knew what to do with it."

She nodded. Good. That was good. Less bodies that she would be responsible for.

"Please let me go," the Duke begged. "I can help you get proof."

"Yes!" The Serpent agreed from behind her. "Bring us proof!"

Iris was still feeling the weight of Arto's dagger in her palm acutely. "That won't be necessary."

The sharpened metal of her dagger cut through the skin of his throat easily and Iris forced herself to watch as the light left the Duke's eyes even while the Serpent screamed at her behind her back.

"Joliette! No, what are you doing?"

The sound of his heavy footsteps came from behind her, and she spun as he grasped his fingers onto her shoulder, burying her blade deep into his gut.

The Serpent's eyes met hers, wide and confused as he looked from the weapon buried in his gut to the face of his daughter.

She didn't even feel anything as his body fell heavily to the floor. She'd managed to turn off any part of her that could feel guilt for what she had just done.

There could be no witnesses to what had just happened, she knew that. There could be no one left to report what they had just heard. Iris had to protect Clay at all costs.

Silently, eyes still focused on the carnage around her, Iris wiped the blade off against the skirt of her already ruined gown. What was a little more blood staining her clothing? She could already feel it moving through her skin to stain her soul.

"Well now, bird."

Her heart lurched as Nikolai's voice sparked through her and she turned in an instant, brandishing her knife at him as he stood casually leaning against the door frame with his arms crossed against his chest.

She'd been so distracted by the Duke's words that she hadn't even heard when he'd opened the door behind her.

"Is this the part where we're finally honest with each other?" he asked.

CAMILLA

The Value of Power

"Aw, are you afraid?"

She'd recognize her cousin's voice anywhere, even if it was layered with a degree of sinisterness that she hadn't quite heard from the girl before. A chill that had absolutely nothing to do with the breezy air traveled down her spine as she slowly turned to face the girl.

Erilea's blue eyes were remarkably wider than normal, and she smiled at Camilla toothily as she tilted her head to examine her cousin. She stood tall, hands tucked behind her back politely, even though her cerulean gown had been torn at her ankles and splattered with a darkness that could only be from one thing.

"Erilea?" Camilla's voice was slow, measured. "What happened?"

"You know why I'm Grandmother's favorite, don't you? It's because I'm more powerful than you."

The words themselves didn't shock her. She'd thought them often enough herself, but it still stung to have those fears validated. After all this time, her grandmother's approval should be the last thing Camilla should long for, but Alina was the only family she had, and it hurt to know that she would never be powerful enough to deserve her love.

"I have the mushrooms," Camilla told her, bending to retrieve them from where she had dropped them once more in her fright.

Erilea laughed, the hollow sound echoing through the woods, and Camilla stilled. There was something not quite right about her cousin. Erilea had always been vicious and hurtful, but she wasn't one to follow Camilla into the woods just to taunt her. She didn't often look so... crazed.

And that was undeniably blood on her dress.

A heavy thump sounded as Erilea dropped something in front of her and Camilla smothered her scream with a hand to her mouth as she took in the mutilated body of Muffin, Erilea's beloved cat.

The girl only smiled down at her as her blue eyes flashed black.

"Being powerful is easy, if you know how to get the power."

Camilla fought the urge to retch as her mind struggled to wrap itself around what was happening in front of her.

This was blood magic.

"What have you done?" She whispered, fingers beginning to shake.

Erilea pulled out the kitchen knife she'd been hiding behind her back, seemingly not at all bothered as it dripped blood onto the grass beneath them. "Power is valuable, Camilla. Sometimes you have to be brave enough to take it."

She lifted her free hand, demonstrating her stolen magic as she allowed a small tendril of shadows to dance between her fingers.

"No Erilea, no power is worth that sacrifice!"

The girl laughed knowingly. "You'll take the power too, Camilla. If I don't take it from you first."

It took her only a few seconds to realize what her cousin meant before she was on her feet, sprinting away from the girl who waved the knife wildly in the air around her. Erilea's manic laughter was all around her as she fled, leaping over trees and bushes.

"Erilea stop this!" she pleaded, glancing back over her shoulder.

"I'm going to kill you," her cousin sang, following her at an impossible pace.

With every passing second, Erilea grew closer, her snarls becoming more and more animalistic. Thorns and branches tore at Camilla's legs, piercing through skin so sharply that she couldn't stop the cries that ripped free of her throat.

"I'm going to get you!"

Erilea swung her weapon, cutting across Camilla's ribcage. Instinct took over and Camilla threw back her elbow even while her skin was burning from the cut. She felt Erilea's bone crack as her elbow connected with the girl's face, but Erilea only laughed harder.

"You'll need more power than that to stop me!" Erilea roared. "You'll need more power than that to stop what's coming!"

Camilla grasped onto her cousin's wrist, struggling to push away the knife that Erilea was jamming towards her. Erilea was everywhere. She was stabbing at her and pulling her hair, all while shadows climbed over her legs and swirled around her waist.

"Get off of me!"

Camilla struck out, landing a decent enough shot at her cousin's kneecap to send the girl falling back a few steps and flopping into the brush. She didn't hesitate, turning the second Erilea hit the ground to continue sprinting towards the house.

"Help!" she screamed madly as the dark brick exterior of Hypatia manor came into view. "Someone help me!"

Camilla clutched at her side, heaving gasps of breath desperately as dampness trickled from the wound down her waist. The pain was alive, firing up and down her body with each ragged step forward she took.

"Help!"

She nearly fell over in relief when the door of the house flew open and her grandmother stepped outside. Alina must have been preparing herself for afternoon tea. She was still in a simple slip gown and her hair was loose around her shoulders, but she hardly seemed to care as her eyes widened and she rushed to Camilla's side.

"Camilla!" Alina grasped onto her, and even though the woman had caused so much of Camilla's pain in the past, she couldn't help but lean into her touch as her grandmother's wrinkled fingers smoothed away the tears that soaked her face. "What is the meaning of this?"

"Erilea," Camilla sobbed, the words coming out a jumbled, hard-to-understand mess. "Erilea's trying to kill me."

Alina frowned. "Erilea is doing no such thing."

She would be upon them any minute. Who knew how much blood magic the girl had done? What if Alina wasn't strong enough to stop her? Camilla grasped onto her grandmother's elbows and pushed, trying to shove her back towards the house.

"Camilla!"

"We have to go. We have to get inside before Erilea-"

"Are you guys talking about me?"

Erilea's high-pitched, cheery voice rattled the world around Camilla and time seemed to stand still as she looked up to see her cousin stepping out of the house wearing a perfectly spotless gown and clutching her beloved Muffin in her arms. The damn beast even started purring after Erilea reached to scratch between his ears.

"No, that can't be," Camilla mumbled. "You were just..."

She spun backwards, waiting to see that monster come bursting forth from the trees, but there was only... nothing.

"There's nothing in those woods, Camilla," Alina told her, running a hand up and down Camilla's arm.

"She cut me," Camilla whispered, but when she pulled her hand from her side, there was no blood on her fingertips. She was unharmed. There wasn't even a stitch loose in her gown.

Alina wrapped an arm around Camilla's shoulders and began leading her back inside. Erilea backed away as they passed her, looking too confused to say anything mean. As they stepped into the manor, the baking heat of it choked Camilla, and a fresh sob shook her chest.

"Hush," Alina patted her arm. "You've just had a fright. Let's get you into bed, dear."

Her grandmother walked with her all the way up the many flights of stairs to her cramped room on the top floor. She sat Camilla on the bed, removed her dirty boots, wiped clean the cuts on her legs, and tucked her under the single blanket. When she was done, she drew the blinds, sat a cup of tea by the bedside, and assured Camilla that she just needed some rest and then she would feel better.

Alina closed the door behind her as she left, but Camilla hardly even noticed her absence. She was too lost in her own mind. It had seemed so real. She'd felt the sting of that knife slicing through her skin. She'd heard the crunch of bone when she broke Erilea's nose. What kind of trickery was this? Was someone cursing her?

Or was she simply losing her mind?

When she lifted the teacup to her mouth, she smelt the valerian root immediately. Still, she drank the sleeping potion greedily and welcomed the darkness when it came to her.

LORELAI

A New Life

The streets were alive with a new excitement as they walked through them for a second time that day and this time, Lorelai allowed herself to examine the world around her with curiosity instead of fear. She marveled at the way the tiny houses all seemed squished together in such odd angles and proportions, and yet no one seemed to mind the lack of space as they sat on porches talking and laughing together. Children ran happily, darting through crowds with unabashed joy, so different from the children at court who stayed quiet and close to their mother's sides. Musicians played songs and magicians showed tricks, drawing crowds of spectators with wide smiles and joyful claps.

"What are you thinking?" Helena asked, watching Lorelai watch everyone else.

She felt a furious blush climb up her chest and neck. "They just seem happy."

Helena tossed her head back to laugh before looking around the street herself. "Did you think they wouldn't?"

Lorelai didn't answer, because the truth was obvious. She hadn't spent many days at all thinking about what life was like for those who lived outside of her immediate vicinity. She'd never really traveled far outside of the castle or her home. Truthfully, had her carriage never been attacked, she likely never would have seen this version of life. She would have simply married a wealthy duke or foreign dignitary and moved from one life of luxury to the next.

She jumped slightly when Helena took hold of her hand and began pulling her to a small brown building with blue shutters that were falling off the windows. As they pushed through the door, the size of the crowd almost choked Lorelai. People pressed into every inch of her, a sensation entirely unlike anything she had experienced before. Helena didn't at all seemed bothered though as she pushed through with her shoulder, keeping a firm grip on Lorelai's hand.

In the far end of the room, a girl spun on the tips of her toes while her fingers flew over fiddle strings, filling the space with a jaunty tune. At her side, a young boy, hardly fifteen, with dirty blonde hair and a sweat-soaked shirt, sat atop an overturned wooden barrel, beating on it in time with her music. The crowd cheered and clapped with them, dancing despite the cramped space.

"Two pints please!" Helena demanded as they reached the bar top, smacking down a golden coin which the barkeep took greedily.

He passed them two overflowing cups of ale, foam splashing out over the tops as Helena took them both and passed one to her. She tried not to make a face as it spilled down the front of her tunic. It was, perhaps, bound to happen in a place this tightly packed with people.

"Drink!" Helena instructed, her voice loud over the roar of the music.

Lorelai did as she was told, letting the room temperature liquid slide over her tongue and down her throat. She nearly choked on the bitter taste of it and the way it lingered on her taste buds long after she has swallowed.

"Gods it tastes like-"

"Piss!" Helena agreed, nodding enthusiastically. "But it's all part of the experience!"

"The experience of what?" Lorelai's throat was beginning to hurt from shouting over the music, but she wasn't quite ready to subject herself to tasting the awful excuse for an ale again.

"The experience of *living.*"

Helena grasped hold of her hand once more, pulling her to the side of the room where the band played. She finished her ale in a long drag while the crowd around her cheered, encouraging her on. As she finished, she held it up triumphantly as applause fell around them before passing it off to someone walking by with a tray collecting empty glasses so that she could stomp her foot and clap in time with the music.

"The little bitty on the fiddle is named Madeline," she told Lorelai, leaning over to her ear. "She's the best player you'll find on this side of the Sea of Palaemon."

Surely that couldn't be true. The palace had the finest performers money could buy. Musicians who had trained for the entire lives at the most prestigious institutes. Still, there was something infinitely more infectious about the way Madeline played. It wasn't perfect, far from it, in fact. Notes from the A-string were slightly under pitch and her bow needed more rosin, but she played with a kind of speed and lightness that was so different from the typically classical pieces performed by the orchestras and quartets that Lorelai was more familiar with.

If she was honest, Lorelai liked this style quite a bit more than the music at the palace.

Unable to stop herself, she felt her head beginning to bob in time with the music. Her foot tapped. Her smile grew.

"Do you want to dance?" Helena asked, her too vigilant eyes analyzing the way Lorelai was responding to the music. Grinning, Helena nodded suggestively to where a small circle had cleared in the crowd and couples darted in and out, swinging and dancing wildly. Their faces were alight with joy, their steps fast but sure.

Lorelai shook her head. "Oh no, I couldn't possibly."

Helena, it seemed, was unwilling to take no for an answer.

She grasped hold of Lorelai's hand once more in an iron grip, pulling her through the sticky air of the room. The scent of sweat and alcohol was thick, but no one seemed to notice. Those that did didn't seem to mind. Everyone was alive with laughter and joy and dancing and *life*. It was the purest display of blatant freedom she had ever seen. She was helpless to do anything but simply marvel at the people around her who looked like they were the same species but seemed so entirely different from anything she had ever known.

"Come on!" Helena demanded, darting into the circle and clapping her hands three times above her head before moving her feet rapidly in a succession of kicks and stomps that impossibly seemed to always stay on beat with the unpredictable melody of the song.

Before long, a man had joined her and they danced in time, exchanging the strange dance pattern between them while Lorelai simply stared with her mouth gaping wide. Growing up, she'd taken all manner of dance and music classes. She knew every variation of the waltz. Her almain was perfect. Even the galliard, which was one of the most challenging dances of the court with its leaps and intricate footwork, had come naturally to her. But this? This seemed to be happening three times as quickly as any dance she had seen done before.

The musicians ended their song and flowed effortlessly into the next, this one beginning with staccato bursts of sound before erupting into rapid note progressions. The crowd around her roared in excitement before all bursting into song. Every single person in the room knew the words except for her. Even Helena, who continued dancing with those around her, chanted along in time with the beat. Laughing, Lorelai strained her ears to catch on to what they were saying.

Long time ago when the Gods walked the Realm,

Their children claimed the power that the Gods gave to them.
The Dragon claimed the throne,
Made a palace a home,
And he left all of us in the town.
Well the Dragon got a Queen,
Had a baby or three.
And he started a big old war,
The men lost the lives, and the Dragon lost his wife,
But he married a brand new whore,
And he left all of us in the town.

The song continued, but suddenly Lorelai couldn't bear to listen to another word. A heavy weight had settled in her gut, physically reminding her how much she didn't belong here.

That song was...treasonous. If the Dragon ever heard it he would imprison everyone in this room. Gods, if her father knew she was here listening to a song like this...

She was suddenly suffocating, unable to breathe as the walls seemed to come closer and closer to caving in on her. What was she doing here? She was a respected member of the Athenian court! She shouldn't be wearing trousers and drinking with criminals.

Turning on her heels, she pushed her way out of the room, ignoring the sounds of frustration that followed as she shoved her elbows into backs and stomachs in her attempt to clear space. All she knew was that she needed to get out of there.

Lorelai burst out of the tavern, desperately gulping in the early evening air, as a wave of nervous hysteria settled over her. She was laughing and panicking all at once. By the Gods, what was she *thinking*? She needed to find her way to a guard somehow. They would be able to safely escort her back to the castle at once.

Back to her real life.

"What happened?" She heard Helena only a moment before the girl had grasped hold of Lorelai's shoulders and spun her around. Helena's brow glistened with sweat and her white-blonde hair was escaping from the braids on her head, curling around the edges.

"I'm sorry," Lorelai panted. "I just really must get home. You've been a great help, but if you could please just point me in the direction of the nearest barracks, I should be able to find myself another escort."

Helena's laugh was bitter. "You think a pretty girl like you walks into a barrack and the men all just happily walk you back to the castle? Please. You're safer in that room than you are within a mile range of army barracks."

"The soldiers keep us safe!"

"Yeah, they do!" Helena replied sharply, voice raised and cheeks flushed with irritation. "And they sacrifice little bits of their souls to do so. No one makes it from this realm into the next without dealing with an infinite amount of pain and tragedy."

Lorelai turned from her, not wanting to see the raw emotion that was on her face even while she wanted to protest. Not everyone needed to experience tragedy. Lorelai hadn't.

"I know what you're thinking," Helena said.

"No, you don't."

"You're thinking that you haven't had to experience anything hard, but you know what *Melanie,*" she spit out the name Lorelai had given her like the obvious lie it was. "I think you're the biggest tragedy in that room. I think one day you're going to die with your nose turned up in a ballroom full of all your wealthy friends and the moment you realize that your passing into the Underworld, you're going to think how sad it is that you never truly allowed yourself to have some genuine fun. You're going to realize how *tragic* your sheltered little life really is."

She spun on her heels, braids flying in the air behind her, and marched back into the tavern without even giving Lorelai a second to generate a response.

Not that Lorelai even could come up with a response.

It felt like she stood there for two whole minutes sputtering as she opened and closed her mouth like a dying fish. She furrowed her brow and contemplated what Helena had said, hating that in her gut, she felt like it was... the truth.

Lorelei's life was rather tragic when she stopped to think about it.

She had laid in bed for days because her friends couldn't come to a party. A stupid party that was one of the few sources of excitement in her life year after year. How pathetic was that? Lorelai got an immeasurable amount of joy from hosting the same party over and over without ever challenging herself to do something new or different. She'd never traveled to new places. She'd never tasted exotic foods. She'd never even allowed herself to fall in love with someone because she was afraid of her father's reaction to the fact that she felt attracted to women.

Lorelai was living, but she wasn't alive.

And she didn't want to die in a ballroom, surrounded by her wealthy friends, thinking that she'd wasted this opportunity to have some genuine fun.

So she took a deep, centering breath, and she walked back inside.

Helena was in the center of the room dancing, but she noticed Lorelai the second the door closed behind her. With a grin, she raised the pint of ale high into the air.

"Cheers to my new friend who's decided to dance with us tonight!"

The room held the glasses high in the air, Lorelai walked to Helena's side, and she danced.

She mimicked the steps of those around her until the rhythm of the steps, hops, and claps embedded itself into her soul and moved through every part of her. She lost herself in it and by the time Helena grasped onto her elbow and they danced in a circle together, she simply laughed.

The celebration went on until the early hours of the morning. When they finally returned to Helena's home, Lorelai rested her head easily on the arm of Helena's couch while the girl retreated to her bedroom. She fell asleep happily, feeling more complete than she ever had before. In the morning, Helena would finish escorting her to the castle and her life would go back to the way it had always been, but Lorelai would be different.

Because for the first time, Lorelai had truly *lived*.

IRIS

Is It Over Now?

S he didn't dare lower her weapon, not when he was watching her with such hardness in his eyes. There was no way of knowing how much he had seen or heard. It didn't matter now, anyway. He had to die, and it was going to have to be by her own hand.

"Admittedly, I am surprised to see you here," she mumbled.

He gave her the same lopsided smile that had made her heart skip a beat just an hour ago. "You should know by now I'll be harder to kill than that."

"No, you won't."

He chuckled under his breath and leaned more firmly against the door, crossing one ankle over the next. The tendrils of copper hair that had escaped from where he tied it back and the speckling of blood on his clothes were the only indication of the fight he had been in. Otherwise, he was a picture of relaxation.

Odd considering she had a weapon pointed at him.

She began stepping towards him.

"You going to tell me your real name now?"

Iris' steps faltered ever so slightly.

He couldn't possibly mean...

Nikolai's eyes danced as he pushed off the wall and walked over to examine the Duke's body with an expression that was both simultaneously disgusted and appreciative. He didn't pull the sword that sat in the scabbard of his hip, but his finger never strayed too far from it, even as he turned his back to her.

"Come now, I thought members of The Order were the finest trained assassins in the world? This is how you chose to end this poor soul?"

"I don't know what you're talking about."

He glanced at her over his shoulder with a disapproving quirk of his brow. "Let's stop lying to each other, bird."

She chewed at her lip, and though she knew better, slowly lowered her blade. "We're not assassins, we're spies."

He smiled and inclined his head to the two bodies on the floor. "So you say, but we both know better."

She was careful to listen to every sound around her, preparing for the onslaught of his men to come pounding into the tiny space they were in. Carefully, she positioned herself closer to the door so that she could be prepared to attack.

"How'd you figure it out?" She asked.

"I knew the second I put you on my horse." Nikolai shrugged. "Not many people know Joliette is a Painweaver. She's extremely close-lipped with that information, but it's actually how she escaped after our wedding. She tried to kill me with it, actually. Thankfully, I had friends nearby who rushed in and she fled."

Iris wanted to kick herself. She wanted to kick Walric for not inspecting Joliette for a Descendant's Mark before he sent her in to this den of vipers. A fucking Painweaver. No wonder the Duke had trembled upon seeing her.

Painweavers were an extremely rare branch of Descendants from House Arto, marked with a jagged blade across their right shoulder, and blessed with the ability to inflict the highest form of agony on their victims. No wonder Nikolai's eyes had so often lingered on her bare skin there.

But then, if Nikolai had known from the very start, then when they had lain together...

"At first I just wanted to know what you were planning," he told her, watching her with an intensity that made her want to shiver. "I didn't expect to feel so drawn to you. That was quite an inconvenience, in fact."

"Well, the feeling is mutual," she admitted.

He grinned softly, almost as if it was against his will. "Right away, I saw so much of myself in you. You were more stubbornly vocal than she was, but that passion reminded me of my own. Every time you furrowed your brow, I could tell you were calculating and scheming. You think almost as constantly as I do."

Iris' grip tightened on her blade. He still hadn't pulled his. He was still the picture of calmness, but she couldn't bear to let her guard down. It was going to hurt enough when they finally came to blows. She didn't want the additional sting of being caught off guard.

"It wasn't part of the scheme," she told him. "What happened between us wasn't planned."

"I know that, bird. It was quite obvious that you enjoyed yourself."

And then she let go of her powers.

All of them.

She wasn't sure why she felt so strongly that she needed to let him see her, the real her that she showed no one, the version of her that was as scarred as he was, but she did. If this was going to end in death, she at least wanted him to finally see her.

Joliette's pale skin faded into her familiar shade of caramel. The straight hair curled. The thin lips thickened.

And Nikolai's eyes never flinched.

"All this time, I was sharing a bed with the girl cousin of the Crown Prince."

The words were like a slap and she couldn't help but turn away from him as she recovered from the sting of that. "I am so much more than that."

"Of course you are, my beautiful bird," he laughed darkly, resting his hands on his hips. For a moment, he looked just as tormented as she felt. "You're fucking exquisite. Why wouldn't you be? Everything about you has made my life more difficult. Of course, you would be only more captivating in your natural form."

Her heart jolted, and she couldn't help the confession that poured from her lips. "I don't know why I fell for you so quickly. That's not like me."

Nikolai stared at her for a long moment. "Maybe you're not used to people seeing the darkness in you. Maybe I was just the first person who saw it, accepted it, and joined you in it."

They were running out of time. Every moment they spent here talking only increased the chances that his men would find them, and as skilled as Iris was, she didn't want to have to see if she could fight off so many criminals by herself.

She needed to put an end to this.

"You won't make it out of here," he told her quietly, as if he was sensing her thoughts.

"And I can't let you leave this room, not after what you heard."

He pursed his lips and nodded, confirming that he had in fact heard what the Duke had implied about Clay. His fingers twitched towards the sword on his hip and she twisted the blade in her wrist so it was at the ready. It was time.

When he stepped towards her, though, there was no hatred in his eyes. No anger. Not the steely indifference that comes in the seconds before the kill.

There was pure, undeniable longing.

He grabbed her on either side of her face and pressed his lips to her, pushing her back until she was pressed between his firm body and the wall. His tongue dipped between her lips and she melted into him, sighing and leaning into his warmth. Her mind was in a fog, unable to focus on anything but the fact that he had kissed her.

Her.

Not Joliette. Not the lie.

He had kissed her, and she had to kill him now.

"I needed to taste you," he whispered. "The real you.

Iris' heart beat wildly in her chest and the blade slipped from her fingers, clattering loudly against the floor.

"I want no part of what happened here today," he breathed against her lips. "I never did. All I wanted was to conduct my business trades without the Crown interfering. Finding out about your cousin was Joliette's mission."

"It doesn't matter," she whimpered, feeling her tears fall against both of their cheeks.

"It does, bird."

"How can it?"

Her fingers were pressed against his chest. All she had to do was reach for the sword on his hip and pull it free. Just that one little motion and this would all be over.

"You've seen too much of my life for me to feel comfortable letting you go," he admitted. "But you keep my secrets, and I'll keep yours. You tell The Order that the Duke was dead when you got here, so you killed the Serpent on your own and my men and I got spooked and fled. No one ever has to know what happened between us. No one ever has to know what happened in this room."

She thought over his words about the risk they carried with them. No one in this world mattered to her as much as Clay. Could she really take a chance with his safety because of some fleeting connection she had built with Nikolai Legum of all people?

"I want you to trust me," he told her.

Iris thought of when she had said those exact words to him only a few days ago. So many lies and secrets had existed between them then and now they stood in their rawest forms before each other.

"Why should I?"

His grin was slow. "Because I'm your husband."

Nikolai stepped backwards, bending at the waist to pick up the blade from the floor and hold it out to her once more. An offering of shared acceptance and understanding between them. She took it gently in her fingertips.

"Go," he commanded.

She didn't turn back, not even when his parting words sent a chill down her spine.

"The next time I see you, Iris, I'll kill you."

KENT

GONE TOO FAR

He slept little that night. After Seralyn had left him, he'd walked to the docks and threw stones into the water for what had felt like hours. By the time he finally made the walk back to his home, the candles had all long been extinguished and the bedroom doors shut.

It was probably better he didn't have to face his mother right away, anyway.

He would have to tell her what had happened and he wasn't sure he could stomach her disappointment but he'd never been very good at keeping secrets from her.

Hours passed in the house's quiet, the only sounds being the gentle snores of his sisters and the wind creaking against the shudders outside. Still, sleep would not come to him. He couldn't shake how odd the entire evening had felt.

Seralyn and Jaxon were to be married, and yet the distance between them was impossible to deny. Despite that, though, she refused to embrace the way she felt for Kent. And though Jaxon had obviously been angry to see them together, he'd proceeding with the evening, anyway.

There was also the shadow of fear that constantly hung over her to consider.

Something was making Seralyn afraid.

He knew what he had to do before the sun reached its resting place in the morning sky. He made his way to Seralyn's home with a purposeful stride as the world around him stirred to life once more. Smoke rose from chimneys as men woke and fed their fires once more. Animals grazed in the fields behind their homes and fishermen began making their way to the docks.

None of that mattered.

Her family's cottage by the lake looked the same as it ever had, unchanged by the years he'd spent away. If he didn't know better, he might have thought himself lost in a memory instead of trapped in this twisted present existence he'd found himself entangled in. But this wasn't the past anymore, and Seralyn deserved to know that she had choices in her future.

He heard the yelling as he made his way up the worn dirt path to the home.

"This is the thanks I get for what I've done for you!" Jaxon's voice yelled.

"It was a mistake, Jaxon. It won't happen again," Seralyn answered, voice thick with tears.

"All you ever seem to do is make *mistakes*, Seralyn."

She was quiet for a moment. "You know how grateful I am to you."

He scoffed. "You're grateful? I'm so glad you're grateful. Knowing you're grateful makes the fact that I have to spend the rest of my life married to a whore so much better."

Kent burst through the door without a second thought, a primal urge to protect her taking over his system. Seralyn sat at the kitchen table, still wearing her nightgown, while Jaxon leered over her, his long hair loose over his shoulders. They both jumped as Kent threw open the door, but neither was a match for his speed, his training. He had his fingers around Jaxon's throat and the man pushed back against the wall before either of them had really registered who had burst into their home.

"I might caution you to mind how you speak to your betrothed."

Jaxon shoved at Kent, pushing him off of him with impressive strength for a mortal. "Exactly! She's *my* betrothed. I can speak to her any way I damn well please."

Once again, that need to defend her outweighed any sense of thought or consideration in him. So, he didn't think. He let his instincts take over and acted on the one urge that had been burning in him since he received the wedding invitation. He punched Jaxon clearly across the face.

"Kent!" Seralyn screamed, rushing towards him.

No.

Not towards him.

Towards Jaxon.

She pulled Jaxon's hand away from his chin to look over where Kent had hit him while the other man muttered he was fine. When she was certain he was, she rested the full weight of her anger on Kent.

"What in all of creation do you think you're doing?" She cried.

"Sera-"

"No!" She stepped forward and shoved him with all her might. With her tiny frame, it did little to move him, but it somehow hurt him worse than any injury he'd ever earned on the battlefield. "Don't you Sera me, Kentoni! You've completely crossed the line."

"I'm trying to protect you!"

"Protect me from what?"

Kent jammed his hand at Jaxon, who leaned against the wall, hands resting in his pockets with an amused expression on his face as if he was waiting for Kent to realize he'd missed out on the punchline of a joke.

"You're terrified of this bastard," Kent reminded her.

"Stop reading my emotions!" She positively screamed at him, shoving him once more for good measure.

Kent felt like his own emotions were about to boil over. As if years of suppressing how much he wanted her, how much he loved her, had only made the feelings that much stronger. And now they were simply waiting to erupt.

He wanted to take her by the shoulders and shake her as if that could make her see reason, make her understand she deserved so much more than a marriage that left her feeling afraid each night. She deserved to be reminded of how beautiful she was when she woke in the morning. She deserved to be taken to bed each night and have her body worshipped. She deserved the kind of marriage that was filled with a love so strong it left you feeling completely safe to be yourself.

"That you don't want me to know it doesn't make it untrue," he told her.

Seralyn laughed, a desperate kind of laugh that sent the hair on the back of his neck on edge. As her chuckles slowed, she ran a hand wildly through her hair and turned towards her betrothed. Jaxon only grinned, and for a moment, they looked at each other and some secret communication somehow passed between them.

"I'm with child," she finally said, spinning back to Kent.

For the second time in as many days, time seemed to stop moving around Kent even while Seralyn continued to speak.

"I got bored living in this small little town waiting for *you* to come and save me from it. So one day I left. I left, and I met Jaxon's brother in a tavern. When I realized I was with child, he took off and no one has seen or heard from him since. So Jaxon offered to marry so that my name isn't tarnished and my child isn't born a bastard. So yes Kent, I *am* afraid. I am terribly afraid to raise a child when I obviously don't have the slightest idea how to take care of myself."

The room was still as her words hung between them. After a moment, Jaxon pushed off the wall and squeezed her shoulder before mumbling something about giving them a moment to say their goodbyes. His shoulder slammed into Kent as he left, but Kent was still too shaken to even feel it.

She was pregnant.

His perfect, beautiful Seralyn was carrying a stranger's baby and marrying his brother to save her reputation.

"Are you happy now?" She demanded. "I had to spend my entire night begging him not to call the whole thing off. Now I can only hope you haven't ruined everything by showing up here."

"I didn't know," he whispered.

He wanted to laugh almost as much as he wanted to cry. How could his powers have led him so astray?

Seralyn laughed darkly, the sound more vicious than anything he had ever heard her make before. "How could you? You don't know *me* Kent. Not anymore. We were childhood friends who fell out of touch. You've deluded yourself into thinking there's anything more than that between us."

He let her words echo in his head, allowing himself to feel the crushing blow of them in every part of his body before he somehow managed to gather enough strength to straighten his shoulders and nod at her.

"Very well," he said. "Good luck Seralyn. I wish you and your family well."

Kent didn't wait to hear her response. He didn't stop to say goodbye to Jaxon in the front yard. He didn't even stop to tell his mother and sisters he was leaving. His emotions were more ragged and fragile than they had ever been. So, he climbed atop his horse and rode out of the little town as fast as the steed would take him.

The only thing on his mind was getting back to the castle as soon as possible and forgetting any of this had ever happened.

RANKOR

To Better Days

It had taken a few days to recover after the healer had stitched up his wounds, and then they'd taken their time traveling through the countryside together. Elaijah pointed out all his favorite animals to Rankor, and Rankor taught him a few tricks for self-defense. They'd spent their meals swapping stories about their childhoods and their parents and were careful to stay on the main roads and sleep in inns.

When they finally pushed their horses towards the long trail that led to their uncle's house, a heavy silence fell between them.

"I guess this is it," Elaijah said softly. "Your responsibility is complete."

Rankor grunted out a noise of agreement, unsure of what words he should say.

"Where will you go next?" Elaijah asked, looking sideways at his brother.

Rankor sighed heavily and looked to the mountain range behind their uncle's farm. "Back to the castle, I suppose. My plan was to be back for the Peace Celebration."

"You'll be late now."

"That I will. I suppose the delay was worth it."

They slowed their horses as they approached the house. Uncle Clydric sat on the porch, waiting for them. The older man sat with hunched shoulders and a furrowed brow. He raised a hand in greeting, and Rankor nodded politely.

"It's good you'll be here with him," Rankor told Elaijah. "He's getting older and can't maintain the farm as well. He could use your help, and I've heard he has quite a few sheep."

"Do you mean that?"

Rankor fought the urge to laugh. "Yes, I exchanged some letters with him before our journey. He hates the sheep. Said he needs someone with an affinity for them."

"I'm not talking about the sheep," Elaijah snapped, sliding off his horse and staring up at his brother with crossed arms. Rankor followed his lead and dismounted. "Do you mean that the delay was worth it?"

Rankor smiled. "It wasn't so bad getting to know my kid brother, after all."

Before Elaijah could protest, Rankor reached over to ruffle his hair before pulling the boy to him in a tight hug. Elaijah groaned but eventually returned the embrace as Rankor patted him heavily on the back.

"Yeah, well, I'm not a kid."

"Well, you don't have to be a stranger either. Maybe one of these days I'll show you around the castle."

Elaijah was quiet, pursing his lips as his Adam's apple bobbed slightly in his throat. Finally, he tucked his hands into his pockets and rocked back and forth on his heels. "Yeah, I'd like that."

For the first time in a long time, Rankor felt a sense of comaraderie with someone without feeling the guilt that he had lived while so many others hadn't. Their sacrifices had not been in vain, and the best way Rankor could honor them was to continue *living*. To embrace his friends and his family and to love with all his heart.

So Rankor would do just that, starting with Elaijah and ending with whatever new soul he was lucky enough to love next.

He left his brother in his uncle's capable hands and started making the journey back home to the castle, but he went with a new lightness in his heart because he knew definitively this wouldn't be the last time he saw Elaijah. This journey that had been such an inconvenience had brought him someone special, and for that he'd always look upon Chrimpranis gratefully.

CAMILLA

THE BEGINNING

C amilla woke in the dark of the night. Shadows hung in every corner of her tiny room, leaving her mind flashing with visions of her cousin chasing her through the woods. Her bedsheets were once again soaked through with sweat and the air around her seemed thick with heat that was more unbearable than it had ever been before.

Was her grandmother trying to kill her?

Her mouth was so dry. Maybe Alina was trying to keep the house so warm that it would kill Camilla!

That must be it. She wasn't safe here!

Camilla padded over to the windows and threw them open, determined to let in fresh air to cool her balmy skin. The wind slapped against her suddenly and she breathed it in greedily, desperate for it to relieve some of the undeniably building tension inside of her. She was on edge, nearly buzzing with anticipation for... something.

Her emotions were a wild storm inside of her, pushing against every part of her mind. Anger at what her grandmother was putting her through. Terror at what was undoubtedly going to happen next. Doubt at whether she could even trust her own mind anymore.

She wanted to scream and cry and pull her hair out and...

"Hello there," she whispered as a small butterfly landed on the sill of her window.

Camilla dropped her finger to where the insect fluttered its wings rapidly and smiled widely as the small creature flew to her, landing on her extended finger. Slowly, she lifted her hand, cradling it to her chest as the butterfly walked over the tiny wrinkles of her palm.

"Are you my friend now?" She wondered aloud. "Are you here to keep me safe?"

The butterfly lifted itself into the air suddenly, flying over Camilla's shoulder with a rapid intensity that left the girl spinning wildly on her heels.

"Wait!" she cried, chasing after the creature as it flew through the narrow opening where her bedroom door cracked open towards the hallway.

Camilla chased the butterfly, not caring how loud or clumsy her footsteps were, not caring that she still wore the muddied dress she'd ran through the woods in hours earlier. All that mattered now was that she'd found the only creature left in this world that would bring joy to her life.

Clay had abandoned her. Her friends would all turn on her. Her grandmother hated her. Her cousin tried to kill her. This little butterfly was the only thing she had left. She had to find it!

"Where did you go?" she demanded in a hushed whisper, eyes scouring through the darkness.

Just when she was about to give up hope, she spotted its little white wings disappearing through the door where her grandmother kept many of the artifacts of House Hypatia, old things that had little magical use like history books and old family portraits.

Alina had never allowed her in the room as a girl. Her grandmother always thought her dirty child fingers would ruin and break things, but Camilla wasn't a girl anymore and she was tired of listening to what her grandmother told her to do.

She stumbled into the room, letting her eyes adjust to the darkness momentarily so she could hunt down her tiny friend.

"There you are!" She spotted the butterfly sitting still atop a wooden crate filled with old parchments. "What have you found?"

She sank to her knees in front of the crate, eyes scanning over the faded ink on the papers.

It only took her a few moments of glancing at them for her to guess at what they were. Prophecies.

"Gods, there must be hundreds of these."

Camilla shuffled as many as she could into her arms and struggled back to her room, momentarily forgetting her new friend. The butterfly had led her to these! Maybe there was something in here that was important for Camilla! Her butterfly friend wanted to help her, she was sure of it.

She closed the door tightly behind her before tossing the prophecies on her bed and scrambling to light a candle. The flame flickered to life, and she sat it carefully onto the wooden floor before shuffling the pages into a neat pile, pulling her crocheted quilt around her shoulders, and lowering herself against her bed to read.

Time passed in a haze as she lost herself to the words on the pages. Only the most powerful of witches could even attempt to harness magic to see into the future. The ancestors who had come before her and written these prophecies had to have been some of the most powerful Witches of all time.

She sorted them into two piles: one filled with prophecies she could tell had already come true and one with predictions she couldn't quite decipher. With movements that were jerky and uncoordinated, she threw the papers into the right piles until all that was left was one. This prophecy, markedly older than the rest, had been *carved* into a single stone. It was heavy to lift, and she traced her fingers against the scratch-like indentations.

"The daughter of Hyrax will shake the Veil," she read aloud, her voice the only sound in the old manor. "And the King of Damnation will rise once more to rule over the children of the Gods. She will create a new death in the mortal realm and will stand at his side as his armies usher in the new age. Prepare for the Final War of the Gods."

Her brow furrowed as she read the prophecy once more, then once again. Well, that... didn't quite make sense. The Descendants of Hyrax were extinct. There were no more children of the God of Death.

Perhaps not all the Witches' prophecies were entirely accurate.

She was just about to set the stone aside when the sound of her Grandmother's croaking voice seemed to surround her.

"What have you found, girl?"

Camilla jumped, looking wide-eyed at the door where Alina stood in an ivory robe, clutching a flickering candlestick with her grey hair in loose curls over her shoulder. At first, Camilla rushed to shuffle the papers behind her back, terrified of being chastised for breaking Alina's rules, but she stilled.

There was no malice in her Grandmother's face.

And she had been so gentle with Camilla earlier...

"Prophecies," Camilla whispered.

Alina jerked her chin, motioning to the stone between Camilla's fingers. "What's that one say?"

"It's nonsense." Camilla shook her head, setting it aside. "It speaks of House Hyrax, but they're extinct."

Alina was quiet, her glossy eyes unblinking as she stared at Camilla. Slowly, she walked toward her, picked up the stone from the floor, and sat it gently on Camilla's bed, seemingly unbothered as she stepped heavily on the ancient parchment that was scattered on the floor.

"It's never wise to dismiss the predictions of a powerful Witch," Alina cautioned. "But for now, why don't we keep this little discovery between you and I? This information could be very dangerous in the wrong hands. We shouldn't trust anyone else, Camilla."

Alina reached down, grasping Camilla's hand in her own and pulling the girl to her feet. A sudden explosive excitement clouded her thoughts and Camilla bit down on her lower lip to stop herself from grinning too widely. Alina had never allowed Camilla to be the granddaughter she shared secrets with. She had never forgiven her for going places she didn't belong. She had never rubbed her hands reassuringly on Camilla's arms like she was now.

She must have done something right, for once!

And now that she had, she wouldn't stop. Camilla would do anything her grandmother asked of her, and maybe, just maybe, she would *finally* be accepted - loved.

Alina tucked Camilla back into her bed and left, clicking the door shut after her and leaving Camilla alone to stare out the open window. She watched her butterfly come in and land on the stone prophecy for only a few moments before the creature flew away once more.

LORELAI

EVERYTHING HAS CHANGED

Helena kept her word and safely escorted her back to the castle the following day. When they arrived, Lorelai walked in without any preamble, instructing the girl to follow. She led her to her suites and paid her a solid twenty gold coins for her help.

"I knew you were lying about working for one of the ladies," Helena confessed. "You acted far too prim to be hired help."

Lorelai shrugged. "Yes, well, you can never be too careful these days. You never know what sort of *odd jobs* people are willing to do."

Helena grinned, tucked the coin away and left shortly thereafter, and even though Lorelai knew she would never see the girl again, she felt surprisingly grateful for the brief moment in time that Helena had been in her life and for the ways she had opened her eyes to the meaning of life.

Her father stopped by shortly afterwards, hugging her tightly. He had heard of the attack and sent search parties out after her immediately, but had naturally feared the worst. Still, he allowed himself only a few minutes to hold her before reverting to his usual self. He reminded her to look appropriate for the upcoming Peace Celebration, in the lucky chance that she potentially meet someone who could be a strong potential for marriage.

She didn't even feel surprised her father couldn't simply celebrate the fact that she was alive without immediately pushing her towards marriage.

Her closet at the castle was filled with options that would be suitable for the Peace Celebration but she ultimately settled on a blue dress, mostly because she knew the dress was one of Iris' favorites and one of the castle staff members had told her that her friend had just returned from her first mission from the Order. The Peace Celebration was already such a hard day for her. Maybe seeing Lorelai in this would brighten her day.

There was a knock at her door and she hurried to open it, grinning upon seeing Camilla standing and waiting for her.

"I'm so glad to see you!" Lorelai squealed happily, pulling Camilla to her for a tight hug.

"Not as glad as I am to see you! I heard bandits attacked you. I haven't been able to sleep at all. I've been terrified for you."

Camilla pulled away and held her at arm's length, glancing over her as if to make sure she was okay before pointing to a trunk that sat in the hall outside of her room. Lorelai recognized it immediately.

"They found this in the woods while they were looking for you," Camilla explained. "Is it yours?"

Lorelai laughed under her breath as she approached the trunk and crouched down to open it and pull out the most lovely lilac dress with the most perfectly applied gemstones and crystals. After everything she'd been through over the past few days, the dress simply didn't hold the same importance it once did.

"That's beautiful. What are you going to wear it to?"

Lorelai simply shrugged and tossed it across the chair in the entryway of her suite before wrapping her arm through Camilla's and pulling her away from her rooms. "I commissioned it for something that doesn't seem all that important anymore. Perhaps I'll let a friend borrow it one day."

"Well, that's awfully kind of you."

Lorelai squeezed her arm. "It's just a dress."

Camilla gave her a suspicious glare over her shoulder. "Who are you and what have you done with my friend?"

They laughed together as they made their way to Iris' rooms. Their group of friends always attended the Peace Celebration together. Rankor was going to miss this year's festival because of an injury, but Clay and Kent would surely meet them in the courtyard. The five of them would watch the performances and mingle like they normally did. Then in the evening, they would gather to swap stories and play cards.

Everything would be the same as it always was, and yet everything was different. Lorelai was different. And she was okay with that.

IRIS

The Calm Before the Storm

B eing back in the castle felt somehow wrong. She had long since bathed the dirt and blood off of herself, reported on the mission to Walric, and returned to sleeping in her room. Now she looked like a version of herself that she recognized, with her hair colored pink and her skin shimmering, but she felt like everything about her had changed in the weeks that she had been gone.

Every night her dreams started with the way his copper hair had first shined under the sunlight in those woods and ended with the sensation of blood drying between her fingers as she ran from him.

That was in the past, though.

She never should have let him go. It went against every principle The Order had tried to drill into her. If she ever saw him again, she'd have no choice but to finish what she started.

So, all that Iris could do now was go back to her life, heal her injured heart, and pray to the Gods that she never saw Nikolai Legum again.

Life would go on. She would find someone new to love and she would forget she had ever met him.

A knock at her door startled her, and she screamed for whoever it was to come in. Clayton didn't hesitate to push the door open and rush to hug her.

"I'm sorry I wasn't able to come sooner," he sighed against her hair. "I've been out of the castle."

"The Alchemist?" she guessed.

She felt his head nod against hers. "I've almost got the location of his port. I'll have it soon."

Iris pulled away from him and turned back towards the looking glass at her vanity. Clay stiffened for a minute, too perceptive for his own good, before seating himself on the foot of her bed.

"My father told me about Walric's report. He's thrilled you eliminated the Serpent."

His words were sending flashes of memories racing through her mind. A dark room. The Duke's lifeless body. The feeling of blood seeping through her fingertips as she jammed her blade into the Serpents stomach.

"Are you alright?" Clay asked, jostling her from her thoughts. "You seem distracted.

She smiled at him over her shoulder. "Oh, just fine."

He frowned. "Did anything happen on your mission that I should know about?"

She weighed the consequences of telling him. Would knowing that his plans had been discovered convince him not to pursue them further? Or would it only push him to become even more reckless than he was already being?

"Nope," she lied. "I did what I was sent there to do, and now I'm ready to get back to my beautifully glamorous life here."

Clay appraised her for a moment. "Something's in the air today."

"What do you mean?"

"I'm not sure," he mused, running a hand through his hair as he looked out her window to where preparations were being made for the annual Peace Celebration. "Just this feeling in my gut that has me on edge."

"This day is always stressful."

Clay didn't turn to look at her. His attention was solely focused on the world outside, on the bridge that led from the village to the palace courtyard. "It's more than that."

"What does it feel like?"

"Like power," he breathed. "It feels like magic is building in the air."

He left shortly thereafter, needing to check in with his father once more before the festivities kicked off, which left Iris only a few precious moments of privacy before Camilla and Lorelai would come to retrieve her before the start of the celebration.

She took one final, lingering look at herself in the mirror before picking up the dress that she had laid out for herself on her bed. The pink gown Iris had commissioned for the day was ridiculously extravagant, which only made her love it that much more.

Don't miss the rest of the House of Hyrax series!

The Rose in the Shadows
To the Edge of Athenia
The Crown of the Dark Prince

If you enjoyed this book, please leave a review here.

Want the latest updates? Subscribe to my newsletter!

AUTHORS NOTE

Writing this book was not in the initial plan for the House of Hyrax series, but I find myself saying that the characters demanded that this book be written and I'm so glad I listened to them.

While working my way through the initial draft of The Rose in Shadows, I found myself incredibly sympathetic to Camilla. In order for me to accurately write her, I had to have a clear idea of what her backstory was and what had led her to the place she was in for RITS. I knew fairly early on that I wanted to share that version of her with others, the version of her that's nothing more than a girl who's been through far more suffering than she deserved. It became so clear though that each of these characters had such rich lives and complex personalities. I wanted to know more about Rankor's family and how his time in the war affected him. I wanted to see what had happened to Kent that led him to be so reserved. I wanted to explore what Iris' job as a spy was like. I wanted to give Lorelai a chance to really live.

I went into this journey thinking I would create a short novella to explore these stories, and ended it with a novel that I am immensely proud of. Throughout the process, I found myself questioning my skills, my ideas, and my characters. By the time I did my final read-through, though, I found myself laughing and crying all at once. It has been an absolute privilege to share the stories of these five characters and I hope you have enjoyed getting to know them all a little better.

There are so many people to thank for both their support of RITS and of TTEA.

To my parents, thank you for embracing this new adventure with me. Thank you for sharing my book with as many people as you can (even when it slightly embarrasses me). Thank you for celebrating the success with me and for always being willing to listen to me talk about how excited I am of an upcoming event or signing.

To the rest of my friends and family, including my very supportive partner Matthew, you all have shown me what a village of support I have and I am forever grateful. Thank you for always asking me how things are going and for always being listen to me talk about all the aspects of writing that I'm most excited about.

To my Beta Readers, thank you for embracing this story and for the feedback that helped it become what it is now.

To my PA, Sarah, I can not begin to express how fun it is to create with you. Thank you so much for your support of my work and for you incredible dedication towards helping to make this series a success.

To my street team, I love our community. I love our conversations. I love us. Thank you for being on this ride with me.

To my readers, thank you for taking your time to give this book a chance. I hope you enjoyed and I hope you're ready for what's next because I'm so ready to share it with you!